CHALLI

TO TERROR

by

RAYMOND ('TURK') WESTERLING

WILLIAM KIMBER
LONDON

CHALLENGE TO TERROR

THE AUTHOR

CONTENTS

Contents

ILLUSTRATIONS

Translated from French
by
Waverley Root

CHAPTER I

A Lively Boyhood

I don't know if child prodigies of other types come as a blessing to their parents. But I am sure, judging from my own case, that a child prodigy destined for a career of adventure is a phenomenon which no one would wish to see inflicted upon a friend.

It was a thought which did not occur to me at the time, but as I look back, I think there must have been many moments during my boyhood when my mother and father regretted that they had not remained single.

I entered this world on August 31, 1919, at Istanbul, then the capital of Turkey, and was given the name of Raymond Paul Pierre Westerling—French being dominant among the four languages most commonly spoken in my family circle. It took me only until 1923 to acquire an unenviable reputation among the respectable friends of my parents. They remarked politely—when they felt it necessary to be polite—that I was very advanced for my age. I certainly was.

Other boys have managed to create scenes of panic in their homes by introducing into them animals which nervous adults would prefer not to meet there. At the age of five I discovered in myself the gifts of animal trainer and snake charmer, and shared my room with several snakes, a troop of mice (who had to dodge the snakes) and a considerable company of lizards. The lizards liked climbing, and as it seemed dull to have them climbing nothing but the walls and the furniture I taught them to climb up my leg. They got around, and one of the first lessons I learned about adults was that gentlemen visitors did not care to have mice running suddenly up inside their trouser legs and that women visitors enjoyed even less the sensation of a lizard scurrying up beneath their skirts.

I was also in advance of my age in my reading. I was only six when I exhausted the stories of pirates, historical romances and Wild West adventures which take most youngsters pretty well into their teens, and began to attack detective stories, preferably bloody. Whenever I discovered an improbability, which, in this sort of literature was often enough, or a point at which an author, perhaps out of decency and desire to spare his readers, had glossed over some of the more horrible details of his plot, I made my father's life a misery by a series of minute questions. I must have considered him an authority on murder and other crimes. How one over-estimates one's parents in childhood!

At seven, I was already a good shot. (How I persuaded my parents to let me amuse myself with firearms at this age I no longer remember. Possibly I didn't mention it to them.) I could hit a coin at twenty yards with a six-millimetre cartridge. I can still bring down a pigeon with a pistol. If that sounds easy, try it.

By the age of eight I really began to worry my mother, my father and my older sister, Palmyre. It was silly of them. All I did was to disappear. We had gone to our summer house at Pendik for the holidays, and I got into the habit of rising at dawn (conveniently ahead of everybody else), slipping two or three pieces of bread into my pocket, and plunging into the mountains, to return at dark—perhaps.

My father felt that eight was too tender an age for a boy to spend the entire day alone, climbing mountainsides, and he tried to impress that idea upon a tender spot. But each application of his cane to my rear was followed by another disappearance the following dawn, and he finally got tired of this sport before I did—and this, in spite of the fact that I actually felt no great enthusiasm for it. His surrender was announced one morning when I rose too late or he rose too early. He caught sight of me as I was slipping out, heaved a resigned sigh, and said: "Have a good time—but be careful!"

A Lively Boyhood

"Be careful!" Ridiculous advice! I have always been careful. If I had been careless, I would have died a hundred deaths by now.

It was thus without parental objection that I was able to prowl through the mountains, to collect insects and butterflies, to discover isolated high-perched hamlets, to become the friend of the mountaineers and the shepherds.

My explorations, instructive though they were, did not constitute my entire education. I had, in fact, been going to school since the age of six. The beginning of my formal education had been the reason for a considerable argument between my parents. That I was to receive normal instruction had been agreed. But in what language?

I already spoke three. Although the Westerlings were Dutch, they had lived in Istanbul for three generations and had acquired the polyglot gift for languages then common to all the inhabitants of the Turkish capital. My father, a dealer in antiques and a manufacturer of furniture, spoke English, French, German and Italian in his shops, Turkish in his workshop, and Greek to my mother, who belonged to a good-class Greek family. My mother rocked me to sleep as a baby with Greek lullabies and had begun to educate me in French. My sister Palmyre and I spoke Turkish with our playmates and with the merchants of the *souks*. One of the few languages of which I had never heard a word was my "native" tongue—Dutch.

The question provoked a major argument between my parents. While my father insisted that I should go to an English school, to receive a "gentleman's" education, my mother favoured rather the solid instruction provided by the French Jesuits. But in this society, where the authority of the head of the family was supreme, there could be only one result. Anyone could have predicted it: I was sent—of course—to an English school; but after a month, when this gesture had sufficiently sustained masculine authority, I was taken away—of course—and sent to the Jesuit school of St. Michel. A little later, I was sent to boarding school at the largest Jesuit college in Asia Minor, St. Joseph's.

11

Challenge to Terror

It was fortunate for me that I learned so readily that it was possible to be simultaneously the laziest student of the school and one of the first in my class. I had only to read a Latin text once or twice to know it by heart. While my schoolmates hunched desperately over their desks, their clenched fists pressed against their temples, as though to push their lessons into their brains, I enjoyed myself in the company of Robinson Crusoe or simply closed my eyes and launched myself into a daydream which might find me on a pirate ship or operating a detective agency. I possessed a regular moving picture show inside my head, projecting fantastic films which Hollywood itself might have envied.

I lived a sort of film in my school life also, casting myself alternately as Haroun al Rashid and as protector of the weak. Two-thirds of my pocket-money went to maintain the former role, serving to realise as if by magic the wishes of my comrades and, I hoped, to dazzle them with my magnificence and munificence. As protector of the weak, I found breaks the most propitious time to undertake the hunt for bullies. It led to some magnificent fights.

I was ten when I first demonstrated my affinity for firearms in a fashion which, for once, was as displeasing for me as for my parents. I was playing in the garden with a friend of my own age and the toy with which we had elected to play was a loaded rifle. It went off and I received the charge in my leg. I spent my holiday in bed.

The lesson was not vivid enough to preserve me from a similar but graver accident three years later, when I was thirteen. By this time I had decided that I was too grown up to be content with so innocuous a weapon as a rifle. I laid hands on my father's big double-barrelled shotgun and prepared for some sport. Unfortunately, I could find no cartridges. But after careful exploration, I discovered a drawer filled with treasure—a large box of powder, loose shot, caps, in short everything necessary to manufacture cartridges for oneself. Preferring not to be disturbed, I transported all these delightful objects to a quiet corner of the garden, and set to work.

12

A Lively Boyhood

The garden was not destined to be quiet for very long. I found it more difficult to achieve a satisfactory cartridge than I had expected. It occurred to me that it might be quite as interesting, and easier, to create a small explosion. An old wall ran around the garden. It was not a very good wall and I saw no reason why I should not blow it up if I felt like it. And I did feel like it.

I packed some powder carefully into a hole in the wall, laid a little trail of powder along the ground away from it, and, leaning forward on my hands and knees, I struck a match and lit it. The whole world seemed to blow up at once. I was bowled over, and as I tried to scramble up I realized that my surroundings had disappeared. I was blind!

My mother was already hurrying towards the site of the explosion, having started with the boom and the tinkle of falling glass as the windows of the house gave way. It was an axiom in our family that any loud disastrous noise meant that I was in some sort of trouble. My screams increased her pace and in a few minutes she had me in bed again. My hand, knees, face and chest were badly burned, and for two months I could not see properly. Then my sight returned, and after another six months of convalescence I was able to resume my studies by myself, and by the time I could return to school I had caught up with the others.

My ability as a scholar caused the school authorities to overlook some of my less desirable characteristics, and when my father's business began to go badly, two years later, and he was obliged to announce that he was taking me away from school, the Director protested. It would be a crime, he said, not to allow so gifted a student to continue his studies, and offered to absolve us of all expenses. But my father was too proud to accept what he considered charity, so I was taken away from school and brought home.

The school did not abandon me even then. One of my professors came to our home regularly, two afternoons a week, for three years. I followed the regular curriculum of my class and he corrected my exercises. In my spare time I practised wrestling and ju-jitsu, in which I had been proficient at school, and made a little pocket money by giving lessons in these sports to other youths and winning occasional prizes at amateur tournaments.

At the age of eighteen I was given a job as cashier in a large shop. The pay was good, but it was no place for a young man of my impatient temperament. Day after day and all day long, I was shut up in a cage, badgered with figures, and faced with no prospect except that of continuing this dull monotonous existence for the rest of my days. I stood it a year. How, I don't know. Then I gave up and took a job with a recently acquired brother-in-law, Palmyre's husband.

The move was only from one shop to another, but this was a different sort of shop. It was a ship chandler's, and a ship chandler is only one step removed from the sea. I found the shop encumbered by cables and ropes, anchors and sextants, motors and rolled-up sails, a romantic spot. I liked the profane fishermen and the often tipsy sailors who were our customers. I sat spellbound as the captains and the marines swapped tales of shipwreck and adventure. Soon they began to mingle tales of war with their recitals, for once again Europe was fighting. Now the ship chandler's began to seem to me as confining as the cashier's cage had been. Great events were going on in the world, men were fighting and dying like the heroes of the romances I had read as a boy, and I was condemned to stay out of it all, tucked away in a country that remained obstinately in a state of non-belligerency. Early in 1941, the strain became too great. Without saying anything to my family, I visited the Dutch consulate, was accepted for the Dutch army, and given my tickets for the trip to Cairo, where I was to enlist officially.

I returned home to break the joyous news to my family, who turned out not to be overjoyed.

My mother and sister burst into tears, while my girl friend, who was hovering timidly at the door, discreetly outside the family conclave, wept too. My father disapproved completely.

"My son," he said, "you are not made for the army. They

14

will tell you what you're supposed to do, and if you don't do it they'll clap you into the guardhouse. In fact, knowing you as I do, I predict that you will spend most of your army career in the guardhouse."

"Have you ever been in the army, Father?" I asked him.

"Certainly not!"

"Was *your* father ever in the army?"

"Of course not!"

"Was *his* father ever in the army?"

"None of our family has ever been so foolish," my father answered, "till you."

"Then," I said crushingly, "how can you tell that I'm not made for the army? You don't know anything about the army. Nobody in our family knows anything about the army. Nobody has ever been in the army."

At this distance, the argument does not seem as unanswerable as I thought it then, but in any case my father did not answer it. He saw I was decided and he let me have my way. Perhaps he thought he might as well let a sergeant worry about me from now on as continue to do so himself.

I kissed my mother and my sister goodbye, stopped at the door to bestow a few more kisses on my girl friend, and ran for the train. I had time, but ran anyway. I could not wait to get away from the dull, humdrum city of Istanbul and be on my way to the glittering exotic cities of western Europe—and to the war.

CHAPTER II

Bedouins and Zulus

Twenty-four hours by train brought me to Mersin, where I took the boat for Egypt. The cuisine was so good that I went down with a bad attack of food poisoning and instead of walking down the gangway at Cairo, a hearty recruit for His Majesty's service, I went feet first on a stretcher when the boat stopped at Haifa. I spent the next eight days in agony in a hospital. But then life, and interest in it, returned to me. I was in Palestine. There were Bedouins in Palestine. I decided that I could not leave Palestine without seeing some Bedouins.

Excursions into the desert were not included in the programme the Dutch Army had arranged for me and I had a feeling that I might not get much co-operation for my plans in that quarter, so I refrained from mentioning them to anyone. I simply hired a lorry-driver and got him to take me into the desert to look for Bedouins.

This might have been putting my head into the lion's mouth. Axis propaganda had had much effect on the tribesmen, who were more or less hostile towards the English, and it was hardly the moment for British soldiers or potential British soldiers to be paying social calls on Bedouins. When I arrived with an Arab guide whom I had hired to find a nomadic encampment for me, I was received with evident surprise, to say the least.

However, I got along with them very well. We talked some English, which several of them could speak a little, but conversed mostly with our hands. I managed to explain that I had been born and brought up in Turkey, and they soon discovered the sympathy which I had always felt for the Moslem religion. I did not speak Arabic, but I did know many surats from the Koran. That was enough for these men of the desert to receive me as a brother.

I had intended to spend a few hours with them. I stayed a week. I shared their life and I joined them in their prayers. I found them a friendly simple people who reminded me of the mountaineers who had been my friends during my boyhood wanderings. They were the kind of people I was to find myself liking everywhere—uncomplicated people, unpretentious people, people not civilized out of man's natural character. Later I was to find much the same sort of person in Indonesia, where the majority of the population also practises the Moslem religion to which I had already been drawn in Turkey.

16

Bedouins and Zulus

I returned to Haifa at about the time when everyone had given me up as having successfully deserted without yet being in the army. I was shipped on to Cairo, where my impatience to get into the war seized me again. I made myself a nuisance to the authorities, wanting to be shipped to England and the war or to be assigned to a unit so that I could really consider myself a soldier at long last. As far as I could make out, the English were practising in my case their famous doctrine of "wait and see".

Having nothing else to do, I explored the city and met a girl. I had had flirtations in Turkey, and had had girl friends there, but this time I felt that everything was different. This was the girl of my life. This was the girl I never wanted to leave. (How did I reconcile that feeling with my ardour to be off to war? I didn't. I didn't try.) I carried on a whirlwind courtship and we decided to marry. The date was set and all the details arranged for the wedding, which was to be celebrated according to Catholic rites. I was deliriously happy.

The day before my wedding, without warning, I received my orders. I was to join an Australian unit camped in the desert.

This, too, would have made me happy if it had occurred two weeks earlier. As it was, it made me miserable.

I thought of desertion. Actually, I had a choice between two desertions—I could desert the army or I could desert my fiancée. It was my father who decided for me. I remembered his words: "My son, you are not made for the army." I had to prove him wrong.

On the following day, instead of going to the church, I took my place in the lorry, which rolled out across the desert. And at the hour when I should have been standing at the altar with my bride, I was instead under a tent pitched in a waste of sand, surrounded by a band of Australian giants speaking a gibberish which I supposed to be English, but which to my ears was entirely incomprehensible.

I had hardly become used to Australians and to the Australian way with the English language, when I received

17

new orders. I was to leave the desert at once to board the *Empress of Russia*, sailing that very day for England. This was the direction I wanted to take. I joined the *Empress of Russia* in happy anticipation of action.

It was not going to be a short trip. The *Empress of Russia* was avoiding the submarine-infested Mediterranean and the dangerous narrow passage through the straits of Gibraltar. Our route was to take us through the Red Sea and around the Cape.

At Port Sudan, the ship stopped long enough for us to be allowed shore leave. With a comrade, I went into a waterside bar for a glass of beer. Under the shade of the burning corrugated iron roof, I fell into conversation with the bar-owner, a Greek, who became very friendly the moment I spoke to him in his native language. I asked him what there was to see in Port Sudan.

"Nothing," he said with conviction. "A thousand times nothing."

I pressed him further. He finally came up with an idea.

"There's a Zulu village about four miles from here," he said. "You might visit that—if you're interested in natives."

"Which way?"

He gave me directions.

"But be careful," he warned. "They're touchy. It's safer to go with a crowd. If you chance it, watch your manners. Be nice and friendly."

With his aid, we persuaded a taxi driver, also a Greek, to take us to the Zulu village. He began by demonstrating extreme unwillingness to go anywhere near the place without escort, an armed escort, but the combined persuasions of his compatriot and of our money finally won him over. He would take us within half a mile of the village, he said, but no further. There he would wait for us to come back—if we came back. An optimist.

We left him on the road, already turning his car ready for a quick getaway, and followed on foot the trail that led us to the thatched huts of the Zulus. The first sight of them was impressive. None of them seemed under six feet; they had

18

muscles like motor-car springs and their expressions seemed to indicate that they could already see us in their stew-pans, staying for dinner. The Greek had told us to be friendly. I wondered if anyone had asked the Zulus to be friendly.

My comrade improved on our instructions. He was too friendly. He took a fancy to the first Zulu maiden he encountered, a young lady the colour of ebony, built like a female Hercules, with crocodile teeth.

She seemed to like him too. As he became more demonstrative, she showed that she was willing to be friendly also. But her boy friends thought differently. My comrade suddenly found himself surrounded by a group of gesticulating giants who clearly intended to teach him his business.

I summoned ju-jitsu to the rescue. Picking the largest of his attackers, I took a running jump and dived headfirst into his solar plexus. As he went down, upsetting one or two of the others, I grabbed my friend's arm and we left. Fast.

I think we must have set some sort of a record for the half mile. As we pounded down the home stretch towards the car, the driver caught sight of us, pelting towards him like mad, pursued by a crazy mob of dervishes waving lances and knives. He decided not to wait, but started up his motor and went into gear.

We put on a last burst of speed and overtook him before he could properly accelerate. With a flying leap, we landed on the car and clung. If it had had no running board, you would not be reading this story.

CHAPTER III

The Art of Silent Murder

The *Empress of Russia* was taking the long way round and I was still fuming with impatience to get to the fighting. Aden, Durban, Capetown—now we were around the Cape

19

and heading for England—the days at sea were long and monotonous. But at last we steamed into a harbour. I had never been to England or anywhere near it, but from what I had heard, it didn't look right to me. I asked where we were.

We were in Puerto Rico!

Submarines, I supposed. Rather than take the *Empress of Russia* the whole way up the West African and European coasts to the British Isles, the Admiralty had no doubt elected to have her cross the Atlantic twice.

But it seemed that the second crossing was doomed to be delayed. At Puerto Rico, our Chinese crew disappeared. Apparently, unlike me, they didn't want to get any nearer the war. For four days we lay in harbour, while the officers tried unsuccessfully to recruit a new crew.

I was not the only one who was impatient to get to the war before it ended. A group of us volunteered to replace the deserters. I became a stoker, a truly infernal job. The *Empress of Russia* was not an oil burner. She ran on coal and for the next week or so, I must have shovelled tons of coal into her boilers. I did not mind the hard work, but being continuously cooped up below decks did bother me. However, I worked with a will. With every shovelful of coal, I reminded myself, I was pushing the ship a few feet nearer England.

When the engine-room bells at last brought the *Empress of Russia* to a stop, I went up on deck. This time the scenery was more along the lines I had expected.

"Liverpool?" I inquired.

We were in Halifax.

I had nothing against Canada, except that there was no war there, but the longer I travelled, the further I seemed to be getting from the fighting. I had been on the way for weeks, and I was now farther from the war than when I had been at home in Istanbul. However, the British Government was not consulting my wishes in determining the route by which I was to arrive at the battlefields, and there was nothing to do but to go with as good grace as possible to

20

the training centre at Stratford, Ontario, to which I was posted.

This was a Dutch training camp, so that it was natural that the British army, having me on its records as Dutch, should have sent me there. There was only one slight difficulty. Although I spoke four European languages, Dutch wasn't one of them.

Fortunately, I have a natural facility for languages, and in two months I was able to discuss military theory and drill my companions in my "native" language.

The training finished, we embarked for England on 19th December 1941, where we were mustered into the Princess Irene Brigade, at Wolverhampton. This unit, which was later to gain fame at the time of the Normandy landings and in the operations which followed, was formed of young Dutchmen who had escaped from occupied Holland. Looking back on the brilliant record it made later, one might consider it a privilege to have belonged to it. The advantages escaped me at the time.

Here I was, almost within smelling distance of the fighting, and I wasn't doing any fighting. I was waiting. I had not yet learned that for the private soldier war is 95 per cent waiting. I was prepared to charge the enemy with a bayonet, but not to charge potatoes with a paring knife. After fifteen days in the gallant Princess Irene Brigade, I felt that I had passed my life with the potato and was likely to spend the rest of it in the company of that homely vegetable. I began to feel that my father had been right. If this was what the army was like, I was definitely not made for the army.

In the morning, potato peeling. In the afternoon, policing the grounds. Morning, afternoon and evening, an interminable series of tongue lashings from a particularly evil-tempered sergeant who had taken a special dislike to me. It could have been no greater than my dislike for him.

He was not a man of great imagination and his insults revolved around a few main themes. One of them was the probable illegitimacy of my birth, a theory which he based on the fact that I was not a real Hollander from Holland, but a mongrel variety from an inferior part of the world. I had not come all the way from Istanbul to Wolverhampton via Canada, to listen to abuse.

My temper gave way at an unfortunate moment for the sergeant. I was sweeping out the latrine. He was superintending in his usual fashion which meant that he was roaring insults at me.

"*Swing* that broom, you bastard son of a Dutch bastard!" the sergeant shouted, his eyes half-closed, his face red, the veins swelling on his neck, his mouth wide open as he yelled at the top of his lungs.

I swung the broom in two movements. Movement one: down into the noisome trench of the latrine. Movement two: up into the sergeant's open mouth. He was cut short in full cry—temporarily.

The deep joy which I experienced from this modification of bayonet drill was moderated by the memory of my father's prophecy that I would spend most of my army career in the guardhouse. I fully expected, when I was called before the Camp Commander, a few minutes later, that I would at once take up residence there. But I described the sergeant's attitude and his remarks in detail, and to my great surprise the result was a sharp reprimand for the sergeant.

I felt better about the army, but not about the potatoes. I still wanted to find some more soldierly employment for my time. I thought the opportunity had come when word went around the camp that a company was being formed for service in India. But I was out of luck. The company went off—but I was not in it.

Then another chance presented itself. The call went out for volunteers for instruction as parachutists. This was more like it. I had my name put down at once, and training began.

Instruction was psychological as well as physiological. Not only were we taught how to land and to absorb the shock of the jump, but from the very beginning, when we jumped from low platforms to the ground, the command was given each time, "Action stations! Go!" This was repeated as we tried jumping from gradually increasing heights: "Action stations! Go! . . . Action stations! Go!" The idea was that we would become so used to jumping at this command that when we made our first jumps from planes, it would be almost automatic for us to respond, and we would launch ourselves naturally into the air through sheer habit.

I was never to get this far—on this occasion at least. Towards the end of the first week of training we were practising jumping from a truck running along at a speed of twenty miles an hour. "Action stations! Go!" the command came. I leaped from the truck, hit the ground at a bad angle, and felt something snap in my foot. I had broken an ankle!

My attempt to get more action kept me inactive for a month. During that time I lay on my back in a hospital bed or sat up in a chair, chafing at my helplessness and almost regretting the potatoes.

Two days after I was returned to camp another call for volunteers went out. This time it was for the Commandos. Once again I signed up and two weeks later I was in the Commando Camp in Achnacarry, Scotland.

Now I was no longer in a Dutch unit. There were men of all nationalities in the camp, volunteers exclusively, instructed and officered by Britishers. They lost no time breaking us in by easy degrees or coddling us. They set us to work with an intensity which made me think at first that they didn't want to train us, they wanted to kill us.

I learned how to cross a river on a thin rope, clinging to it with knees and elbows, upside down, like a sloth. I became an expert at passing obstacles of any kind, hiding myself, using all sorts of weapons or fighting without any.

The ordeals through which we ourselves were put were nothing compared to what we were taught to apply to the enemy. We studied the art of silent murder. Firearms were of minor importance in our curriculum. We preferred to kill quietly.

We learned how to creep up on a sentry and strangle him before he could cry out, without even letting him drop his rifle, to prevent the clatter from giving the alarm. We practised knife-play until we were as expert as Sicilian bandits. We were taught how to slip into the quarters of an enemy officer, chloroform him and carry him away without waking his orderly in the next room.

If murder was the most important of the crimes we were taught, it was not the only one. We ran the whole gamut of misdoing. Arson: how to burn a house, a camp or a forest. Theft: how to steal documents or arms. Sabotage: how to destroy buildings, blow up bridges, de-rail trains.

At the end of eight weeks of high-powered instruction, we were ready to operate behind the enemy lines, to prepare the way for ordinary troops to break through the enemy front, and especially to land on enemy coasts and conduct raids against them. We were chiefly men of the night.

Our operations were destined to be carried out usually under cover of darkness. We knew how to make ourselves absolutely invisible at night to the eyes of our enemies, while we kept our own eyes sharp by opening and closing them rapidly and continuously, till we could see in the dark like bats. We had been instructed how to commit the perfect crime and how to hide a corpse without leaving a trace. In case of capture, we knew how to adopt false identities and how to answer interrogations. In short, we knew how to serve the country as the most expert of male-factors. I sometimes shudder today as I consider how many graduates of the Commando camps are walking about the streets, endowed with a first-rate training in crime, in case they should be tempted to make illegitimate use of it.

Let me say at this point that I do not think that there is any soldier in the world better trained for the toughest tasks or the most disconcerting surprises than the British Commando.

Having escaped death by the skin of my teeth a dozen times during my training, I left Achnacarry in top form, tough, hardened and anxious to come to grips with the enemy. Perhaps my form was too good. I had hardly left the training camp, ready and eager for action, than I was sent back to it. I had a corporal's stripes and a job as instructor in silent murder and in fighting unarmed. One month later, after I had given a demonstration of this art at an inspection, I was called to Commando No. 10, and promoted to the post of instructor for the entire unit. It was flattering, but at the same time, it wasn't what I wanted. Instructing wasn't fighting. I didn't want to prepare other people to get into the scrap. I wanted to get into it myself.

Early in 1943, No. 2 Dutch Commando troop was called to go to India. I applied for permission to join them. It was not without difficulty that I was able to get out of my training assignment, but I finally succeeded in getting myself attached to my old troop. Before sailing, we were granted an unusual amount of leave; and it was one evening when we were enjoying this privilege, that we had an opportunity for a little preliminary practice of what we had learned.

We ran into a group of Scotch Commandos, excellent fellows as a rule, but on this occasion over-inspired by indulgence in their national drink. It must be admitted that we were not exceptionally sober either. The Scots took it into their heads to show themselves highly critical of Holland, of the Dutch, and finally of the Royal Family. We felt it necessary to contradict them—not subtly, I'm afraid. The next fifteen minutes were rather lively. They were devoted to a demonstration, by both sides, of Commando tactics. The Dutch remained in possession of the field.

The next morning a captain of Dutch General Staff had me called in.

"Corporal," he said, "the Commander has been informed that a number of our allies were rendered somewhat the worse for wear last night by a group of our men. Do you know anything about it?"

"Yes, sir," I said.

I was cursing myself for having got into the brawl. After trying so hard to get to India, would I be punished now by having my posting withdrawn?

"Ah—how were the two sides compared, Corporal?" the officer asked. "Did you outnumber them?"

"No, sir," I said. "If anything, there were a few more of them."

"Then we—I mean, you won?"

I ventured to smile.

"I believe we did, sir," I said.

"Most reprehensible," said the officer. "Most reprehensible. The Colonel wants me to tell you . . ." he paused and grinned, "that this little episode will not be held against you. Dismissed."

CHAPTER IV

Rocket Bombs

A month later I found myself, as I had hoped, in India—but the war was still eluding me.

I was sent first, for no particular reason that I could discern, to Kedgoon, near Poona, and then, again for no particular reason I could discern, to Coconado, near Pondicherry. The closest I came to seeing any action was to be chosen after a visit of inspection to act as personal bodyguard to Lord Louis Mountbatten, Allied Commander in this area, when he visited our camp.

I had hopes that something exciting might happen when I was sent to Belgau, near Goa. Here we went through six weeks' special training for service in the jungle, which made it appear that the powers which directed our destinies had some specific service in mind for us. I learned how to make my way through the densest forest, to penetrate thick undergrowth noiselessly, to cross swamps, to live off the jungle, distinguish edible plants from poisonous ones, to protect myself against wild animals, snakes and, what was often more important in the tropics, insects.

The plan, we understood, was to send us into Burma. Burma sounded interesting and I waited with impatience for the orders which would finally lead me to actual combat. But when the time came, it turned out that only six of us were to be attached to No. 5 Commando. In order to determine which six should go, the names of the whole group were put in a hat, shaken up together, and drawn one by one. By the time the fourth name had been reached, I was convinced that the fatality which had so far kept me out of the war was going once more to refuse me a chance of action. The fifth name was drawn. It was not mine. Clearly, my bad luck was going to hold. But hope dies hard, and I listened, holding my breath, for the the sixth name. Again I lost. Fate, I decided, had it in for me. I was not destined for a life of adventure. I was so discouraged that if at that moment I had been offered a chance to get out of the army, I would have snapped it up at once.

Even worse was to come. I was returned to England!

It was the end of 1943. I had spent nearly three years trying to get into the war and the war was still eluding me. I had travelled a distance roughly equal to going completely round the world and I had only got to Eastbourne, England. When, fifteen days later, we were lined up for review, and it was announced that four of us were to be sent on a special mission, I hardly paid any attention to the names that were read out. I had become a fatalist about the war and myself. I was resigned to being counted out again.

I was counted in! One of the four names was mine. We were taken to London, to the headquarters of the Intelligence Service, where we were told that our new job would consist of "operations behind the lines" and would necessitate additional special training. No further information was given us.

I plunged with enthusiasm into the new course of training. It seemed that I had been training, training, training indefinitely, without ever being given a chance to use what I had learned. Now I anticipated the first opportunity to make practical use of my achievements. If it had not seemed evident that at last all this training was actually to be used for something, I might have undertaken these exercises with less interest. As it was, I entered into them with zest. There was, besides, a new and electric atmosphere in the camp. Something big was preparing. We sensed it from the attitude of our officers and from the specific nature of our training, evidently directed towards carrying out some precise projected operation.

The new training I was getting caused me to resume a course I had taken up before and been forced to abandon—parachute jumping. That meant, I knew, Europe again. It was obvious that if it were suddenly decided that I must learn to jump from a plane, it was not for landing in England. I sensed more missions ahead of me, like the first—deep, perhaps, into enemy territory, since I would have to be delivered by plane and not, as on the first occasion, by boat.

My new training began with nine days intensive exercise in jumping. During its course, I made six jumps from planes, and found myself a natural enough parachutist. The first time, the leap into nothingness was a disagreeable necessity, but after the jerk caused by the opening of the parachute, the sensation of floating down through the air was actually pleasant. Once or twice I hit the ground rather hard, but never as roughly as when I jumped from the truck. I decided that I had no objection whatsoever to the parachute as a means for reaching my zone of operations.

My superiors also must have been satisfied with my progress, for at this time I was made a sergeant. The parachute training was followed by forty days of practice in the arts of destruction, sabotage and counter-espionage. I became so thoroughly indoctrinated with the technique of using explosives that I could hardly look at a bridge without wanting to blow it up.

One night the orders came—I was to have a chance to assuage my newly inculcated thirst for explosions. I was given instructions as to the region in which I was to operate and supplied with false papers, false ration cards, false banknotes and false explanations for the benefit of any curious persons who might come in contact with me.

At 5 p.m. we were called for final briefing. There were four men in our team. We were to be dropped south of Groeningen, where we were to take charge of the resistance forces. We could organize them, train them in the use of modern weapons and prepare them to take their part more effectively in any future operation.

One objection was raised in this briefing session. It was that none of the four of us was acquainted with this particular region. The observation passed without comment. Apparently no one considered it important. The meeting ended with the order to be ready to leave at 7 p.m.

It was about 6.30 p.m. when the fatality which seemed to be trying to keep me out of the war gained one more trick. Word came through that we were not to leave after all. The objection which had apparently been disregarded when we had been briefed was now upheld. Another team, containing men who knew the Groeningen territory, was to take our place. At seven, when we should have been taking off for Holland, it was they who left instead—left in what we thought of, resentfully, as *our* plane.

I was thoroughly dejected. I had prepared so long for this, I had been ready, anxious, keyed up—all for nothing! While others succeeded in getting the fighting fronts, I remained behind, stranded, eternally stranded in England.

I was fed up with this war which would let me have no part in it. I had been trained, over-trained, gone stale with training. The fighting was reserved for the other chaps.

My depression lifted slightly when, after the invasion, I was ordered to Belgium, to join Prince Bernhard's headquarters. It dropped over me again like a wet blanket when I learned what my assignment was to be. I was to stay behind the lines and train Dutch resistance fighters in the Commando tactics I knew. Training again, nothing but training!

But this time I found a means of cheating my undistinguished destiny. Our training included "practical exercises". Having a real enemy handy, there seemed no particular need to carry out the exercises against a theoretical enemy. We used Germans as the foils for our training. We practised by going through the lines and keeping the enemy from getting bored waiting for us. As it was up to me to designate the teams that made these expeditions, I ordered myself out on them.

With some of my resistance fighters, I made a number of excursions into enemy territory in the Brabant and Limburg districts, and began at last to see a little action. As a result, I began to enjoy the war.

These sorties by men who were supposed still to be trainees were not strictly regular, but that did not seem to bother the military authorities, who made me a sergeant-major just the same.

Our operations were carried out from the camp whose location kept life from being dull and, especially, from being quiet. We were so close to the front that we had as neighbour a launching ramp for German V-1 flying-bombs which were being fired from Holland towards England. They went off with a whoosh and a roar which made it hard to believe that we were only on the sending end, not the receiving end, of these formidable missiles. As a matter of fact, we managed to find ourselves sometimes on the receiving end as well.

Located next to us was another noisy neighbour—an artillery battery whose job it was to try to shoot down the V-1's before they picked up too much speed and thus prevent them from hitting London. This was nice for London but occasionally hard on us. Every time one of the shells got a rocket while it was on its way over our heads, we were gratified with a shower of shrapnel from the exploded V-1. We were in the open country but we were enjoying all the delights of the bombing of London.

This periodic peppering with bomb and shell fragments was not sufficient for our happiness, however. We took it into our heads to hunt the V-1's ourselves, popping away at them with small arms as they flew overhead. Our cook got in a beautiful shot with an automatic rifle. It destroyed the rocket, but the rocket returned the compliment to the kitchen. We had to eat cold meals until the cook could get new equipment to replace what his lucky shot had demolished.

A few days later, while we were at lunch—this time the cook has to be exonerated—we received an even more impressive sample of the efficiency of the V-1. The neighbouring battery hit one of the rockets directly over our mess. Usually a hit meant that the rocket exploded in midair and all we had to do was to dodge the metal fragments which came showering down. This time the battery brought the rocket down so adroitly that it didn't explode until it hit our roof.

Once again there was an impressive amount of broken tableware to be seen, but I didn't see it. For the second time in my life, an explosion had blinded me.

CHAPTER V

Chaos in Indonesia

It was three weeks before I recovered my sight and five months before I was fit for service again. My convalescence was hastened by my pleasure in receiving a commission as lieutenant; but it seemed likely that that would be the end of my military career. The war was drawing to a close and although I had been a casualty in it, I did not feel that I had seen much of it. It was finished in Europe. Would I get back into the fight in time to help end it in Asia?

It seemed that I would at the beginning of July, when I left England on a special plane for a special mission in the Far East. But the planes which carried the atomic bombs were faster than mine. I was still in Colombo, a member of Force 136, when the Japanese surrendered on August 14th.

While the world was joyfully celebrating the end of hostilities, I was plunged into gloom. My thirst for adventure had not been sated. The taste I had had of war was only sufficient to stimulate my craving for excitement. And now it was definitely too late. Hostilities were over, peace had come, the world would settle down to a quiet, tranquil, humdrum existence again, welcome no doubt to most of its inhabitants, but intensely boring to a nature like mine, which demanded excitement, activity, danger.

I overestimated the capacity of the world for peace. The official war was over, but in the part of the world where I found myself, unofficial hostilities were just beginning. It was to be my curious destiny to begin really to wage war, to put into full use at last the training destined for use in war, only after the war was over—or theoretically over.

Sitting becalmed—I thought—in Colombo, I did not even suspect what area was to give me all the adventure I desired. It began about a thousand miles to the east, across the Indian Ocean, and ran eastward for about 2,500 miles more—the mysterious, distorted, luxuriant archipelago of the Netherlands East Indies, the Spice Islands of the early navigators, source of rubber and oil for our modern industrial civilisation which these islands had served but of which they had not become a part. For me, their romantic names—Sumatra, Java, Borneo, the Celebes, the Moluccas, Bali, Timor, Amboina—were still only names, the names of places, vaguely unreal, placed on authentic maps but still, it seemed, in another world, a world the average Westerner hardly hopes to discover for himself.

Yet I was to discover this world and to find it the land of my destiny.

Peace came like a conflagration to the Dutch East Indies. After their capture by the Japanese, order had been maintained, but with the Japanese surrender that order began to break down. There was no authority to take its place. Anarchy became the order of the day. The Japanese did not attempt to check the marauding bands which formed spontaneously in the confusion of the end of the war. On the contrary, they supported and encouraged many of them.

For the surrender, in this far-flung territory, distant from the occupiers' capital and even more so from the victors' homeland, had curious and confused results. This was no case of a surrendering authority handing over intact to its conqueror the organisations and forms for the continuous maintenance of public order; it was a case of the collapse of the old system for the preservation of order, and a new system could only be established by conquering the forces of disorder. The Allies, with the surrender of Japan, had ended the need for fighting any longer against the Japanese Army—officially, at least—but in the Dutch East Indies the fight was far from over. The prize had been conceded, but still had to be won. The party giving it up was not handing it over, but simply dropping it into a mêlée of conflicting forces from which it had still to be snatched.

No doubt, in spite of the repercussions of the surrender, the Japanese could have maintained order if they had wanted to, so as to permit unopposed landings of Allied forces, to whom the authority could then have been turned over, but they did not want to. The Japanese had no intention of making things easy for the Allies.

Their reactions to the surrender were diverse. In some sectors, Japanese officers simply refused to believe the news. They were far from home, it was difficult to reach all of them with irrefutable evidence that Japan had surrendered and that their orders were to submit to the Allies, and it was possible for them to maintain that what reports did reach them were an Allied ruse to trick them into accepting a Japanese capitulation which had never occurred. Then there were the bitter-enders who believed that even if Japan had surrendered, Japanese forces would still hold out, independently, in territories such as those they held. And, finally, there were those to whose methods the others were sooner or later to rally in practice, who saw an opportunity to wrest political victory from the jaws of military defeat. Their armies had been beaten, but the ideology which those armies had served might still gain the day. Conquered, they still plotted to leave the islands as conquerors. If they themselves could not hold them, they could leave a situation which would make it impossible for the Europeans to hold them either.

They had already found a popular slogan in "Asia for the Asiatics". During the war, the other peoples of Asia had been given reason to suspect that this meant "Asia for the Japanese." But now the Japanese were going. Should they accept meekly the return of their islands to the sovereignty of the white colonists? A vacuum in authority was about to occur, and this was their chance to move into it. "Asia for the Asiatics" might now mean Indonesia for the Indonesians and not for the Japanese.

The Japanese encouraged this tendency, which could prevent the prize they were being forced to give up from being acquired by their enemies. They also encouraged more violent developments. They wanted bloodshed, they wanted terror, they wanted excesses and outrages, so that a hatred would develop between natives and Europeans too fierce and too bitter for reconciliation ever to be possible.

The native movements of opposition to a simple return to the *status quo ante* were not limited to what could have been orderly and disciplined organisations for the achievement of independence. The Japanese stirred up hate against the whites, encouraged the formation of terrorist bands to take "revenge" on their former governors, and refrained from restraining their ravages. There were groups which had a special interest in opposing any peaceful entry of the Allies, because they had collaborated with the Japanese under the occupation. There were gangs led or partly constituted of Japanese deserters. There were hordes of fanatics who looked upon the crusade against Europeans as a sort of holy war. There were the bandits who emerge in in any time of disorder, when police power fails, ordinary criminals, riff-raff without political motives, inspired only by the chance to rob, murder and rape with impunity.

The peaceful people of Indonesia, the great majority of the population, which wanted only an end to fighting and a chance to start living their quiet industrious pre-war life again, were certainly victims of the pillaging and raiding bands the Japanese permitted to roam about the country unchecked, but their first and most helpless targets were the European prisoners. The civilians in the Japanese prison camps, men, women, children and old people, were already in a miserable state from hunger and from the brutality of guards whose favourite means of reproving prisoners was to break their arms or legs. With the Japanese surrender they were at last able to look forward to freedom, but they were instead suddenly exposed to attacks by mobs of howling fanatics, who massacred them without resistance from the Japanese guards—these last having no interest in taking risks for the sake of their charges, even assuming they were not in a plot to let themselves be "overpowered" and their prisoners murdered.

It was no easy problem for the Allies, with limited forces in this area, to get control of the situation in time to save the prisoners. In so widespread an area, even the establishment of an unopposed police force would have required large numbers of men. But it was not an insoluble problem. Though it was perhaps no easy job to gain control of the entire archipelago, we did have the means to save the prisoners and there were enough ways in which they might have been done.

For some unknown reason, no really serious effort was made to rescue these unfortunate victims of the war. If these strange tactics were part of some calculated plan, if thousands of prisoners were deliberately left in the hands of our enemies, it must be admitted that those tactics were effective. Their continued presence in the prison camps provided the Indonesians with a powerful weapon in the political struggle which was to follow. The threat which hung constantly over these unfortunate pawns in the bloody game which was being played in Indonesia constituted a means of pressure which terrorists could hardly be expected to be too scrupulous to employ.

So these hapless people remained confined, at the mercy of the many lawless and uncontrollable, or at any rate un- controlled, forces which were devastating the country about them—the guerrillas, the terrorists, the bandits and still, at this period, the Japanese. To these last, Lord Mount- batten, speaking as representative of the conquerors to the conquered, could theoretically issue orders; but he had few means of enforcing them.

Against this chaotic background, the Republic of Indonesia had its birth. Three days after the Japanese surrender, on August 17th, 1945, a Javanese engineer named Sukarno proclaimed the Republic and on the following day was named its President.

Sukarno had not taken this step without persuasion. His own desire had been less to push himself forward than to go into hiding. The coming of the Allies boded no good for him. He had in 1943 first paid a visit to the Japanese South Pacific Commander, Marshal Terauchi, at Saigon, and had then gone on to Tokio where he was received by the Mikado. With the news of the Japanese surrender, Sukarno went into hiding near Batavia. There he was ferreted out by a group of Communists and fellow-travelling students, who brought him to Batavia by force. On the way, their twisted daggers were brought into play, and it was with a kriss at his throat that Sukarno agreed to proclaim the Republic.

He must have been surprised himself at the later gains of a movement which he initiated with so little enthusiasm.

The Republic had hardly been announced when the confusion, disagreements and cross purposes which various nations and individuals were to demonstrate in regard to the Indonesian Republic first made themselves apparent. On September 3rd, Lord Mountbatten ordered the Japanese to dissolve the Republic immediately and on the 28th he followed this up by forbidding them to hand over the authority in Java to any political party.

The Japanese did nothing.

On the 28th September British troops landed at Batavia, and while General Sir Philip Christison was referring to the Sukarno government as the "de facto" authority, Vice Admiral Patterson was declaring that it would not be acknowledged. When the Dutch representative Dr. H. J. van Mook stated that he was willing to talk with Sukarno on the relation of Indonesia to the Kingdom of the

Netherlands, the Dutch government immediately disavowed the statement.

On October 20th, British troops landed at Semarang and on October 25th at Surabaya. Heavy fighting occurred after the second landing and General Mallaby was murdered by Indonesians in Surabaya. The British had now made landings at three points in Java, accompanied by statements that they had no interest in non-British territories and that Britain recognized no authority but the Dutch, but Dutch troops were still being kept out.

The Dutch government had sent a brigade to Singapore to take part in any landings, and thus provide a token force, at least, to signify the re-establishment of Dutch sovereignty. The Allied command did not appear nearly as interested as the Dutch, despite the statements made in London, in this gesture being made. For some time the Dutch troops were held on land, and when they were finally embarked in warships, they found themselves cruising idly back and forth along the shores of the archipelago, while British forces alone made the three landings in Java. Finally, on November 19th, the Allied command forbade the landing of Dutch troops "to prevent complications". The Netherlands brigade was returned to Singapore.

Although the motives may have been different, everyone seemed in agreement to keep the Dutch out of the Dutch East Indies. The Japanese and the Russians, the Americans and the English, the Australians and the Indonesians all demonstrated, by words or actions, their agreement in this policy. Whatever the reasons for this position, its practical result was to prevent Holland from regaining the possession of a territory which before the war had produced great riches and which had often been described as a model colony.

The first landings had been made in Java. But the much larger island of Sumatra, whose situation was particularly interesting to the British, since it lay just across the narrow strait of Malacca from their own Malay States, was still inviolate. Preparations were under way for a landing in Sumatra, but it seemed likely to be a difficult operation.

The Japanese were showing themselves hostile to acceptance of their government's capitulation and terrorism was increasing daily. The gentle inhabitants of this rich and peaceful island were exposed to bandit depredations, while the European prisoners of the Japanese were in daily danger of massacre.

It seemed essential to get someone into Sumatra ahead of the Allied forces. That was my first mission.

CHAPTER VI

By Parachute to Sumatra

The first Allied soldiers to enter Sumatra after the Japanese capitulation were a team of five parachutists who were dropped at Medan, in north-east Sumatra, to prepare the way for the Allied landings. This is the happiest part of Indonesia, the country of the great tea and tobacco plantations. It did not impress our first envoys, however, as a complete paradise. Hardly had they landed, than they called for help. The Japanese, they reported, had adopted a menacing attitude, and terrorist bands were roaming the countryside, burning, robbing and killing.

The answer to this call for help was the dispatching of myself with four men, also by parachute. My second in command, an English captain, theoretically outranked me, but because of my special training and my nationality, in practice I was chief of the team. It was not much of a force to control a territory pillaged by lawless bands, in which the Japanese, who had surrendered on paper, still seemed undecided as to whether they should really give up. But my instructions were to organise a native police force of two hundred men and with them to take control of Medan just before the disembarkment of the Allied Landing Forces.

We were dropped on the airfield of Medan. The men of the first team were there waiting for us. Also waiting were several officers of the Japanese general staff. They might have come to meet us, or even to ask for orders, as the conquered's greeting to the conquerors. But they made no move to greet us, and their expressions were by no means welcoming. Their manners were entirely correct but at the same time very cool. So were ours.

"What are they doing here?" I asked one of the men who had preceded us.

"They have come to make sure you didn't bring any arms," he answered.

I glanced uneasily upward, to the cases winging below the parachutes which our plane had just discharged after us. Half of them I knew, should contain arms, the other half be filled with food and cigarettes.

One of the parachutes failed to open, and its burden dropped rapidly a few feet from us. As it approached the ground, the Japanese officers hurried towards it. At the shock of landing, the container broke. There was an explosion of cigarettes. I breathed again.

I set up my headquarters in the Deboor Hotel, the most comfortable in Medan. Here the Japanese were polite enough to evacuate a whole floor for us. I quickly discovered that they had also pushed politeness so far as to surround us with guards, who might have been explained, no doubt, as having been provided for our protection, but who seemed principally interested in spying on everything we did.

The day after my arrival I took a walk through Medan to become acquainted with the city. I found it a charming place, with many handsome villas set in brilliant flower-gardens. But against this beautiful background, the general misery and disorder were thrown into the greater relief.

The Japanese army seemed to have given itself over to pillage. Everywhere Japanese soldiers were carting furniture out of the houses and loading it into lorries. Some of them stopped in their task to salute as I passed, in accordance with the orders that had been given them. Others stared at me insolently, apparently hoping that I would object and thus provoke an incident. I ignored them.

I came across one band of pillagers which was being directed by an officer.

"Why are you taking the furniture out of these houses?" I asked.

"Orders from Headquarters," he said. "We are making room for your troops."

"Do you think our men are coming in carrying their furniture on their backs?" I asked him.

I filed an energetic protest against the pillaging and it stopped—at least in the neighbourhood of my hotel.

I noticed that the sight of the uniform which I wore provoked two completely opposed reactions from two different sections of the population. The *tani*, the Indonesian peasant who works his own land, was happy to see me. I represented the end of the war, the end of terrorism, the return to the orderly tranquil life he desired. Many a peasant stopped in the street to smile at me, joining his hands in the Oriental salutation and bowing to me in greeting. The little merchants, chiefly Chinese, also showed they were glad to see me. As the herald of their deliverance.

In contrast, the small group of semi-intellectuals who maintained a continuous violent activity in the city were quite as demonstrative in the opposite sense. They glared at me with hatred as I approached and then spat on the ground in sign of contempt.

Medan was in the grip of terror. The Japanese were maintaining only a semblance or order, and in secret were giving arms to the terrorists.

The basis of the terrorist bands were the militiamen whom the Japanese had been using for the last three years to police their fellow-countrymen. Having oppressed their fellows in the name of the Japanese and committed every outrage and excess under the protection of the occupying power, these militiamen were both hated and feared by the population. They could not expect forgiveness either from their own people or from the incoming Allies. It was thus to their interest to prevent the establishment of order, and the functioning of an effective police force, whose first task would inevitably be their own suppression. They were doomed by their past records to become outlaws, and outlaws was what they had become. It was with joy that the Japanese afforded these bandits the means to continue harassing the enemy before whom they had themselves been obliged to bow.

The worst of these terrorists were mere boys. The Japanese had taken youths of twelve and thirteen, recruited them into their militia formations, and made fanatics of them. The very names of their groups were indications of the reckless, ruthless character which it had been easy to stamp upon these youngsters of an impressionable age. One of them called itself the "Death Battalion". Another was the "Suicide Company".

Some of these unscrupulous, unmanageable bands were being converted into the instruments of extremist parties, and were increasing their membership by taking in adherents of these groups. Some became affiliated with the *Tentara Keamanan Rakjat*, the People's Army—but its actions were no boon to the people. Others attached themselves to the P.K.I.—the Indonesian Communist Party.

So, building up my own force, trying to keep an eye on everything, taking frequent walks throughout the region to see for myself what was going on, I moved through this convulsed society.

One day, during one of my explorations, I saw smoke and flames in the direction of the airfield. I hurried towards it, wondering what could have happened. Was it a plane burning? Or a hangar?

It was a bonfire. A Japanese bonfire. Japanese soldiers were busy feeding the flames. They were feeding it with a curious sort of fuel.

What was burning was a great pyre of packages of banknotes—Indonesian occupation florins. The soldiers were tossing sheaf after sheaf of bills into the flames. There must have been tens of millions of dollars burning there.

I stood there watching. I could have intervened. I could have carried away as much money as I wanted. But

I supposed that what was burning was worthless paper, the money of the conquered, which would no longer be honoured. Tomorrow it would be replaced by the solid currencies of the Allies. So I watched the banknotes burn. I was young and foolish. I let the money burn and took no action, merely reporting this Japanese action to the proper authorities.

I was only twenty-four and inexperienced. I had not yet learned one of the lessons of war—that the institutions of the conquered often survive the arrival of the conquerors. I was to discover later that the Japanese occupation currency would remain good throughout the archipelago for a long time to come. And even when it was at last called in, it was exchanged for native florins. By standing idly by and watching that money burn, I lost a chance to change the course of history. In January 1950, I was to fail to capture the capital of Java for the lack of a few hundred weapons, purchasable with a few thousand dollars. I could have carried away in my pockets enough money to have made the difference, in that attempt, between failure and success.

Fires were no unusual sight in Medan those days, though money was not their usual fuel. Every night the sky was red with the light of burning villages. Every night the staccato crack of machine-guns could be heard in the region about Medan. The terrorists were everywhere, falling on peaceable *kampongs*, or native villagers, shooting down the inhabitants, pillaging their dwellings and finally putting the torch to them before taking flight. Even the palace of the Sultan of Delhi was half destroyed by fire.

Bloodshed and anarchy were the order of the day. No one was safe. The Chinese and the Hindus in particular were robbed, tortured, their daughters carried away and raped. Even in Medan itself, there was no security.

Not far from my hotel lived a Swiss family, the Thielles, who, because of their neutral nationality and their personal popularity, had not been put in concentration camps with the other Europeans, and had never been the object of any sort of persecution or annoyance either by the Japanese or the natives. One morning I was summoned hastily at my hotel to come to the Thielles. Something had happened there.

I crossed the street, in the middle of this smiling seemingly safe and civilised city, and I saw at once why I had been sent for. From under the door flowed a thick red viscous liquid. It was blood. It took a great deal of blood to form the tell-tale stream which was oozing under that door.

I pushed the door open and entered. The whole Thielle family (with the exception of one daughter who had not been home at the time) was there—or what remained of it: a pile of little lumps of bleeding shapeless human flesh. It was the first time I had seen the result of a form of torture killing widely known in the Far East—the cutting of victims, alive, into the smallest possible pieces.

CHAPTER VII

The Flag Stays Up

We were still awaiting landings in Sumatra when I received a radio message from the Headquarters of Force 136, in Colombo. I was asked if I could find out what had happened to the Dutch General Over Akker. Interned in a prison camp by the Japanese, he had organised a resistance movement there and had consequently been transferred to a regular prison. Since then there had been no news of him.

I set out therefore for Japanese headquarters, taking with me as interpreter a half-caste who spoke Japanese. The Japanese had plenty of English-speaking officers, but it pleased them to pretend that none of them understood English.

Once at headquarters, I asked for the major who commanded the prison where Over Akker had been sent. I was led into a hall where the Japanese officers were holding a banquet, celebrating one of their national holidays. The *sake* (rice wine) had been flowing freely, and most of the banqueters seemed in an ugly mood.

The prison director was a fat slug of a man with the neck of a bull. He rose and glared at me insolently while the interpreter put my request. Behind him several other Japanese officers got up too and tried to stare me out of countenance.

The major said a few words in Japanese and then took hold of him by the wrist. The interpreter turned an embarrassed and apologetic face towards me.

"He says for you to come back tomorrow," he explained. "As for me, I'm invited to stay."

It seemed a moment admirably suited to the direct methods I had learned as a Commando.

My fist connected with the major's jaw and he landed on the floor some feet away. His aide, one of the group just behind the fallen major, sprang towards me. I rolled him under the table just behind his superior officer and clapped my hand to my revolver. The others immediately decided to pass over the little incident as a good joke all around.

Miraculously, several of the officers present suddenly discovered they could speak English and used this language to offer excuses for their colleague. They attributed his unfriendliness solely to the effects of the *sake*.

I didn't bother with their excuses. I grabbed the major, who still had no very clear idea of what was going on around him, by the collar, dragged him outside, packed him into my car and went off to the prison with him to conduct my investigation.

I found General Over Akker—but only on the prison records. He had been decapitated.

He was luckier than many. Having one's head cut off was a quick death—more merciful than the sort of thing that had happened to the Thielles for instance. And many occupants of the Japanese prisons and prison camps died horribly when their places of confinement were attacked by

terrorists against whom the Japanese had no intention of
defending them.

Yet sometimes curious things happened. In another
prison, a young man who was later to become my right
hand man, Sergeant Colson, had his life saved by the
Japanese—only incidentally, it is true, and not with any
intention of serving anyone but themselves. Yet the fact
remained that but for the Japanese I would never have had
the services of Colson.

A Dutch officer, he was shut up in a cell with a number
of other prisoners, in the most horrible circumstances.
They were all half-dead from starvation, their bodies were
covered with ulcers and they were suffering from all the
maladies which privation and hardship engender. Although
the Japanese surrender had taken place, they were nevertheless kept imprisoned and at the mercy of the vanquished,
who made no attempt to alleviate their torturing regime.

One day, a band of terrorists attacked the jail. The
Japanese offered no resistance. Instead they opened the
gates to the bandits, let them help themselves to arms and
urged them cordially on to the massacre of the defenceless
prisoners. Their treachery was repaid in kind. The terrorists,
having taken the arms of the Japanese guards, locked them
into a courtyard and promised to return to kill them as soon
as they had disposed of the Europeans. They passed from
cell to cell, pulling open the doors, and pumping machine-
gun bullets into the bodies of the prisoners, many of them
so ill that they could not even move or make the slightest
gesture of defence.

The Japanese, in desperation, began boosting and hoisting
one another to the top of their surrounding wall, where,
arming themselves with bricks torn from it, they bombarded
the terrorists with these, the only weapons they had left,
although their opponents had automatic firearms. But the
terrorist bands were not usually valiant in the face of resistance, their speciality being murdering the unresisting.
Under the hail of bricks, they ran away. Those prisoners
whose cells had not yet been reached were thus saved—

and among the fortunate survivors was my future aide, Colson.

But this was a highly exceptional case. Throughout the Dutch East Indies, prisoners who were looking forward hopefully to release after years of confinement, were being murdered by hundreds. In Java alone, during this period, three thousand Dutch and Anglo-Saxon prisoners had been killed and the butchery was only beginning. It seemed to me that one of my most urgent tasks was to get European prisoners to safety before the terrorists could assassinate them. This was more easily said than done.

There were, for instance, in eastern Sumatra, three camps whose inmates I wanted to bring into Medan, where we would be better able to protect them. They were located at Pakanbary, Ronaprapat and Sihantar, ranging from seventy to a hundred and forty miles from Medan.

As one of the representatives of the victorious powers, I was authorized to issue orders to the Japanese. I could have told them to bring the prisoners to Medan under the protection of their arms. But I knew very well what would happen. The Japanese might indeed have organized convoys for the transport of the prisoners—only to let the terrorists know when and by what route the convoys were to pass. The terrorists would have attacked, and, after firing a few shots in the air in token resistance, the Japanese would have permitted themselves to be "overpowered" and the men, women and children, the infirm and the sick from the prison camps would have been horribly murdered.

This was no mere supposition but had already happened, several attempts made in Java to bring prisoners to safety under Japanese escort having been defeated in this fashion.

I should point out here that not all of the Japanese behaved in this manner. There were areas in which they did their best to protect convoys removing prisoners from the camps. But I dared not trust the lives of these persons, for whom I was responsible, to the chance that the Japanese in the Medan region might be co-operative, as they had been in some places, rather than hostile, as they had been in others. I had my reasons for not depending in this case on the dubious benevolence of the Japanese.

I felt that it was necessary that we should bring the prisoners to safety ourselves, without the "co-operation" such as it might be, of the Japanese. But how? My efforts to form a native police force were being only very slowly rewarded. It was understandable that volunteers were hesitant about coming forward from this terrorised population, surrounded by Japanese and bandits, against whom there were exactly nine of us to protect them. True, Allied forces were due to land later, but potential volunteers could be excused for doubting whether they would survive as long as that.

Moreover, with the exception of the few pistols we had brought with us, we had no arms for those few volunteers who were beginning to join us. I had asked the Japanese for weapons, but they took the attitude, legally irreproachable, that as they were still responsible for maintaining order, they had to keep them to be surrendered later to the official Disarmament Commission, when it arrived for the formal ceremony of the transmission of power.

This was correct enough but while they were thus solemnly protesting to us the impossibility of failing in this duty of keeping their arms until the future arrival of the Commission, they were opening the doors of their arsenals nightly to the guerrillas who raided them to take the very arms which were denied to us. The bandits would arrive in lorries, and the Japanese sentinels fire a few shots into the air for the benefit of anyone within hearing, thus establishing the fact that they had resisted. Thereupon they leaned their rifles against the walls, conducted their "attackers" to the gun racks and watched tranquilly while they loaded their lorries with weapons and drove away.

If this was the way to get arms, I decided, two could play at that game.

A few nights later, a group of terrorists were treated to a surprise. They had carried out a raid on a Japanese arsenal and were driving triumphantly along in their loaded lorries when the headlights struck suddenly on a tree which had apparently fallen across the road. The driver jammed on the brakes, the lorry came to a halt and the guerrillas piled out to remove the obstacle.

At this moment, half a dozen of us leaped out of the ditches at the sides of the road where we had been hiding and attacked. Half a dozen shots were enough to put the terrorists to flight. We moved the obstacle we had put on the road, climbed into the lorry, and drove off.

After this operation had been repeated a few times, we began to have a fairly substantial stock of arms. This indirect disarming of the Japanese worked excellently. The terrorists got the weapons from the Japanese and we got them from the terrorists.

We still did not have enough men, however, nor were they well enough equipped to evacuate hundreds of prisoners from the three camps and escort them the considerable distance to Medan. Moreover, the matter was getting urgent. I had been building up my force as quietly as possible, for it was necessary not to show my hand until I had sufficient strength to keep control of the situation. If I had let it be known that I intended to move the prisoners, it would have been equivalent to signing their death warrant. That would have given the terrorists a reason for wiping them out before I could evacuate them. Similarly, my growing strength was dangerous to the prisoners. As long as I was still not able to protect them by force, the nearer I came to being able to do so, openly, the more likely was it that the bandits would try to beat me to it.

There seemed only one way of moving the prisoners to safety, despite the superior numbers and better arms of the terrorists. That was to do it by surprise—to evacuate the prisoners while the terrorists were otherwise occupied. I proceeded to see to it that they would be kept busy for a while.

My great asset in the campaign I was about to undertake was the rivalry and ill feeling among the different bands. They were agreed only on one thing—the European was Enemy Number One. For the moment they seemed to be acting by common accord in massacring the whites, pillaging villages, violating women, attacking Chinese and Hindus, but in the fight for power among themselves, they represented all sorts of clashing tendencies. Some of the former militiamen of the Japanese considered themselves as belonging to the Republican army of Sukarno, others described themselves as Communists—and among these thre were those ready to follow the directions of Soviet Russia, as well as the Trotskyist and the nationalist Communists. There were Mohammedan groups who wanted to make of Indonesia a purely Islamic state. And there were piratical bands which cared nothing at all for any political principles whatsoever, but whose activities, like those of all the others, were camouflaged by the pretext of the struggle for independence.

It was a standing tactic of mine in my activities in Indonesia always to plant my own men in the ranks of the enemy in order to be informed fully from the inside of everything that was going on in the hostile camp. I had my spies in the different groups and they reported to me on the state of mind of the bandits, who seemed dominated usually by a curious mixture of ferocity and childishness, on the conflict among them and on the brushes and incidents which occurred from time to time. My men also procured for me copies of the rubber stamps with which these guerrillas identified their "official" communications—for even those whose sole interest was booty pretended to political motives and gave themselves high-sounding titles.

I then proceeded to dictate a few violently insulting notes which were turned into the native tongue and delivered to the different bands, as if they had been sent to them by their rivals.

It did not occur to any of the recipients of these *billets doux* to doubt their authenticity. Why should they? They were signed with the names they knew as those of the chiefs of rival bands, which they certainly considered unknown to Europeans. They bore the official stamps of the groups from which they were supposed to have emanated. They showed intimate knowledge of incidents supposedly known only to the persons involved. And they carefully prodded certain sore points reported to me by my agents among them. These agents helped also to inflame the anger this exchange of missives aroused. They urged the insulted to take revenge. In no time a lively civil war was going on among the guerrillas, who postponed temporarily the extermination of the whites in an attempt to exterminate each other. By the time they returned to normal, the operation was nearly over. With a handful of men, we had removed practically all the ex-prisoners from the three camps, transported them into Medan without once being attacked, and installed them in a walled enclosure in the centre of the city where a very small force would be sufficient to hold off a considerably larger mob of attackers—particularly such easily discouraged attackers as the terrorists had usually shown themselves to be.

The camp where I had installed the liberated Europeans was more a hospital than anything else. Half of its inmates were suffering from beri-beri. Others had dysentery and hunger *oedema*. Almost all of them were covered with ulcers. Most of the men could hardly stand up. Many of them dragged broken limbs about or had twisted arms or legs, whose bones had grown together again badly after they had been broken by their Japanese jailers. The children were skeletons. Everyone was dressed in shreds of cloth, the merest rags pieced together any old way. The place was a scene of a nightmare.

It was obvious that these people were not going to be able to defend themselves against any attack and I had very little means with which to defend them myself. I had Japanese sentinels posted around the place outside, but I had no confidence in them if the terrorists attacked. I knew they would betray us at the first alarm. My chief trust was placed in the handful of natives I stationed inside the barbed wire, most of them Amboinese, from that Indonesian island whose men are renowned warriors. They were backed by a few of the stronger prisoners. Still the situation remained extremely weak and I thought the best defence was to try to avoid attack at least until a few more of the men could be fed back into the semblance of human beings. It was my intention to remain tactfully quiet, to give the terrorists no provocation, to try to persuade them to forget, if possible, the very presence of this camp in Medan.

In every group, however, there are always a few fools with a gift for suicide. We had them among our ex-prisoners.

Hardly removed from their extremely dangerous position to one that was only slightly less so, some of the European dignitaries—high civil servants or bankers—apparently in their haste to recover their former positions, found nothing better to do than to try to bring new dangers on their heads. The first thing they wanted to do was to hoist the Dutch flag above the camp—the national colours which so far had not been seen again anywhere in Indonesia except on our cars. It would have been an obvious provocation. Having raised them halfway out of the grave, I did not want to see them slide back into it again. My thanks for this service was abuse. It was due to me that they had been removed from an almost fatal situation, but they did not trust my judgment as to the measures necessary to maintain the comparative safety I had won for them. I was a coward. I was not a real Dutchman. I had been born abroad, I wore the British uniform. I wonder that they didn't accuse me of treason.

One day three rather rickety old Dutch gentlemen called on me. They all had high-sounding colonial titles from pre-war days, and they were prepared to be rather stiff with me—as stiff as these lately resuscitated corpses could be.

"We are among Dutchmen here," they told me. "We are on the soil of a Dutch colony. We must fly the Royal colours."

"Can't be done," I said. "You mustn't aggravate the situation unless you have the means of protecting yourselves. We have no such means."

They went away apparently convinced. But in fact they weren't. It was from the Republican guerrillas that I learnt they had put up a pole and hoisted a flag.

A native brought a note to me, which turned out to be an ultimatum. If the Dutch flag were not pulled down at once, the camp would be considered an enemy fortress and would be attacked by Republican forces. All its occupants would be treated as defenders of colonialism—which in less polite words meant, I knew, that they would be slaughtered.

I called in my three worthies and said to them:

"I understand you raised the Dutch flag contrary to my instructions."

One of the old fellows drew himself up as if he were making a speech and said:

"Yes, sir! Her Majesty's flag is flying again over Her Majesty's colony."

I tossed the ultimatum across the desk to him.

They read the ultimatum and turned even paler than their natural colour.

"What are you going to do, Lieutenant?" one of them asked.

"That is what I planned to ask you," I said. "This is your show. You hoisted the flag."

"You won't abandon us to these thugs!" one of them cried indignantly.

"Of course not," I said. "If they attack they will be met. We have half a dozen men, a few rifles and one Bren gun. I suppose they will send a few hundred men with machine guns against us."

The three old chaps started whispering together. Finally one of them spoke up.

"We think under these circumstances," he announced, "that it is advisable to take down the flag. After all, there are the women . . ."

"And the children," one of the others added.

I called an orderly.

"Go to the camp," I said. "Put two armed men at the

flagpole. Their orders are to permit no one to haul down the flag."

I turned to the delegation.

"Gentlemen," I said, "I did not want that flag raised. But since it has been raised it will not be pulled down. It's a question of prestige now."

"Will you let us all be massacred for a question of prestige?" one of them quavered.

"Not at all," I said. "If you are all massacred, it will be against my most determined opposition."

I put a man with our single Bren gun into our car, beside the driver, and kept it rushing about, in and out of the camp, to make it look as though we had a few dozen of them. An old bugle which we dug up was sounded almost continuously from different points of the camp. Our few men were instructed to move about and keep showing themselves from different angles, and those ex-prisoners who were able to move about were given rifles and the same instructions. The whole idea was to make it look from outside as if we had plenty of force to make it unpleasant for any attacker. I knew the terrorists didn't like real resistance.

In fact, the much-feared attack did not take place, though I don't know whether I had called their bluff or they had decided not to call mine. Whether their original threat was a bluff or not, they didn't follow it up. I still don't know whether their ultimatum was a bluff, but I know that my manœuvres were. Fortunately they didn't realise this, so the flag stayed up.

I had a sample a few days later of the kind of operation the terrorists preferred to affronting armed men. A Chinaman and his wife burst into my office one evening with tears in their eyes. They implored my help to recover their daughters, aged nine and eleven, who had been kidnapped and carried off to a neighbouring village, whose location they were able to give me.

Taking two men, I got into our car and we made for the village. When we entered it, we fired a few shots in the air. Militiamen appeared from everywhere and scattered, running. There were only three of us, but that was enough to scare them anyway. Three men with guns were too many for them. Little girls were as far as they dared to go.

Villagers led us to the native hut where the girls had been taken. They were lying on the floor. The younger one was dead. She had been assaulted by practically a whole company, the villagers told us. We drove the other girl to the hospital, where, shortly after her arrival, she died.

CHAPTER VIII

Freezing Out the Dutch

The Allied landings which I had been sent to prepare took place on Sumatra on October 13th, 1945. The British came ashore at Pandang and Medan, on opposite sides of the island, on the same day that they occupied Bandung in Java. It was also on that day that the red and white Republican flag was hoisted over the Medan Post Office. Very few Indonesians were present.

The local population witnessed the arrival of the Allied troops with the greatest relief. To them it meant the end of terrorism, the end of the robbery, rape, murders, extortion and tortures the guerrillas and the bandits had visited upon them ever since the Japanese collapse.

They were doomed to a bitter disappointment. Since the terrorists had guarded themselves from treatment as simple criminals by assuming, as a sort of protective colouring, some political complexion or another—the great majority of the bands represented themselves as a part of the Indonesian Republican army—a systematic campaign against them might have been interpreted as aiding the Dutch, against whom all of them had taken their stand. So they continued to operate with a high degree of impunity. Meanwhile the Dutch troops, which though few would undoubtedly have regarded the situation differently, were being kept out of Indonesia.

It had been assumed almost as a matter of course, before the Allied landings, that one of the first things that the Allies would do would be to arrest Sukarno. It had also been assumed that the militiamen who had been guilty of atrocities during the war in the service of the Japanese would be prosecuted as war criminals.

The first to believe this were the militiamen themselves. Transformed into terrorist bands of the "Republican army", they turned the savagery which they had been exercising against the population towards the new arrivals whom they accepted automatically as their enemies. The first Gurkhas who arrived at Surabaya, in Java, died in flames when the building in which they had barricaded themselves was burned down in the night. Brigadier-General Mallaby was murdered in Surabaya; and several English officers, who had passed an evening at the Society Club with a group of Dutchmen who had escaped from the death camps of the Japanese, were waylaid on their way home by heavily armed fanatics, who killed them by cutting them into the customary small pieces.

It is very hard to make a fair judgment here. Lord Mountbatten's first orders, forbidding all political activity to Sukarno, were sufficiently explicit. But here lay the tragedy: there had been so much high level tension between America and Britain about the liberation of this economically and strategically all-important Pacific area, that Indonesia was in practice left a no-man's-land. In vain the Dutch had requested to let their own planes and experts gather intelligence information about how things were shaping under the effects of Japanese racial incitement. So when Mountbatten threw out his first feelers he found himself confronted by an entirely unexpected situation, and asked for new instructions. These were given by a government entirely new to the job, without any insight into Indonesian affairs, which were in no way comparable to the situation in India.

Challenge to Terror

When the terrorists realized that they had little to fear from the Allies, they abandoned all restraint. The last remnants of the discipline maintained by the Japanese disappeared completely. The soldiers of the Mikado deserted en masse, taking their arms with them, and joined the guerrillas. Acting as instructors, they trained the native terrorists in even more effective tactics of brigandage.

The little people, the *tanis*, the peasants, were in despair, while the merchants, and inhabitants of the cities hardly dared leave their homes. The high hopes which had been placed in the Allies were dashed to the ground. Their coming had been so eagerly awaited as a deliverance, and now that they had arrived, things were worse than ever, and infinitely worse than they had been under the Japanese.

Meanwhile Sukarno's agents in Sumatra were working busily to enlist as many of the terrorist bands as possible as units of the Republican army which would later be called upon, it was assumed, to oppose the return of the Dutch to Indonesia. They gained, indeed, a mass success—perhaps of a nature likely to become a boomerang—when the Communist gangs of the P.K.I. were ordered to join the Republican army. Their tactics were to infiltrate it and gain control of it—in other words, to make of an ostensibly non-Communist Republican army a tool of Communist policy.

In my opinion, this objective was pursued with great success. Whole regions, for instance Eastern Java, fell under the control of Communist officers, theoretically under the orders of the Republican government. Actually, they gave only lip service to the government, and used the official status their affiliation gave them as an aid to their systematic liquidation of the whites and the more prosperous natives and their maintenance of a state of anarchy.

The Republican government of Indonesia, in whose service these men were supposedly enrolled, was powerless to prevent their massacres and extortions. In the regions they controlled, terrorism was the order of the day. The plantations, refineries and industrial installations which it was to the interest of the government to preserve, were

being destroyed. It is my belief that these tactics were
followed on the orders of Moscow, to create a situation
which may make it possible for Indonesia to be proclaimed
some day an out-and-out Communist state—although the
existing government has never shown hostility to the idea.

The excesses of the guerrillas aroused indignation and
disgust among the English and Hindu officers and ranks
in Indonesia, whatever their orders, dictated from above
by high policy, may have been. Sometimes they violated
their instructions against intervening and took individual
initiative against the terrorists; but such acts could be no
more than palliatives for this sorry situation.

One such irregular reaction occurred one evening in
Medan, where there was a barrack of Sikh troops. One
night the Sikhs were aroused by terrified screams. They
learned that the four daughters of an Indian merchant from
Madras had just been kidnapped by a guerrilla band.

Kidnappings of young girls, followed by rape and often
by murder as well, were frequent enough. If the victims
had been whites or natives, no doubt they would have been
left to their fate. But these were Indian girls who had been
attacked under the very noses of Indian troops. Orders or
no orders, the Sikhs were not prepared to stand for it.

Their Hindu colonel woke up the local governor, Tangkoe
Hassan, and told him that if the girls were not returned to
their homes that night, he would not answer for the reaction
of his troops. Two hours later they were brought back
unharmed.

They were the lucky ones, for they had benefited by a
protection not offered to many. How many Indonesians,
half-castes, whites, who did not enjoy the same luck, were
obliged to suffer whatever torments their ravishers chose
to inflict upon them! And yet how easy, as this incident
proved, would it have been to protect the helpless against
their persecutors!

But it was an epoch of utter madness. As though the
local terrorists were not bad enough, the Chinese Communists whom the British had driven out of the Malay

States crossed the straits to join them. Like Sukarno's Republicans, they had no ties with the natives of Sumatra and no scruples about martyrising them. For those unacquainted with Indonesia it is important to realise that this is by no means a unified region, and that Sukarno, even assuming his contestable right to speak for Java, where he had proclaimed his Republican government, had no title to speak for Sumatra.

Long before the Dutch conquest, the people of Sumatra had suffered from Javanese tyranny. Inhabitants of a very different island, with traditions of their own, they had always been hostile to Java. The establishment of a Republic in Java did not strike them, therefore, as a move towards liberation for themselves. It was rather a promise to replace domination by the Dutch with domination by the Javanese. Of the two, many of them no doubt preferred the Dutch, who had established in the East Indies what was often regarded as a model colony and who could be counted on to protect them from such outrages as those with which they were now only too familiar.

Dealing with a population already unfriendly, the Republican leaders, sent from Java by Sukarno to rally the guerrillas to the Republican flag, saw no necessity to concern themselves with the misfortunes of the people. Indeed, they considered terror their only means of subjecting them to the control of the Indonesian Republic. Daily the number of raids, of cases and rape and murder increased. Sumatra, like the greater part of Indonesia for that matter, was plunged into a state of bloody anarchy.

With an apparent lack of vigilance the British stood aside in Sumatra and elsewhere, allowing chaos to develop and indiscriminate killing to go on, notably of Eurasians—between whom and the pure-bred natives they made, curiously enough, no distinction. I should not like to nail down responsibility. Quite possibly the British Government never knew exactly what was happening, but this much is certain: the authorities in Singapore and in the Malay States had every interest to see prosperity restored. In adjoining

Freezing Out the Dutch

Sumatra, Indonesia's richest island, huge stocks from the Dutch estates were available, which for almost two years the crippled Japanese merchant navy had been unable to handle. Chinese merchants began to aid smuggling on the vastest scale, payment as often as not being made in the weapons which were to be had for next to nothing out of Japanese dumps, but for which the extremists gladly paid top prices in rubber, tobacco, etc. . . .

There was no normal commerce in either Java or Sumatra. The terrorists were simply seizing the crops—latex, tobacco, tea—and smuggling them into the free port of Singapore, where they were bartered for arms and ammunition. It was excellent business for the Malay States. The stocks of arms which the Japanese had left in Malaya were sold to the Indonesian terrorists at fancy prices. Arriving by the junk load in Sumatra, they enabled the terrorists the more easily to raid farms and plantations and steal more crops. These robbers, given official status by the Republican government, were building up enormous fortunes, and so of course were their opposite numbers in the Malay States.

Thus an end was being put to the old rivalry between Indonesia and Malaya, and the Dutch, kept out of their former islands while they were thus being pillaged, were at last paying for the long monopoly which they had enjoyed for three centuries in the exploitation of the fantastic riches of the Spice Islands.

The Australians showed themselves no less indifferent to any return of order in Indonesia, although they must have known that order was a first condition to make emancipation on a Philippine basis possible. The slogan among some sections of them became "Ditch the Dutch", not a very loyal slogan, considering that the Dutch authorities, by flatly refusing to give any preference to Japan, notably concerning oil, once World War II had started, and declaring war upon Japan on their own accord immediately after Pearl Harbour, had drawn the first attack upon themselves. But whatever the merits of these arguments, the Australians declared themselves, first at Singapore, then in Java and finally at Lake Success, violent opponents of the "capitalists of Amsterdam"; while on a more practical plane they sold arms to Sukarno and constituted themselves advocates of his Republic. If today the nature of his régime has begun to frighten them, and tomorrow they find it replaced by the Communism of which it is the fore-runner, they will have only themselves to thank. They will have been among the artisans of that structure.

Another factor which worked for Sukarno was the position of the British in India. Faced with a Hindu nationalism which felt a natural sympathy for the Indonesian nationalism which Sukarno appeared to represent, the British may have thought it preferable not to exasperate the Indian Congress Party by opposing its favourites in Indonesia.

Up to the end of 1946 America adopted a neutral attitude, the trust President Roosevelt had put in Queen Wilhelmina, when she gave her royal word as to Indonesia's emancipation (her so-called Pearl Harbour speech), being still felt. But as the smuggling of arms out of Japanese dumps in Malaya and in Indonesia itself went on and the extremists continued in their opposition to any agreement, however reasonable, public opinion in the States started to change.

With the English landings in Sumatra, I assumed that my mission in Sumatra was over. But Brigadier-General Kelly, who was in command of the forces which had landed in the island, asked me to continue to work with the Counter-Intelligence Service.

In spite of their easy-going attitude to the guerrillas, the Allied forces could not ignore completely the acts of terrorism which were committed under their very noses, particularly when these acts were directed specifically against English officers.

CHAPTER IX

Capture of the Terakan

It was not surprising, in the face of this mildness of the English, that terrorism continued to mount in Sumatra. Emboldened by the perseverance of the British in turning the other cheek, the guerrillas took to attacking Allied soldiers themselves. Shots were fired daily against British jeeps. Perhaps the loss of several English lives could have been traced directly to the effect on the terrorists of examples of lenience.

But even British patience is not inexhaustible. When several British officers and soldiers were murdered one after another and the crimes traced to the same band, it was too much. The leader of the band was known. He was a Terakan—that is to say, half-Chinese, half-Japanese—and his headquarters were in a *kampong*, or native village, near Medan. His arrest was ordered.

But planning to arrest the Terakan and succeeding in the attempt were two different matters. The *kampong* was in difficult jungle country, which the Terakan never left. He sent his men out on their sniping and raiding expeditions, but stayed behind himself, the entire village area being guarded day and night. If anyone approached, tom-toms gave warning of the arrival of an intruder while he was still miles away. At night, luminous signals were used as well.

Ordinary methods of getting the Terakan proved useless. Although the British shelled the whole village, as usual it was only the innocent who suffered, and the British objective was still unattained. It was the arrest of one man they desired and that one man seemed uncapturable.

One day, an English major came to my office and put the problem before me.

"How can we get hold of this fellow?" he asked.

61

Challenge to Terror

"Order me to arrest him," I said. "I'll have him for you in twenty-four hours."

"How are you going to go about it?"

"I'll just go and get him," I said.

The major roared with laughter.

"I'll bet you a bottle of Scotch you won't get him before tomorrow night," he said.

"I'll take that bet," I said. "Come here for dinner tomorrow."

I hadn't guaranteed to produce the Terakan in twenty-four hours blindly. I knew what I was talking about. I made it my business to have my men planted everywhere, to keep me thoroughly informed about the movements of everyone against whom we might have to act. I had one spy in the Terakan's own *kampong*, which was only five miles from Medan. He was a Batak warrior of Sumatra, whom I had provided with some trade goods and sent into the Terakan's village to reconnoitre on the pretence of being interested only in trade. He had visited it several times and knew all about the place—most important, he knew which hut the Terakan slept in.

The ordinary method of trying to arrest the Terakan would have been to take a squad of men and march towards the village. Long before they reached it, the tom-toms would have informed the Terakan of the size of the party, the direction to take to avoid it, and any other information necessary to enable him to be elsewhere when the squad arrived. I knew that a descent in force would be worse than useless. This was a job for a small party, the fewer the better, and it could succeed only if we could reach the village without being seen on the way.

I selected two men to go with me—the spy who knew the village and a Madrassy. We put on black clothes and blackened our faces and our hands. The purpose was not only to make it difficult to see us in the dark. We were also disguising ourselves as "spirits of the night".

Indonesians are afraid of the dark. They believe that after the dark, the spirits of the night come out, evil demons

whom it is wiser for men—especially guilty men—to avoid.
Even the terrorists, in spite of the advantage the dark
gave them in their attacks, seldom operated long after the
sun went down or long before it came up. The later we
worked, the less likely were we to meet anyone. And if
we did come upon someone unexpectedly, the fearsome
spectacle we offered would help to strike terror into his
soul—and paralyze his reactions just long enough. We
would not need long to tranquillize him.

We expected to have to do some tranquillizing, for we
knew that sentinels were always posted about the village
and the Terakan's hut. But it had to be done silently.
Therefore we took as our chief weapons a dagger, a bottle
of chloroform and handcuffs. We did also have a pistol and
a hand grenade, but we hoped we would not have to use them.

From the reports of my informer, I knew that the *kampong*
was heavily guarded except on one side, where it was
protected by an "impassable" swamp. I proposed to cross
the swamp. I had learned in my Commando training that
for those who know how to go about it, impassable ground
virtually does not exist.

I must admit that this swamp came pretty close to it.
It would have been easier to cross by daylight, when I
could have had the help of my eyes in spotting a solid lump
of soil here, a supporting root there. But we crossed it all
the same. We started at nine in the evening, and it was
one in the morning when we reached the other side, only
about half a mile from our starting point. We looked even
more formidable when we emerged from it than we had
before. We had added considerable quantities of evil-
smelling mud to our disguise.

Not too much time remained for we meant to get away
before dawn surprised us. We had avoided most of the
sentinels by going through the marsh, but we knew that
there were three more between us and the Terakan's hut.
Taking care of sentinels is one of the most elementary lessons
a Commando learns. Not one of the three uttered a sound.
I believe in doing a neat job, so we took the trouble to

dump the three bodies into a stream which happened to be handy. It was not only tidiness that impelled me. I did not want unexpected visitors stumbling over dead bodies while I was busy with the Terakan—it might have led them to assume that something out of the ordinary was going on. I also had in mind the psychological effect on the terrorists the next day. They might be impressed by finding a few corpses in their midst, but then they were pretty well hardened to corpses. I figured they would be more impressed by not finding the corpses. Disappearance is more mysterious than murder. It allows the imagination full play, unlimited by known facts.

The dogs were more of a problem than the sentinels. But there is one little trick to keep a dog from barking. You go down on your hands and knees, open your mouth and bare your teeth, and glare at him as if you were a dog yourself. I won't pretend to explain why that keeps a dog from barking. I only know it does.

You can also keep a dog from barking by rubbing yourself with panther grease—if you happen to have any panther grease about you.

Once we were past the swamp, past the sentinels and past the dogs, we had only the Terakan himself to worry about. I expected that to be easy and it was.

I knew for one thing that the Terakan would be alone in his hut. The feeling for caste, for rank is so strong in Indonesia that the leader of a band could not permit a peasant or one of his followers to sleep under the same roof as himself. It would be as unthinkable as for a New York banker to share his bedroom with a pig or half a dozen chickens.

Another advantage is that the natives of this part of the world are heavy sleepers. It is hard to wake one of them even when you want to, and this time that was the last thing I wanted.

I left one of my two men outside the hut, to keep an eye on the surroundings and took the other with me, in case of trouble. But there was no trouble. I doused a rag with chloroform and pressed it over the Terakan's nose and mouth. He made a few instinctive movements, but there were four strong wrists holding him. I doubt if he even woke up. In a few minutes it was clear that he wasn't going to wake up for some little time. I took him on my back and we reached the swamp again without meeting anyone and returned by the route we had taken.

I did not have to carry him all the way. Halfway home, he regained consciousness—to my great relief, but not to his. He found himself surrounded by three Spirits of the Night, or so it seemed to him, who hurried him back to my office where I began questioning him. Perhaps it was because he had received from the groggy state caused by the chloroform sufficiently to realize that he was being interrogated not by avenging spirits but by soldiers in the British service, that he confessed readily, not only to the murders of a number of English officers, but also to a score of other murders, arsons and rapes committed by his hand.

In conducting the questioning, I had him sit down in the fashion customary in native questionings of prisoners—with his legs stretched out straight in front of him. It is not uncommon for prisoners in this country, in their desperation or fear, to make a sudden assault against their jailers. The danger of such an attack is increased by the fact that if you want to get anything out of an Indonesian, you cannot handcuff him or tie his arms—if he cannot use gestures, he simply cannot express himself. You might just as well gag him and then ask your questions.

A man sitting in the ordinary fashion, with his feet planted flat on the floor, can spring from his chair in a single movement. If his legs are stretched out before him, he has to pull them in before he can rise. The difference between a single movement and a double movement is the difference between having the time to counter a sudden attack and not having that time. So I had the Terakan seated in this fashion. Beside him stood my Madrassy with his sword ready in his hand.

It was well that we took this precaution. As the fumes

of the chloroform gradually cleared from his brain, the Terakan suddenly pulled in his legs and bounded at me. My Madrassy was as quick as he was. The naked sword swished through the air as the Terakan rose from the chair. His body brushed against me as it fell, but it was no longer capable of harm. The Terakan's head, neatly severed from his shoulders, took the opposite direction and bumped erratically over the floor. There was one terrorist who would not be released by the British.

I picked up the head which I had to keep for identification, packed it in banana leaves, and stowed it away in a biscuit tin.

My major arrived for dinner. The table was set in my office, where the Terakan had been questioned several hours earlier. We sat down to eat. I said nothing about the terrorist. I waited.

Finally the major grew impatient.

"Well," he said, "where's my bottle of Scotch?"

"I don't owe you any Scotch," I said.

"You don't mean to say you got him?"

"Yes," I said.

"Where is he?"

"Here," I said.

The major looked at me incredulously.

"Here?" he echoed. "Where?"

"In this room."

The major inspected the surroundings again.

"Oh, come, old boy," he said. "You're pulling my leg, aren't you?"

"Not at all," I said. "Look."

I reached under the table, pulled the Terakan's head out of the biscuit tin and put it on the table.

It spoiled his dinner.

The episode of the Terakan was not quite finished. We set out again at two o'clock the next morning (a few hours after a bottle of Black and White had been delivered to me, compliments of the major) and crossed the swamp once more. We had with us a present for the Terakan's band: their leader's head.

It had occurred to me that the disappearance of the Terakan and the three sentinels might be ascribed to a simple desertion by the members of his band. I proposed to demonstrate to them that the Terakan had not departed of his own free will. They could thereafter amuse themselves by making any assumptions they wished about the fate of the sentries. I judged the exercise would be salutary for them. The Terakan had done no good during his life. He might as well serve a worthy purpose after his death, that of a warning to evildoers.

We planted a stake in the middle of the village and on top of it we impaled the head of the Terakan. Beneath it we nailed a polite warning to the members of his band that if they persisted in their evildoing, their heads would join his. Following the nomenclative procedure of the bandits themselves, who loved to operate under such names, I signed the note: "The White Tiger."

Its effect was magical. On the following day, the entire gang cleared out of the *kampong*, leaving it to its original peaceful inhabitants. That evening, the rightful occupants of the village held a little ceremony. Facing the marsh, from which they judged their deliverer had come, they held a sort of thanksgiving service in honour of the White Tiger, that supernatural being who had freed them from the yoke of the Terakan and his bandits.

CHAPTER X

A Price on My Head

There are times when human judgments appear to me to be very strange. I have found myself described as bloodthirsty, tyrannical, oppressive, for having taken such actions as that against the Terakan. What did I do? I killed four men, all murderers. By doing so, I put an end to their crimes, which had hundreds of innocent victims.

67

Challenge to Terror

There are other methods of repression, more commonly followed than mine. It was more in the normal order of things, when terrorists based on a certain village had to be checked, to burn the village or bomb it from the air. The soldiers or airmen who carried out such missions or the officers who ordered them, were not represented as being particularly ferocious characters. They were simply carrying out the duty entrusted to them.

Suppose the case of the Terakan had been handled in this fashion. If the village had been destroyed, there would have been not four deaths, all of guilty persons, but several hundreds, a minority of the guilty plus a majority of the innocent. Yet this would have been a simple police operation, for which no one would have been condemned. For my much milder operations, I was sometimes described as a monster. Was it because I executed personally the measures which I considered necessary? Because I did not shrink from seeing in person, face to face, the human consequences of the execution of those measures? Whatever the reason, I find it difficult to follow the logic of those who condemned me for ending terrorism by executing a few carefully chosen victims who richly deserved their fate, but saw nothing out of the way in a general impersonal holocaust which, because it was impersonal, sacrificed the blameless along with the culprits.

It must be remembered also that in the East it is not the execution itself which impresses and deters other would-be murderers. It is the method of execution. To execute a criminal behind prison walls has absolutely no effect on the population. To execute him in the market place has.

I consider myself that punitive actions levelled against a locality rather than against individuals are not only detestable but impolitic. They cause the population in general to confuse their interests with those of the criminals. Thus when, in retaliation for outrages committed by the Indonesian terrorists, the Allies attacked the area from which they operated, it was as if they said to the inhabitants of that area that they considered them all, bandits and peaceful citizens alike, as included in the same hostile group. As a result the peaceful citizens, attacked together with the bandits, tended to make common cause with them. If the Allies did not discriminate between them, why should they hold themselves aloof from the terrorists? The result of such tactics was to make law-abiding inhabitants of Indonesia detest the forces which were supposed to be those of order.

As evidence that my tactics were better suited to the situation than those automatically adopted in such circumstances by professional military men, I can only offer the esteem in which I was held by the natives. I was safe in Indonesia. I had no need of arms in the most unsettled parts of the country. I went alone, without weapons, into regions considered fatal even for the Japanese.

I proved early that it was possible for a peaceful white man to move with impunity among the natives when I entered Atjeh, reputed as the "country from which no one returns alive", with no other bodyguard than a young half-caste woman! I had been instructed from Colombo to locate all the airfields the Japanese had established during the occupation and to make detailed reports on them. So I posed as a doctor making a tour of inspection of the villages, to ascertain health conditions there. I carried a large supply of medicine, and the young woman who served me as interpreter helped to maintain the fiction by playing the role of nurse. With no other companion I explored this whole region, inhabited by savage warriors usually reputed unapproachable, and returned without having had the slightest adventure.

How did I win the friendship of the Indonesians? First of all, by giving them mine. Did they believe in Indonesia for the Indonesians? So did I. And by that I did not mean, nor did they, Indonesia for the Javanese terrorists.

I did not approach them as a superior being who looked down upon them and intended to mete out justice to them, as I saw it, from above. I met them on their own level and I took the trouble to learn their customs and way of life.

Challenge to Terror

When I entered a native cabin, if they brought me a chair, while the Indonesians sat on the floor, I refused it and took my place on the floor with them. I understood the meaning of the difference. Indonesian society is built upon a pyramid of castes hardly less complicated than that of India. The *tani*, the peasant, must always sit on a lower level than the warriors, the nobles or the intellectuals. By offering me a chair, they were showing a willingness to accept my superiority. By refusing it, I renounced the claim to superiority and made myself one with them. It was a gesture of fraternity which touched them deeply. It made them at once my friends and my allies.

By the same token, when a native came to my office to make a complaint or to ask for help, I always gave him a chair—which the officials of the Republican government claiming to represent the people of Indonesia would never have done. Conversely, when a terrorist came to submit to my authority or to confess his crimes, I made him crawl on his knees to my desk. It was what he expected. If I had received him otherwise, he would have deduced from my incomprehensible lenity that he was not in disfavour in spite of his crimes and that he might therefore commit others with impunity.

I made it a rule also never to refuse help to any native who came to ask it of me. If a father came to me to ask me to try to recover his daughter, carried away by bandits —it was the most common case in which my assistance was sought—even though I was alone, even though I or my men might be overcome with fatigue, I always made an effort, too often alas, in vain, to save the victim. I never dismissed a native who came to me with a complaint, even though it might be against one of my own soldiers. I always listened attentively and fraternally, and if redress was justified, the plaintiff received it. When I made a promise to a native, I always kept it, however much I may have wished later that I had not committed myself. Finally, the detail in which my technique differed perhaps most startingly from that of certain of my colleagues was that I did not give whites priority over natives. In some places, if a white entered an Allied office while a native was there, the native's business was immediately adjourned until the white had been attended to. But if a white entered my office while I was talking to a native, I asked him to wait until my Indonesian brother had finished with his business. The Indonesians marvelled at this. For that matter, so did the whites, if that is quite the word for it.

It was thus that the Westerling legend grew in Indonesia. The little people of Sumatra, and as my fame spread, over the archipelago as a whole, began to demonstrate an extraordinary confidence in me. Sometimes this became embarrassing. Peasants would come to consult me on matters far removed from my jurisdiction, which took time that I could ill spare from my pressing duties. They came to complain to me that their wives were shrews or to ask my advice about the measures to take to prevent a threatened failure of their crops. I spent hours listening to matters of this kind; but what I lost in time was made up a thousand-fold in what I gained in prestige and in the many intangible results of the affection I won among this people, so gentle, so unfortunate, so sadly tried, simply because in me they had found someone willing to listen to their troubles and, when he could, to help them out of them.

One of the very tangible results of the esteem I won from the natives was the fidelity of my Indonesian soldiers. I always had more Indonesians than Europeans under my orders. I have never been abandoned or betrayed by any of them. I made dozens of raids with Indonesian soldiers or militiamen alone. They never failed me, and their loyalty was absolute.

I remember one occasion when we were attacking a dangerous murderer named Sihita, whose presence in our vicinity had been reported by some of our friends. I had with me only three natives, two militiamen of our anti-terrorist groups, and one of my spies. We walked straight into an ambush. The terrorists threw grenades at us. A splinter from the first one struck me behind the ear, and I fell unconscious. My native followers, not knowing whether I was dead or alive, deprived of their leader and caught in a disadvantageous position by superior numbers, might have been excused for taking to their heels and leaving me behind. Instead, they fought like demons until they succeeded in carrying me, still unconscious, back to safety. I owe my life today to their courage.

I still carry a souvenir of the gratitude I owe to them. When they got me to Medan, the doctor who examined me, said: "That piece of shrapnel is so firmly stuck in your skull that it has practically become part of it. I think it is safer not to try to remove it." It is still with me today, a little protuberance behind the right ear, which means I can never wear a city hat.

If I took pride in the testimony to the popularity of my methods provided by the affection of the simple Indonesians, I also considered as a tribute the great unpopularity I enjoyed among the terrorists.

One of their most important organizations was the secret society known as the "Black Buffalo". Its speciality was the quiet assassination, generally by poison, of those of its enemies whom the guerrillas did not dare to attack directly. Early in 1946, the "Black Buffalo" honoured me by putting a price of £20,000 sterling on my head.

In this period of political chaos and its consequent accompaniment of misery and poverty, £20,000 was more than enough to give ideas to some kitchen boy who might be tempted to add an extra ingredient to my meal or to a band of professional killers who might consider it good enough pay to justify considerable risk. As their special contribution to my security, the newspapers gave the reward wide publicity by reporting it extensively.

Nevertheless so far as I know no attempt was ever made by anyone to collect that imposing sum.

I was protected by a shield more powerful than any force of bodyguards I might have organized—my reputation as a just avenger.

A Price on My Head

The friendship of the common people surrounded me with a protective screen. As for the terrorists, they, who terrorized others, were themselves in terror of me. They did not dare attack me directly. They had been too much impressed by our lightning raids, our nocturnal kidnappings of criminals. The fact that I always acted by night increased their horror of me. Afraid of the dark and the spirits it enfolded, they thought me at least half-supernatural myself. This superstitious awe they felt for me was increased by the mystery, for them, of my methods founded on my Commando training plus the special jungle exercises I had gone through in India. In their eyes, I was one of the demons of the night.

But if they did not dare to strike at me, some of them dared once to strike at someone very dear to me—and with success.

I had become acquainted with a half-breed girl, an adorable woman as beautiful as she was gentle, whom I intended to make my wife. One night she disappeared, kidnapped.

It was a bitterly ironical fact that I, who had rescued so many women who were strangers to me from the bandits, who had solved so many crimes in which I had no personal interest, found myself without the slightest clue on which to act in this case, which touched me so closely. The disappearance was complete, absolute, without trace of its authors, without indication of the direction in which to search for the victim. I put all my informers, all my spies, all my scouts to work to look for the tracks of the criminals. None of them turned up even the vaguest hint of what had happened to her, of who had spirited her away.

To this day, the mystery remains complete. I still shudder when I think of what must have been her fate.

CHAPTER XI

Intrigue and Error

Of all the members of the British occupation forces in Sumatra, only two had prices placed upon their heads. One was Captain Orum (who, like myself, had been born in Turkey) and I was the other. In my own case at least, I considered that the fact that I had been singled out by the terrorists as a particular enemy, was a symbol of the differences of opinion which existed between my British superiors and myself.

I was unable to accept the spectacle of a whole population of one of the gentlest peoples in the world delivered without defence to the outrages of Javanese guerrillas and former collaborationist militiamen, trained in atrocities by their Japanese masters. The instructions given by higher authorities to the British troops prevented them from restoring order. The Dutch military authorities, I was sure, would have acted differently. But a situation was being created which would make it difficult for them, when they were finally admitted to their former territory, to regain possession of it.

Prime Minister Attlee declared before the House of Commons on October 17th, 1945:

"Meanwhile not only have we a strong moral obligation towards our Dutch Allies as the sovereign Power until they are in a position to resume control; but also the maintenance of law and order is essential to the fulfilment of the military tasks which arise out of the termination of the war with Japan and in particular to the safety of the several thousand Dutch nationals interned in the interior of the country."

But law and order were not being maintained, for at this time the British forces were not cracking down on the guerrillas, who were subjecting the archipelago to a

Intrigue and Error

régime of fire and blood. The longer this situation continued, the less likely was it that "the sovereign Power" would ever be able to "resume control".

Mr. Bevin, the Foreign Secretary, said on November 23rd, 1945: "It is quite clear that His Majesty's Government have a definite agreement with them [the Netherlands] to provide for the Dutch Netherlands Indies Government to resume as rapidly as practicable full responsibility for the adminstration of the Netherlands Indian territories."

Meanwhile time was being allowed for the Republican government to gain strength and become, at last, to some extent, the government which it had claimed to be at the beginning when actually it governed nothing. The Sukarno "government" originally was a cork tossed wildly about on the boiling currents and cross-currents of terrorism and anarchy. Sukarno was induced to put himself forward in the first place, as I have already related, by terrorist threats, and when he was temporarily out of the premiership terrorist methods led to his return to it. Clearly he could not be independent of the forces which put him in office and kept him there.

When Sukarno's cabinet resigned on November 14th, 1945, after fruitless negotiations with the Dutch, Soetan Sjahrir formed the new government. On December 27th, an attempt was made to murder Sjahrir, but it failed. On February 1st, 1946, the "People's Front" was established, one of whose leaders was the dissident Communist Tan Malakka. Its declared aims, the foundation of one sovereign Indonesian Republic, were in tune with those of the Sjahrir government and seemed to be a bid for inclusion in it. But when Sjahrir formed a revised second cabinet on March 12th, the People's Front was not represented in it.

Tan Malakka's faction therefore returned to direct methods. Discovered to be plotting a *coup d'état* against the Republican government, he was arrested, along with several others, on March 23rd. But two weeks later he was released, an action whose lack of wisdom was demonstrated on June 27th when Malakka's men kidnapped Sjahrir. With Sjahrir

75

thus eliminated, Sukarno came back again. On June 29th, he took the power back into his own hands (tied though they were by the terrorists) and proclaimed a state of siege for all Indonesia. When his new régime had been consolidated, Sjahrir was freed, on July 1st. Not until October 2nd did Sukarno return to a third Sjahrir cabinet the special powers he had been exercising, by which time his own position had been consolidated. Contrary to the rule in most governments where there is both a President and a Premier, the President was in this case politically the more powerful of the two.

While these squabbles for power were going on in Indonesia, the situation there was also causing manœuvres in the international field. Before the United Nations, Ukrainian delegate Manuilsky was accusing the British of maintaining a state of war in Indonesia, and called on that international organization to prevent Dutch colonialists from drowning the new-born independent state of Indonesia in blood. These colonialists did not at the moment possess the means of doing much drowning, as their forces in Indonesia only consisted of eight hundred marines who had landed with the British at Batavia.

This Ukrainian action was something of a boomerang for the Soviet diplomats, for an attempt to get the United Nations to pass a resolution calling for the withdrawal of British troops failed and the Indonesian question was removed from the agenda. A week afterwards, Australia, persuaded perhaps by the stand taken by the Soviet bloc that she had been on the wrong side of the fence, lifted a shipping ban which had been opposed against material for the Dutch in Indonesia. But nevertheless, the general picture was one in which all the great powers, often for very different reasons, took the side of the still largely fictitious government formed with the connivance of the former Japanese régime, and prevented the Dutch from regaining their East Indian empire, while the reign of terrorism and anarchy spread rapidly to the most remote islands of the archipelago.

The one exception to this rule was France, which because of her situation in Indo-China experienced a fellow-feeling for the Dutch and had no desire to add fuel to the flames of native terrorism camouflaged as a movement for independence. Or was it perhaps because the French could see further ahead than anyone else?

Russia's motives, of course, were simple enough. A large proportion of the terrorists were Communists and the corollary of the Soviet desire for a native government detached from Dutch influence was for a native government attached to Soviet influence. For the same reason, Soviet weight was thrown on to the side of a single Republican government, controlled from Java, in preference to a federal government, in which the many very different regions of Indonesia would enjoy a large degree of local autonomy, because Russia considered, and considers, that it will be easier for Communism to pick up Indonesia in one piece, if it has first been subjected to a strong centralized government, than to win it over to the Soviet island by island.

When Lord Killearn (then Special Commissioner in South-East Asia) arrived in Indonesia as mediator the Dutch had hardly any troops in as yet, but nevertheless, they had started to organize the federal states of Indonesia, which they knew was the only basis on which a democratic development in Indonesia might have a chance. The Malino Conference (July 1946) held to that effect was temporarily proving a great success, spontaneous support being given especially in Eastern Indonesia.

While all these intrigues were being directed against her, Holland herself was losing no opportunity for making mistakes. Instead of depending on the sane and peaceful masses of the country, on the traditional institutions of the region based on the Sultans and the great families which still exercised much influence, they abandoned their natural allies to treat with their worst enemies. In the light of European Socialist doctrine, the Dutch Socialist government ignored the age-old structure of a society very different from anything which existed in Europe, to deal with the Indonesians as if they had been Europeans.

Holland, moreover, wanted to buy too much with too little. The Dutch did not send enough troops for effective action. True, those which they did send were held back from Indonesia by the British—but this was in part precisely because they were insufficiently numerous. If Holland had made a larger contribution to the occupying forces, she would have been able to speak with a louder voice in the negotiations. Holland also was not willing to forego Marshall Plan aid and had therefore to accept the loss of her power of independent action which inevitably went with it.

Finally, Dutch tactics towards the Indonesians and Dutch policy in general showed a lack of flexibility at some times, of firmness at others, which led their negotiators from one retreat to another. Again and again they refused all concessions on some secondary point, only to grant in the end much more than they had been asked for at first. Finally, they had to abandon the federal constitution which Sukarno had once been led to accept and, by 1950, Indonesia was given over entirely to the depredations of the bandits who had been martyrizing it, against the illusory hope that the Dutch property would be respected and Dutch economic and financial ties with Indonesia maintained.

It was a tragic capitulation, which leaves the fabulous riches of the Spice Islands open today for Soviet domination.

For my part, as an Indonesian at heart and, I hope, one day an Indonesian by nationality, I desire ardently real independence for Indonesia. I want to see a true Indonesian government, not a dictatorship of puppets, themselves either tyrannized by terrorists or at the orders of a foreign despotism. I want to see an Indonesian government which will be the expression of a democracy based on legal elections in the various islands. I want to see a Federal government, which will respect the diversity of races, of tongues and religions, in this once paradisiacal region of the earth.

CHAPTER XII

The Martyrdom of Batavia

I knew that I could not continue much longer to serve a policy which was keeping Sumatra and the rest of Indonesia in chaos and nightmare. As long as I could concentrate on the details of my work, on the carrying out of the missions entrusted to me, all was well. But as soon as my activities overlapped the sphere of policy, as they so regularly did, I found myself the unhappy instrument of a policy I detested.

I was not alone in having these sentiments. Many of my comrades among the English and Indian officers, and for that matter, many of the ordinary rankers of the occupation forces also, were horrified by the misdoings of a régime which they were obliged to tolerate, and disgusted by having to stand idle in the face of guerrilla provocations.

One of the last straws, so far as I was concerned, was the following incident involving the occupying forces—not that it was of any great importance, but because it was humiliating and because the humiliation was so unnecessary.

The Indian soldiers of the 26th Division—the "Tiger Heads"—to which I was attached as Intelligence Officer, had hoisted their regimental flag above the water reservoir which supplied their camp at Medan. Almost at once the water mains leading from the reservoir were demolished and an insulting ultimatum received to the effect that either the flag must come down or the troops would continue to be deprived of water.

There was no need to give way to this. A simple military demonstration would have sufficed to keep the terrorists quiet. I had demonstrated in a precisely similar case—that of the flag hoisted over the camp of the rescued prisoners— that a bluff of this kind could be called. And I had not even possessed the force to back up my defence, if the terrorists

79

had dared challenge it. The 26th Division was quite capable of backing up any action it chose to take. But what it chose to do—or more exactly, what it had to do, in face of orders forbidding all use of force, unless it was completely unavoidable—was to pull down the flag.

For days, the fly-by-night papers edited by the various vaguely political bands exulted in this demonstration of "British cowardice". The men and officers of the Division were deeply ashamed of their surrender. So was I. I chafed with the desire to get out of this non-combatant army.

It must be credited to the honour of individual English and Hindu officers that from time to time, when particularly unjustified massacres or particularly hideous violences occurred under their very eyes, they took repressive action on their own individual responsibility, contrary to the directives they had received. Thus a few of the Indonesian bandits were eliminated from the scene. But such reactions were rare and exceptional. They were not sufficient to cleanse my mouth of the bad taste the whole situation had left in it.

I was therefore highly pleased when in July 1946 the Dutch invited me to join the Royal Indonesian Army, of which a few contingents had at last been authorized to land at Batavia. It was with regret that I said goodbye to my comrades.

On July 26th, 1946, a plane of the K.N.I.L.—the Royal Indonesian Army came to Medan to pick me up. On the same day I landed in Batavia.

Batavia had always been vaunted as the modern Baghdad of the South Seas. I found it sadly changed.

Before the war, there had been no more eloquent testimony to the benefits of Dutch rule in Indonesia than the capital of Java. Along its lazy canals, seemingly imported from Holland, the beautiful Javanese women washed their clothes or bathed in their multi-coloured sarongs. The streets were flanked with model buildings for a model city, from the villas set in their brilliant gardens, through the big office buildings, the colossal banks and the white

The Martyrdom of Batavia

palaces of officialdom, to the splendid India Hotel, one of the most famous hostelries in the Orient.

Now this monument of civilization had become a sinister No Man's Land, whose silences were punctuated by the explosion of grenades, frequented by suspicious armed men. Once, at night, the characteristic sound of Batavia had been the croaking of the bull frogs. Now they could no longer be heard. Their voices were drowned nightly by the crackle of machine-gun fire.

The people of Batavia had once been happy, prosperous, picturesque. Now they dragged through the street in rags, half-starved and eaten by disease. They were the innocent bystanders, the non-participating victims, who paid the toll for the rivalries of the conflicting powers around them, who had made a battlefield of their home. There were the English, who occupied the region, but failed to keep order in it. There were the Dutch, who had at last been permitted to land, but were not yet permitted to attempt to maintain order themselves and were too few to do so even if it had been permitted. There were the terrorist bands, belonging to six different and mutually hostile political groups. And there were the bandits pure and simple.

The city was jammed with a population far beyond its capacity. It had been overwhelmed by swarms of refugees, who flocked in from the countryside in hopes of finding a relative security in the presence of the occupation troops: Chinese, who were being systematically massacred by the bandits; Europeans; half-breeds; and Indonesians proper. Every Dutch villa, designed for habitation of a single family, harboured at least fifty persons.

The Indonesians had been awaiting the Allied victory for months, in a fever of hope and expectancy. With it, they had hoped for the arrival of the many things they needed so bitterly, after four years of Japanese confiscations and requisitions: medicine, food, clothing. All they had seen were strips of bunting stretched across the fronts of buildings, shouting the word: "Liberty! Liberty!" By this, the extremists who had put up these signs seemed to mean liberty

81

for themselves to pillage in their turn, and deprive the unfortunate people of what few possessions the Japanese might have left them.

The Dutch, it is true, had been prepared to bring needed supplies into Indonesia. Sizeable convoys of Dutch ships were in Australia, assigned to this mission of relief. But the Australian dockworkers had declared an embargo[1] against the Dutch ships and they remained tied up uselessly to the wharves, while people in Indonesia died for want of the cargoes they might have been carrying. The Australians were supposedly motivated by opposition to the Dutch colonizers, as exploiters of the natives, and, therefore, by sympathy for the latter. But the result of their "sympathy" was to keep the natives in misery. Thousands of whites, removed from the Japanese concentration camps in a dying condition, expired also for want of the medicines which the becalmed Dutch ships could have brought them.

But while the whites were dying by thousands, the Indonesians were dying by tens of thousands.

To the horrors of privation had been added the horrors of terrorism. They were exercised even in the midst of this great capital city of Java.

Passing by one of the numerous canals, I saw a group of men engaged in drawing some heavy cumbrous object out of it. I stopped to see what they were doing.

As they strained at their task, there rose slowly from the waters of the canal, the dripping shape of a massive cross. Nailed to it, naked, was a young Eurasian girl, arms and legs widespread in the form of the letter X, great spikes driven through her hands and feet. Thus crucified, she had been raped on her cross, and then thrown, cross and all, into the canal, to die by drowning if she were not already dead. It was not a rare sight. This was a torture the terrorists seemed to delight especially in applying to Eurasians. Every day such crucified bodies were removed from the canals.

[1] August 1945, and continued for two and a half years.

It was only a few weeks before my arrival in Java, on June 5th, 1946, that extremists had slaughtered the entire Chinese population at Tangerang, just before that city was occupied by Dutch troops. In that mass murder, about ten thousand persons lost their lives—men, women and children, the women being all raped, even the littlest girls.

CHAPTER XIII

Making Commandos

It seems to be the rule of every new régime that it should rename everything capable of being renamed. Thus, at the time when I arrived in Batavia, it was already beginning to be called by its new title, Djakarta. It also often seems to be the rule with new regimes to assume that a change of name has a magic effect which by itself will produce reforms with no further effort on the part of the baptizers.

Changing the name of Batavia to Djakarta, however, had had no such magical effect. The new name did not produce a new order. There was, in fact, no order at all in Batavia-Djakarta. It was not the capital of Java, it was the capital of chaos.

I had my first small sample of that the day after I arrived, when it took three whole hours even to find out where the Commando camp was located. Nobody knew, including those officials supposedly in control of it. I finally discovered that it was at a place called Polonia, about four miles outside Djakarta proper.

I took a bicycle-rickshaw to go to Polonia, being careful to sit sideways in order to be able to keep an eye on the cyclist who propelled the little vehicle. One of the favourite tricks of the terrorists was to deck out some of their killers as rickshaw cyclists. When a European hired one of them, his driver, pretending he was using a short cut, took him through some little frequented district, and at a favourable moment, leaned over and slit the throat of the unsuspecting passenger from the rear. I knew about this little trick and I did not propose to be welcomed to Djakarta—and dispatched from it—in this fashion.

I found the Commandos under the direction of an old friend, Captain Scheepens. He had been in the same group as myself at Colombo. He was engaged in planning an action for the next day and showed me, on the map, how he proposed to operate.

He was charged with protecting a bridge, which it had been learned, the Republicans planned to dynamite on the morrow. He explained how he proposed to dispose his men. It was not the way I would have done it. I told him I disagreed and warned him that he would have heavy casualties.

I learned what had happened the next day about noon, when Mrs. Scheepens called at my hotel. She was in tears. The action had been catastrophic. The captain himself had been seriously wounded. Of the nineteen men placed at the bridge, eleven were casualties, wounded or dead.

That same day, I was ordered to take over command at Polonia.

The so-called camp was actually a group of three or four buildings in which about fifty men were billeted. I found their morale frightful. The action of the day before had been only one of a series of disasters. They had been operating against the guerrillas of Indonesia as if they were facing regular soldiers of a European army, operating according to the laws of war in a highly developed country. There had been no adaptability to the different conditions of Indonesia, to the different type of enemy and his different tactics. The result had been a series of failures and a group of thoroughly discouraged men.

I could do nothing with men in that state. I needed resolute men, determined men, daring men for the sort of operations I proposed to carry out. I had rather have half a dozen men like that than a hundred of the half-hearted. With six men of the right type, I knew I could get the better of a hundred apprehensive adversaries, who felt themselves half-defeated in advance.

I lined my fifty men up and told them that I proposed to operate in a new fashion. The assignments would be tough and dangerous and would demand every ounce of a man's energy, strength and courage. Therefore, I wanted no one but volunteers under my command. Those who didn't want to stay were free to leave the Commandos.

Of the fifty men I had before I opened my mouth, twenty were left when I finished talking. This suited me perfectly. Twenty men ready to follow me after I had warned them I was going to demand the utmost of them were twenty men of the kind I wanted. The other thirty I would rather not have around. They would simply be a drag on the others. I didn't want thirty men who needed to be protected plus twenty men to do the protecting. I preferred twenty men who could take care of themselves, unencumbered by the necessity of taking care of someone else as well.

However, if I preferred twenty good men to twenty good plus thirty bad, that didn't mean that I considered twenty a large enough force to handle hundreds of terrorists. I wanted more men, but of the same kind as the faithful twenty. I secured from the High Command the authorization to recruit additional Commandos under a special régime. Within a few weeks, I had a force of a hundred and fifty men. Some of them, volunteers from the regular Dutch units which had now been allowed to land, had been trained by me in Holland, at the time when I had been stationed near the V-1 launching ramp. It was gratifying to find them eager to serve under me again and the instruction they had already had was invaluable in giving me sub-instructors to help train the green men.

I began by lecturing my troop on the principle which was to be the basis of the type of training we would undergo and of the operations to follow it. It was that we were not faced by a hostile population—far from it. Our basic assumption was that we were working on behalf of a friendly population, as anxious to be freed from the terrorism of

the bandits as we ourselves were anxious to end their depredations. It was among the population that we would find
our most valuable supporters. It would be they who would
be our best informers, for they could move about unsuspected
where a white man would be immediately conspicuous, and
it was they who knew intimately the terrain, an indispensable
condition to the success of our enterprise.

Since our enemies were the bandits alone and not the
population some of them claimed to represent, we must
never fire a village or burn the hut of an innocent native.
We would attack only the leaders of the bands and armed
guerrillas. These bandits, these pseudo-soldiers had terrorized the people of the *kampongs*, and for that matter
those of the cities. At first, the local people might be afraid
to help us. But as they saw that we attacked only their
oppressors and never themselves, we would win their confidence and, particularly if we showed ourselves capable of
protecting them against the bandits, we would eventually
receive precious aid from them.

Even in the Republican "soldiers", the bandits and
gangsters with whom we had to deal, I continued, we should
not necessarily see enemies. Many of their followers were
misled. Many of them, inspired by a sincere desire for
independence, had allowed themselves to be made the tools
of the terrorists in the belief that by so doing they were
serving the ends of national independence, even though the
means used might be personally repugnant to them. Some
of them might have been sucked into these bands and
obliged to remain with them through fear of reprisals if they
attempted to get out. Joining a terrorist band was, after all,
one way of escaping attack by the terrorists. We would find
in these bands, I said, individuals who could be redeemed
and converted from destroyers of order into supporters of it.
Indeed, later on, I very often appointed former terrorists
(not their leaders of course) as the official police of villages
which they had once looted, with excellent results.

It was the bandit leaders alone against whom we were
declaring implacable war, I concluded. The way to seize

86

them was to make ourselves men of the jungle. Always surprise, ambush, ruse, never frontal attacks. We would never operate by day. (As a matter of fact, during three years, I never started an action by daylight). We would be the soldiers of the night, taking our enemies by surprise in the dark. We would thus be aided by the powerful psychological factor of the terror Indonesians have for the dark.

Having given these preliminary explanations, I set to work to impart to my men all the knowledge of Commando tactics which had been taught to me, plus what I had added to it by practical experience. I taught them how to fight without arms, particularly without firearms. When they used weapons at all, they were to be silent weapons. I trained them in the tactics of night fighting with forced marches and crossings of swamps, and by familiarizing them with the use of collapsible rubber boats, like those used by airmen forced down at sea. These last, carried deflated and folded on our expeditions, we would blow up when we wanted to slip silently along the water-courses under the shelter of the palms and land, silent as shadows, in the midst of the lake- or river-side village which were our objectives.

In all this instruction, I combined my training as a British Commando, my course in jungle fighting in India and my newly-gained knowledge of the Indonesian bush and of the Indonesian people. This last was perhaps the most important of all. In this way I impressed on my men the importance of establishing sources of information among the natives and of carefully preparing all our operations by means of preliminary scouting carried out by natives. I also trained them in methods of questioning prisoners—how to disconcert them, and lead them to confess, without touching them or even threatening them. I told them, among other things, how susceptible Indonesians are to a very simple preliminary to questioning—simply look at them in silence for half an hour before the interrogation begins. During that period of silence, the prisoner's apprehension reduces his resistance much more effectively than any questions might have done.

He welcomes with relief the final breaking of silence, as an opportunity to end the tension by confessing.

This period of training lasted until November 1946. But it was not confined to training alone. Our practical exercises were actually operations against the terrorists. As in Holland, I made the carrying out of missions part of the training. We conducted raids on bandits in localities surrounding Djakarta, in which my Commandos learned to act alone, to keep their heads under all circumstances and above all, never to let themselves be surrounded.

This training was conceived with the purpose of producing instructors in these tactics, who could then form new groups of Commandos throughout the Royal Indonesian Army. But it was suddenly ended by new orders from my superiors, inspired by a new danger.

In the Celebes, terrorism had broken out with even more violence than in Java. The whole island was aflame. By the end of 1946, the situation had got completely out of control. The local government was helpless before the mounting wave of violence.

My orders were to leave for the Celebes as soon as possible. It was my assignment to try to put an end to terrorism there.

CHAPTER XIV

Terrorism in the Celebes

The situation in the Celebes at the time when I was called to that island, was basically simple: the contending forces were engaged in a race against time.

The Celebes is one of the major islands in the Indonesian archipelago. Its people lived under the nominal authority of their Rajahs, but for all practical purposes under that of their village chieftains. They were a people of peasants, gentle and peaceful, owners of the land they tilled. Neither Japanese, anti-white, nationalist or Communist propaganda had had any effect upon them. The reason was simple. They were well off and content as they were. They had no reason for desiring a change.

In the Celebes, even more completely than in Indonesia in general (though these factors existed in all the islands) extremist and Communist agitation had been ineffective for three main reasons:

(1) In general, the land belonged to the peasants. Agrarian reform, one of the strongest talking points of the Communists in many countries—China, for instance—had no meaning here. The man who tilled the land owned it already. Communism had nothing to offer him.

(2) The immense majority of Indonesians are Moslems. The Moslems are in general anti-Communist almost by instinct. On the other hand Russia has tried, by laying emphasis on her own Moslem populations, to represent herself, in Moslem countries and for Moslem consumption, as a champion of Islam. She has also attempted to twist some of the surats of the Koran into interpretations that would seem to make it appear that Mohammed was a forerunner of Lenin. In some parts of Indonesia, those tactics met with a certain success.

(3) Finally, and this was no doubt the most important fact of all, up to the time of the Japanese occupation, seventy-five million inhabitants of Indonesia had never known hunger. This fact alone speaks volumes for the enlightened nature of the Dutch administration in this territory. So does the number of inhabitants, for when the Dutch first took over this territory, the population was no more than five million.

The phenomenon of dwindling native populations under repressive colonialization is common. It is remarkable that, under Dutch rule, the population of Indonesia was multiplied fifteen times in three centuries, and that without any consequent hardship.

It was, then, a happy people—before the Japanese occupation—which was subjected to the chaos resultant upon political dissensions.

89

The Celebes, like those other sections of Indonesia which had not been yet occupied by the Republican hordes, were anxious for the establishment upon their territory of a legally-constituted power capable of preserving order which would save them from the excesses visited upon Java and Sumatra. In an attempt to establish such a legality, a conference was held in Malino, from July 16th to July 22nd 1946, in which representatives of Holland sat with delegates from Borneo, the Celebes, Pasundan (Western Java), the Mollucas and the Indonesian Republic—which meant at that time eastern and central Java.

Although the Republic was represented at the Malino Conference, its presence seemed chiefly intended to obstruct any tendency towards the creation of a rival power to its own in Indonesia. Sukarno opposed the creation of a Federal Indonesia. Nevertheless, the logic of federalism for a group of islands so diverse was so evident that within a week the basis for a Federation of Indonesia had been created. Local governments were established in those parts of the archipelago which were still free. They benefited immediately from the protection of the Royal Indonesian Army, the only legal force in the archipelago.

Although the Republicans were present at the conference which had arrived at this result, they showed their pique at it by stopping the liberation of European prisoners of the Japanese immediately after the Malino agreement. They gave as a pretext for this action the assertion that the K.N.I.L. was enlisting Japanese ex-soldiers in its ranks. There was no very good reason why, even if this had been true, the European prisoners should have suffered for it. But it was not even true. The K.N.I.L. immediately issued a denial from its staff headquarters, but the Republicans paid no attention to this. The unfortunate prisoners, who had already suffered tortures at the hands of their Japanese jailors, were to spend another year in the dreaded concentration camps, under even worse conditions than those which had been imposed upon them by the Japanese.

As a result of the Malino Conference, a local government

had been set up in Makassar, the capital of the Celebes, but it was extremely weak, having no effective police power of its own. It could resort only to the Royal Indonesian Army, but this authority was also insufficient. The Dutch troops had been very well received in the Celebes. Great hopes had been placed in them for the restoration of order after the Japanese repression and for the improvement of the economic situation, which had deteriorated badly during the occupation.

Unfortunately, the Dutch disappointed the Celebes on both counts and quickly fell into discredit on the island. To begin with, because of the troubles in Java, large numbers of the officers who had originally landed in the Celebes were called to that island, and not enough remained in Makassar to organize an effective police and civil admin-istration. In the second place, no serious effort ever got under way to improve the economic situation by importing necessary food and supplies, providing for the distribution of cloth, and so forth.

This delay in restoring the Celebes to normal conditions was utilized by the Republican government of Java in its fight against time for control of the Celebes. What the Republicans wanted to do was to gain control of the region for their single centralized government of the whole archi-pelago as against the federalization envisaged at Malino. This in spite of the fact that on November 15th 1946, a draft agreement had been initialled at Linggadjati which provided for a United States of Indonesia. This would have been a Federation, of which the Republican government would have been only one member, along with a number of others, linked to Holland and her other possessions in a union created by a common allegiance to the Dutch crown.

Even though Republican representatives may have felt it necessary, for psychological reasons, to pretend to accept this federalization of Indonesia, they intended on the prac-tical plane to bring about its collapse in favour of the centralized government—which would amount in reality to the domination of Java over the other islands. It was therefore their strategy in the Celebes to attempt to gain control of the island under the very noses of the Dutch troops before the weak government of Makassar could consolidate its authority and be in a position to cope with the Republic.

Thus, for six months before the moment when I was called in—in other words, even before the Malino Conference—Java had been pouring guerrilla fighters into the Celebes to combat the tendency towards a local government for that island, in the general framework of a Federal Indonesia. Some of them were Javanese. Others were recruits from the Celebes, who had been taken to Java, trained in terrorist tactics there, and then brought back to their native island to prey on their own countrymen.

The Javanese terrorists arrived by junks, crammed with men and arms. They landed in Polembankong and Baroe, which they controlled, about seventy miles from Makassar. It was difficult country, a terrain which it was practically impossible to attack with the limited forces at our command, and from that base they infiltrated the whole island, particularly Makassar, the capital.

This was the political background at the time when I arrived in the Celebes.

I pursued my usual tactics in preparing for operations in this region. Before leaving for the Celebes myself, I sent scouts ahead—about twelve of my men, not in uniform themselves but in ordinary native costume, to inform themselves, and me, on the exact situation in the island. Not until I had received reports from them and knew exactly what to expect did I leave myself, with the rest of my command. We arrived on December 5th 1946—a hundred and twenty-three men. Not a large force with which to end a reign of terror which was being carried on by many hundreds of well-armed fanatics.

I met with a surprise on my arrival at Makassar. I was handed there my commission as captain. I was twenty-seven years old—the youngest captain in the Dutch Indian Army.

Terrorism in the Celebes

Immediately upon my arrival, I was called into conference with the Commander-in-Chief of the Dutch troops in Eastern Indonesia, and with the officers of his staff. I discovered that, in view of my work in Sumatra and Java, I was expected to establish the operational plan for the entire island. It might have been embarrassing to have been confronted unexpectedly with such a demand if I had arrived in the island without preparation or previous knowledge of the situation. My preliminary explorations stood me in good stead in this first conference. I was happy that I had proceeded in this fashion. For that matter, it was my invariable method, and I had had many other occasions, and was to have more in the future, to be thankful that I had made it a rule always to explore the ground before I ventured upon it. I know from actual experience that preparation is vastly preferable to improvisation—or to put it otherwise, that improvisation is more effective when it is based on preparation.

Although I had been prepared by the reports of my scouts for a bad situation in Makassar, I found the reality just a trifle worse than I had expected. This exquisite city, bathed in the shade of coconut palms, in whose shops the subtlest craftsmen of the East created their delicate jewels of fine silver wire and mother-of-pearl, had become a kingdom of cut-throats.

There was a Dutch garrison in Makassar, but it might as well have been in the Hague for all the protection it was able to give to Europeans. It was hardly possible for a white to sit down on the terrace of the Society Club without having a grenade thrown at him.

The merchants were as usual the victims of daily extortions. Everywhere in the Pacific, the business streets are usually gay late into the night from the perpetual blaze of the Chinese bazaars, with their wealth of variegated merchandise on display. But in Makassar, the shops were closed as soon as twilight approached. The dullness of the evening streets, so foreign to this part of the world, was one symptom of the terror which weighed upon the city.

93

Challenge to Terror

Young girls, as in Sumatra and Java, were constantly being kidnapped and raped. Murder was a commonplace. The first sight that greeted me when I entered the barracks on the night of my arrival at Makassar, was the decapitated body of a native soldier from the island of Amboina. His head had been cut off by the cyclist of a rickshaw which he had taken, and in which he had imprudently failed to seat himself so that he could keep a vigilant eye on his employee.

The evidences of fear which could be seen in the city were even clearer in the surrounding countryside. The green shoots which should have been rising from the rice fields were nowhere to be seen. Culture had been abandoned. Peasants dared not to work in the isolation of their fields for fear of being murdered on their own land. Nor was there any point in toiling to raise a crop which would inevitably be stolen in the end by the bandits. Agriculture was at a standstill, work of any kind impossible. Trade with the neighbouring islands had stopped.

The local police made no effort to combat this state of affairs. One reason for this was that it was paralysed from within. Extremists from Java had infiltrated into the police organizations and neutralized the attempts of all those who might have desired to resist by threatening them with reprisals if they dared oppose the Republicans.

The native mayors, the *besturs*, were also afraid to act, for fear of having their throats cut. Tax collectors dared not leave the shelter of the capital. No revenues were brought in to the helpless Makassar government. It was therefore without funds to pay its officials. Thus administrative activity was breaking down.

In short, the chaos which the Republicans had set out six months earlier to produce in the Celebes had been achieved with virtually complete success.

CHAPTER XV

Death of a Terrorist

One of the first things I learned about the acts of my predecessors in the Celebes was that they had proceeded according to the same policy of conciliation applied by the British in Java and Sumatra, and with the same bad results.

When a series of crimes had disclosed that a group of terrorists was based on a certain village, the Dutch troops would make a raid on that village, round up the population in the main square, and demand that the terrorists among them be denounced and handed over to the authorities. At first the *tanis*, anxious themselves to end the banditry which was making normal life impossible for them, pointed out the offenders to the soldiers. As the guilty were led away, the peasants breathed more easily, imagining they had been delivered from their tormentors.

Unfortunately, they were wrong. The policy of the Dutch was to hold the evildoers for several days, during which I suppose they were considered as having time to repent. The guilty were then lectured paternally, like naughty boys, told not to do it again, and released!

Their first act was to return to the village where they had been captured and take frightful vengeance on those who had given them away. Not only did they murder the actual denouncers, but often their family, their friends, sometimes even the members of the same caste.

Naturally, the peasants lost all confidence in the Dutch Army. They also ceased to co-operate with it. They did not dare. Terrorism had won another round in the struggle for the Celebes.

As my basic instructions to my men had already indicated, I was not dedicated to the opposite policy to that of conciliation—repression. On the contrary, I sought to work with the population and to spare even the small fry among the bandits. But I disapproved strongly of letting genuine criminals go scotfree.

Immunity for them could only be granted at the price of the martyrdom of the common people on whom they preyed. When it came to dealing with them, the firmest hand was the kindest hand. One execution of a criminal might mean the saving of hundreds of lives among the innocent.

It was on this basis of protection for the common man, and inexorable justice for the real criminals, that I went to work on my task of pacifying the Celebes.

It was obvious that the first thing to do was to clean up the capital. If we could not maintain order in the centre of administration, where our troops were garrisoned, how could we expect to maintain it anywhere? If only for the psychological effect, we had to demonstrate that where Dutch troops were stationed, murder and pillaging could not be carried on with impunity. It was also important that the city be made untenable for the bandits before we could hope to clean up the countryside. For so far, whenever military action had been undertaken against any region where terrorist activity was particularly great, the criminals had simply taken refuge with their accomplices in the city, where it was easier for them to lose themselves. By cleaning up Makassar itself, we would automatically reduce the chances of terrorists from outside the capital who tried to hide there with the aid of sympathisers.

Simultaneously I set up a system to keep tabs on all suspicious elements coming into the Celebes. In Makassar, we registered all Javanese who had arrived in the capital recently—for it was chiefly Javanese sent into the island by Sukarno who were responsible for the anarchy which reigned there. At the same time, the chiefs of the outlying villages were ordered to report to us on all Javanese who passed through their settlements.

Meanwhile, I got some of my men (not, of course, identified as belonging to my organization) into the city police. They quickly gained the confidence of their colleagues and were able in a short time to give me a list of the terrorist agents who had infiltrated the police. Some of them had managed to work their way into important positions, and at the same time that they were directing criminal activities, they were using their police connections to paralyse any official reaction.

We quickly eliminated these false policemen. Some, who were convicted of being actually responsible for crimes, were executed. I did not want to order any more executions than were absolutely necessary. But those few I intended to make striking, so that the effect of the example would be as great as possible. This objective was achieved. In a few days the atmosphere in the city had changed completely. The police were again performing their functions. The people felt that they were once more protected. Makassar was beginning to become unhealthy for terrorists.

As I had predicted to my men, I found many followers of the chief criminals were not beyond redemption. Even the actual perpetrators of some of the crimes did not seem to me to be those really responsible for them. They were obeying the orders of unscrupulous chiefs, but they themselves were simply misled. They justified their acts as necessary evils committed in the service of the greater good, for those slogans of "liberty" and "independence" which their cynical leaders, who had no belief whatsoever in either, dangled before them to convert them into the instruments of their malevolent purposes. Some of these lesser bandits I warned. I gave them a chance. I advised them to disappear if they wanted to escape punishment. But if they failed to take advantage of the opportunity, if they persisted in stirring up trouble after I had warned them, then I was pitiless. To have acted otherwise would have been to court the same reaction as that which had greeted the "conciliatory" releases of criminals which my predecessors had practised so unsuccessfully.

One such incident of retribution following an ignored warning occurred in spectacular circumstances which shocked many Europeans and caused sharp criticism of my methods. I think perhaps some of my critics might have been less harsh if they had had a full appreciation of the facts of the case, if they had been acquainted with the basic principles on which my entire action was based and if they had realized, in particular, the use I made of psychological factors precisely in order to reduce the need for the strong measures which were charged against me.

It was my custom at this time to take my meals at the Society Club. It was frequented by an Indonesian who had had extensive business relations with Dutch inhabitants of Makassar before the war, and who was using his acquaintanceships to gather information which permitted the terrorists to carry out successful raids. His work as a spy had cost us dearly. He had been responsible for the creation of several ambushes in which Dutch soldiers had been killed.

We had all the proof necessary to have him arrested, tried and executed. But I thought him one of the persons capable of being saved. He was indisputably a criminal in the eyes of the law, particularly the law of a state of siege (which had been declared for the territory) but I considered him a sincere nationalist, whose convictions were worthy of respect. So, instead of arresting him, I drew him aside, one day in the Society Club, and told him:

"I know everything you have done and everything that you are doing. I am giving you fair warning. Don't let me see you here again."

He paled, nodded and left the Club. I did not see him for a few days. But then I learned that he was still operating as a spy and that he had even dared to disregard my warning and was appearing again at the Society Club and talking with his old friends, though he was taking care to go there only in the mornings, when I was not normally there, as I never came before lunch.

Therefore I made it a point to go to the Society Club in the morning. I found him there, sitting around a table with a few others.

I walked up to him.

Death of a Terrorist

"Do you remember what I told you?" I asked.

He nodded, without rising.

I drew my revolver and shot him through the head where he sat.

The hullaballoo which this act caused among the Europeans of Makassar was terrific. "Murderer" was the politest word they applied to me. I have no doubt that the reader's first reaction also is that I am some sort of monster. But let me put the case before you. My act was not unpremeditated. It was calculated for definite reasons, to produce certain results. It produced them.

What was the alternative?

A course which would have shocked no one, which would not have shocked you who are reading these words, was open to me. I could have had him arrested and tried. I am able to state flatly that there would have been no doubt about the result. He would have been executed.

Thus, so far as he was concerned, the result would have been no different. Personally, I feel that the way in which he did die was preferable to the other. He was spared some days of anguish during which he would have lived only to contemplate the coming of death. As it was, he died quickly and mercifully.

But if he had been tried and then executed, if we had gone through the approved legal forms, themselves certainly cold and inhuman enough, his death would have been accepted as in the normal order of things. It would not have shocked public opinion.

The point is that *I wanted to shock public opinion.*

Not European public opinion, which expressed itself so violently against me. But what the Europeans failed to consider at the time was that if this manner of execution was so spectacular that it shocked them, it must also have shocked the Indonesians—and in particular, those I wanted to shock, the criminals, the terrorists, the employers of the executed spy.

If the proof of the pudding is in the eating, the merits of this spectacular execution can be said to have been demonstrated.

On the following day, there was not a terrorist in Makassar. They had got out like the proverbial rats abandoning a sinking ship. Assaults ceased. There were no more murders, no more rapes. Grenades were no longer thrown at the Society Club, even though its terrace might be thronged with Europeans. It may be that some of those who railed against me so bitterly lived to do so because of the very act they criticized.

It had its effects. The most deserted streets became as safe as the Fifth Avenue. At night, the lights gleamed once more in the windows of the Chinese shops. Under their lamps, the jewellers worked peacefully at their jewels in filigree. Makassar had recovered the calm and tranquillity of pre-war times.

How many lives were saved by the sacrifice of this one life? Or not even by its sacrifice, for it was a life lost in any case, but only by the fact that I elected to take it in public, suddenly, brutally, instead of committing the terrorist spy to the more routine processes of the courts.

Hundreds of lives, surely, were saved by that one act, the lives of other criminals as well as those of the innocent and of our soldiers who would otherwise have had to pursue slowly and for no one knows how many long weeks the task of ending terrorism in Makassar. The shot in the Society Club ended it overnight.

I think it was justified.

CHAPTER XVI

Cleaning Up the Celebes

Makassar had been freed of terrorism. But in the country districts it continued to rage unchecked. My new task was to clean up the countryside, using the now purified city as a base.

I continued to follow my invariable tactics, undertaking no operation without complete preparation.

I knew very well that if my Commandos started out in their lorries for any destination, they would no sooner find themselves on the roads towards a certain *kampong* than their arrival would be announced by the tomtoms while we were still twenty or twenty-five miles away. By the time we arrived, the terrorists would have disappeared and their arms would have been hidden. Probably the villagers would have taken to the bush also, either because they feared themselves compromised by having been the hosts, however unwilling, of the bandits, or because they did not wish to be questioned. On the basis of their experiences so far, they expected reprisals from the bandits if they gave us information and perhaps punishment from us if they didn't. Clearing out was safer.

I knew that in such circumstances all I could expect to find in my village on arriving there in force would be a few weaklings, left behind because they were unable to keep up with the flight of the others. And I was not interested in these dregs of the *kampong* population. For that matter, I was not interested in the population itself, which I knew had sheltered and perhaps aided the bandits only out of fear of their threats. I was not even particularly interested in the bandits. I was really interested only in their chiefs.

This was the way in which I operated:

When we learned that a band of terrorists had established itself in a certain *kampong*, I sent several native scouts to the village to insinuate themselves into its population and remain there for several days, to find out the things I needed to know. These scouts were not known to each other, each man imagining that he was working for me alone. Thus I had checks on the reports I received from each man in the reports of the others, and if by any chance a terrorist had infiltrated into my own organization, which was a possibility I had to take into account, he would quickly have been revealed by his disagreement with my loyal men.

Challenge to Terror

What I wanted my informers to find out particularly was which of the band was its leader, what hut he lived in, what his names were (all the terrorist chiefs had several aliases), who his right-hand men were and where their arms were kept. I also required them to learn all about the alarm system, whether by luminous signals, tomtoms or messengers.

Another important thing to know, in case we failed to take them entirely by surprise, was where they hid their arms in case of alarm. This we discovered very simply. While my men were in the village, I would start a troop of men in the direction of the *kampong*. We never attempted to go all the way to it. We created only a false alarm. But false or not, it was an alarm, and all my scouts had to do, in order to inform me on where weapons would be hidden when I really arrived, was to watch the reactions of the bandits when they only thought I was arriving.

When I had all the information I needed, I passed to the real attack.

We always set out at night. We always started, too, in a different direction from that we really intended to take, circling back on to our genuine route after we reached some point at which we could find cover for this manœuvre. We never approached a village by a road. We took the way which our informants had indicated to us as the least likely to be guarded. Sometimes we crossed ricefields, sometimes we ploughed through swamps, sometimes we glided among the trees of a wood, but always we sought to reach the village undetected, to surround it, and then go directly to the spot where we knew the bandit chief customarily slept.

Often he was our prisoner before he awoke. But sometimes we did not find him in his usual quarters. Then I had recourse to another method. I assembled everybody in the village in its central square and proceeded to gaze intently into the eyes of each of them, one after the other.

I have been told many times that there is something peculiarly penetrating about my eyes. I do not pretend to explain it. I make no conscious effort to hypnotize anyone, to impose my will on others simply by staring at them;

but it has been reported back to me so often that few persons can stand my gaze that I assume it must be true. I know that when my soldiers committed some breach of the regulations—absence without leave, for instance—they were totally unable to meet my eyes. And yet my men were no schoolboys. They were a tough lot. I would not have advised most persons to try to stare them out of countenance.

With Indonesians, the effect of my gaze was even more marked. When I had to interrogate a prisoner, I always began by looking steadily into his eyes, without saying a word. Generally it took no longer than a minute before he began to tremble—and in a few minutes more, he would be pouring out his confession in terror.

My officers and my men asked me dozens of times what my method was, what the secret was, so that they could employ it themselves. Possibly they may have thought that I was holding something back from them when I told them that I had no method and no secret, that I was conscious of doing nothing except looking steadily, in quite normal fashion, into the eyes of my prisoners. But whether they accepted that explanation or not, it was the simple truth. I did nothing to intensify the effect of my gaze. It was completely natural.

Since I possessed this gift, there was every reason for putting it to work. So in my surrounded village I would walk from one man to another, looking fixedly into the eyes of each. Ninety times out of a hundred, the criminals could not meet my gaze. They turned their heads away, betrayed their confusion, and even jumped to their feet and ran—straight into the arms of my waiting men. Sometimes they simply confessed on the spot.

I questioned the criminals there and then, before the villagers. Then I asked the villagers to judge them.

Indonesians have an extraordinary sense of justice. Confident in me to protect them from reprisals if they answered truthfully, they judged the terrorist leaders with the greatest accuracy.

"Does this man deserve death?" I would ask.

If the answer was "No," I knew I could trust it. Here
was a man who could be redeemed. This improvised jury
of his peers, knowing him intimately, had pronounced its
verdict, and I accepted it.

If they answered "Yes," we took the bandit away. We
saw to it that he did not return to take vengeance on his
accusers.

I learned by experience that I could put complete faith
in these communal judgments. So far as I know, never
once was there any miscarriage of justice in these village
trials. That is more than can be said for the more formal
processes of the courts of our highly organized western
societies.

It was rare that more than three or four leaders of these
bands would be condemned as deserving death by these
village councils. Often I would find twenty of the bandits
exonerated by the villagers. What was to be done with
them?

This was a problem which the inhabitants of the villages
found it too difficult to solve. I had my own solution.

Once the real criminals, the leaders, had been dealt with,
I chose from the remainder of the band the boldest and the
least corrupted of its members. With the assent of the
peasants, I made him chief of a village militia, charged with
keeping order and protecting the *kampong* against other
bandits. The other members of the band became his police
force. Then I had the former bandits and the inhabitants of
the village take an oath according to the rites of Islam and
I left the village to uphold constituted authority, to manage
its own defence thereafter.

Thus each time I cleared the terrorist chiefs out of a
kampong I left behind me an organization for self-defence
which guaranteed the village against coming under the
power of another group of bandits. Once purged of male-
factors, the *kampong* remained purged for good. It could
take care of itself for the future. I was no longer obliged to
worry about that particular area. I could pass on to others
confident that what had been done would not be undone the

next day or the next week or the next month, confident that the process of cleaning up the Celebes was cumulative, and that where a success had once been gained it would never be necessary to do the same job in the same place all over again.

The results I achieved by converting bandits into policemen were astonishing. Not only did these reformed recruits often warn me of the approach of new bands, similar to those to which they had themselves once belonged, and which we were stalking, but they often fought magnificently themselves against terrorists, though the village militiamen were armed only with lances and with *machetes*. More than one of them died in the defence of the order which they had once menaced. By their sacrifices, they redeemed all the errors into which they had been drawn earlier by the lies and deceptions of those who had misled them.

CHAPTER XVII

Ruse and Persuasion

I have already spoken of the childlike character of the Indonesians including even the terrorists with whom I had to deal. That quality made it easy sometimes to unmask them with comparatively transparent devices.

At one time, for instance, I had to arrest a bandit of a particularly bloody reputation named Malik. Ordinarily, it might have seemed that to apprehend a man with his record for ferocity would have been a difficult and dangerous operation. No doubt it would have been, if I had attempted to take him by force. But it turned out to be extremely easy to catch him by a trick—not an especially complicated one, either. In fact, the bandit gave himself away with a singular lack of guile.

I knew the *kampong* in which he had taken refuge, but I had no idea what he looked like. I did not expect that in this case the other villagers would be likely to denounce him. He was too dreaded a character for that.

My method therefore was to go to the village, assemble everyone in it and begin to question them.

"I am looking for Hamid," I told them. "I have orders to arrest Hamid. Which one of you is Hamid?"

The villagers assured me that there was no Hamid among them. This I was quite willing to believe. I would have been somewhat disconcerted, indeed, if they had produced a Hamid. However, I pretended incredulity, and turned to the villager nearest me.

"Are you Hamid?" I demanded. He denied it.

"Are you sure?" I asked. "What is your name?"

He told me. I glared at him suspiciously, but turned to the next man.

"What is your name?" I demanded.

Thus I continued, questioning one after the other, until I had reached about the tenth or twelfth of the villagers. Then I got the answer I was asking for:

"I'm not Hamid. My name is Malik."

Once again I put on my most suspicious air.

"You are sure you are not Hamid? You are really Malik?"

"I swear it! Ask the others! They all know I am Malik."

I did ask the others. They confirmed the fact that the man before me was Malik.

"Very well," I said. "I won't bother about Hamid today. Malik will do."

And nothing remained for me to do except to check to make sure that this Malik was the Malik I wanted, for thousands of Indonesians bore this name.

Sometimes more complicated ruses were necessary. On one occasion, in a particularly dangerous corner of the island, where it had not been possible to send in agents in advance, since all strangers were executed, I entered a village I knew to be infested by bandits. The real villagers were terrorized, and dared not reveal which among them were the terrorists. I had no luck at all trying to find out who were the chief gangsters. Ordinary methods of persuasion got me nowhere. I decided to resort to stronger ones.

I picked out four young men. I chose expressly those who were manifestly inoffensive, certainly not bandits. I hoped they were among the most popular inhabitants of the *kampong*. Certainly they seemed as if they ought to be. I had my men take them into a hut where I could talk to them privately.

"I am going to have you shot," I told them.

It would be an exaggeration to say that they were happy about it. But they still refused to give any information. It was clear that they feared reprisals against their families if they denounced the terrorists. It could hardly have been on their own account that they continued to keep silent, since the alternative for them was death in any case.

"I am going to have you shot," I repeated, "but you will be safe if you want to be."

They showed keen interest in this amendment of my original proposition.

"All you have to do," I said, "is to co-operate with me. When the firing squad shoots, fall down and remain perfectly motionless until I tell you to get up. All right?"

They were as happy as children who were being permitted to act out a play.

I had my four men led out into an open space not too near the assembled villagers. Indonesians have a gift for remaining as still as a wild animal hiding from a hunter, but I thought nevertheless that a little distance between my actors and the audience for this comedy would be a wise precaution.

"These four men are going to be shot," I told the villagers sternly. "After that, we will shoot four more, and so on until you give up the bandits who are hiding among you."

The first of the four young men was placed before the firing squad.

"Ready! Aim! Fire!"

Challenge to Terror

The bullets whistled over the "victim's" head. He slumped to the ground with excellent effect.

The villagers looked far from happy, but no one spoke up. The second man was put in position and "executed" also. Still no reaction. I began to wonder whether the trick was going to work.

Execution number three occurred. By now the villagers were exchanging uneasy glances and whispering to one another.

Man number four was led up. At this moment one of the village elders rose to his feet:

"Are we going to let ourselves all be shot, one after the other, because we are afraid to accuse criminals who don't even belong here?" he asked.

The question provoked a riot. Shouting, yelling, gesticulating, the villagers fell upon some twenty of the men among them, overpowered them and hauled them before me, denouncing their crimes as they did so. I managed to quiet them down after a moment and persuade them to talk one at a time. It did not take much questioning to establish the fact that four of them were their chiefs, the real outlaws of the band. These four men were placed against the wall and another volley was fired. This time the aim was not high.

As the bandits fell, I turned to the imaginary victims.

"Get up!" I ordered.

They rose. The whole village broke into roars of laughter. Even the followers of the four dead men chortled with glee. Apparently they had never in their lives heard of anything as funny as this macabre comedy. The Indonesian sense of humour may be somewhat peculiar, but we had certainly managed to appeal to it. The villagers were still laughing when we left the *kampong*.

It was a more direct appeal which worked on another occasion, at Kampong Baru, about fifty miles north of Makassar. It was in this region that the armed agitators sent from Java were accustomed to land.

This time I was trying to identify the members of a secret

organization which called itself "The Black Tiger." The villagers had been brought together in the market place as usual. This time also none of them would talk. I decided to try the effect of a little speech.

"I came here," I said to the group of men who stared at me silently, "to meet the very brave men of 'The Black Tiger.' I know what they have done, but I wish them no harm. If they come forward themselves, they will have nothing to fear from me. Is there anyone here who can say that I have ever failed to keep a promise—or to carry out a threat? No! The whole island knows that they can depend on my word as well as on my warnings.

"No one wants to step forward?

"Very well. I will give you five minutes. Afterwards, I will use different methods. I am well informed, and if the eighteen men of 'The Black Tiger' who are here show themselves too cowardly to speak up, there will be no pardon for them.

"The five minutes start now."

I looked at my watch and waited. A minute seems a long time under such circumstances. After a time, I spoke:

"One minute."

Nothing happened. I announced two minutes. Then three minutes. As I said "Three minutes," a man rose.

"I belong to 'The Black Tiger,' " he said.

"You are a man of courage!" I said to him. " Also you are my friend. Come and sit here beside me."

He obeyed. I looked at my watch.

"Four minutes," I said.

Twenty-three men got up!

I seated them about me in a little group.

"I am sure," I said to them, "that you are all real nationalists, real patriots. I understand that and I approve of it. Your country has a right to be independent. It will be. But what connection is there between independence and the banditry you have been carrying on? What connection is there between independence and murder, robbery, rape, extortion?

"You are dishonouring your own cause. I will give you a piece of good advice: give up terrorism. Instead of that, stay here and become a militia to defend this village against bandits."

Two weeks later, a group of Javanese tried to land near the village. The Javanese had automatic weapons, rifles, explosives, even mortars made in Java. My Black Tigers had spears and krisses. With these primitive arms, they held the Javanese long enough for a military patrol to come to their rescue.

CHAPTER XVIII

Mission Completed

By using the methods I have just described, I brought about the pacification of the Celebes with astonishing rapidity. In doing so, I was careful never to violate the legal fiction which held that we were not at war with the Republican government in Java.

True, that government was sending terrorists to the Celebes to prevent the local government from consolidating itself, in the hope of establishing the authority of Java over the Celebes. True, also, Java was indulging in what would have been recognized anywhere as acts of war. And true, finally, the bandits represented themselves as being part of the Republican army.

But at the same time the official situation, the legal situation, was that of two supposedly friendly and equal local governments, the Republican "shadow" government of Java and the Celebes government centred at Makassar, both of them members of the Federal government which was theoretically developing as a result of the agreements reached at Malino, and later at Linggadjati, to which both governments were parties. It may be that Java had accepted these agreements in bad faith—in fact, she had—with the intention of rendering impossible in practice the Federation she had accepted in principle, but that was a matter outside my competence. In any case, I was serving the cause of the Federal idea. It would have been bad policy to have retaliated in kind to Javanese aggression. That would have meant accepting Java's thesis, and acting like the Republican government, as though the Federal idea had already been abandoned.

My tactics, therefore, were based on the premise that I was just a policeman repressing crime. I arrested terrorists, not because they were operating at the instigation of the Republican government—though they were—but because they were committing plain unvarnished crimes. Whenever I found among them, as I often did, an officer of the Republican army, whom I considered to be a genuine nationalist, I did not arrest him, which would have been the proper procedure if I had admitted that the Celebes government and the Javanese government were carrying on an undeclared war, as they were. I treated him as though he, similarly to myself, were serving the common cause of the pacification of Indonesia in preparation for the establishment of the Federal government to which both the Celebes and Java had agreed.

I added these officers to my own staff, inviting them to help me in restoring order. Officially, they could only approve of this attitude. They were servants of the government of Java and the government of Java was on record as having recognized the independence of the Celebes within the framework of the future confederation.

I allowed these apprehended officers full freedom of movement—though of course I was never ignorant of what they were doing. I informed them conscientiously and daily of our operations—after the event, of course. I think I confused some of them pretty thoroughly. Here they had come over from Java with the idea that I was the enemy, and I refused to be the enemy. I professed to take the public declarations of their government at their face value (though I knew better) and they could hardly do less. Some of them were even induced to take part in radio broadcasts, in which they have their impressions of our activities—and under the circumstances, they had to be favourable.

I know definitely that I did confuse some of our other prisoners, when I invited Republican officers to join me in questioning them. When a terrorist who had been sent by a Republican officer from Java to prey on the Celebes found himself being interrogated after his capture in the Celebes by a Republican colonel from Java, his expressions were something to see. Sometimes the colonel's face was worth studying as well.

Meanwhile, terror in the Celebes was dying down. In the villages which we had liberated from the bandits and had provided with self-defence units, the inhabitants had taken seriously the duty of preventing any recurrence of the crimes which had been troubling the island.

There were times, indeed, when I had a really tough time saving terrorists from villagers who wanted to lynch them. The natives were severer than my Commandos. Once freed from the exactions of the Javanese Republicans, they had no intention of allowing them to regain a foothold in the region, and they showed themselves implacable towards these murderers and dynamiters.

The effect on the latter was magical. Once they found that their enterprises were turning out badly, once they found that the villagers themselves had organized to combat them and were not disposed to be lenient towards them, they began to get out of the Celebes. They no longer had to cope only with the inadequate Dutch forces. They had to face a whole population, which was more than they cared to do.

The pacification of the Celebes proper was completed in just two months. It began on December 15th 1946, and was ended on February 15th 1947. During that period, I directed eleven operations, in the course of which less than six hundred terrorists were killed in the fighting or executed. Of my own hundred and twenty-three men, I lost exactly three.

This, however, was not quite the end of the job. The

large island of the Celebes was cleared. But the guerrilla
fighters who had fled from the Celebes when the peasants
joined the struggle against them had not all returned to
Java. They had taken refuge in the smaller islands surrounding the Celebes and there, naturally, they had continued their criminal activities. So I took my men to these
other islands and spent another month in ridding them of
terrorists also and in setting up the same sort of self-
defence systems in the villages which had been established
in the Celebes proper to guarantee them against a possible
return of the Javanese.

It was during this part of my campaign that I committed
a slight violation of military regulations concerning which
my conscience does not particularly trouble me. Sailing
towards a small island called Barangkompo, I came across a
smuggler's junk. We captured it, and found it loaded with
arms and cloth.

According to the rules, the cargo should have been handed
over to the military high command. I did turn in the
weapons. But when I looked at the cloth and remembered
how bitterly it was needed by my friends of the *kampongs*,
rendered destitute by the reign of terror to which they
had been subjected, I could not bring myself to give it up
to the military authorities who would doubtless have stored
it away somewhere, carefully protected by miles of red tape
which would have effectually prevented it from ever being
any good to anyone.

I did not mention this part of my prize to my superiors.
I distributed it instead among those natives who had
been most loyal to us and who needed it most. Their
gratitude was touching. I am sure the goodwill we
gained among the natives by this gesture amply repaid
the gift.

The final phase of the cleaning up of the islands surrounding the Celebes was entrusted largely to the natives
themselves. If we had tried from without to penetrate into
every inaccessible nook and cranny of this difficult country,
the task would have been interminable. We had recourse

to the aeroplane, which could fly above these dangerous seas, broken by islands and reefs, and these jungle-covered mountains which guarded the bandits' refuges. We dropped pamphlets from the planes into all the villages, describing the misdeeds of the bandits who had come to those islands from the Celebes. We told how they had been made to suffer heavy losses by the self-defence tactics used in the Celebes, and thus encouraged the islanders to follow that example.

To our propaganda we added the reports of the "jungle telegraph" which spread far and wide, mysteriously, the news of everything that had been happening in the Celebes, even to these islands separated from it often by considerable stretches of water. The peasants took courage and refused to allow the malefactors to settle in their islands after they had been driven out of the Celebes. Their last refuges were rendered untenable. They took their boats and set sail, defeated, for Java.

Thus ended successfully a mission which had been decided upon in desperation to aid a local government which found itself powerless to cope with internal disorder. When I arrived in Makassar, I found chaos and anarchy there. When I left, early in March 1947, only three months after my arrival, peace and calm had been restored. Communications were operating once more, by land and by sea. The fields about the city, deserted when I had come, were again under cultivation, the green rice-stalks reflected in the water of the paddy-fields. The Celebes was its normal self once more. It had been pacified.

It was a sad blow for the Republican government of Java. A demonstration had been made of the weakness of the authority of that government over the other parts of Indonesia. It could have meant the liberation of Java also. The cardboard Republic of Java might have been swept away, as easily as its agents had been swept out of the Celebes.

Might have been, that is, if the Dutch had been allowed a free hand, as they had had a free hand in the Celebes. But

Java, alarmed, called her friends at Moscow to the rescue. When these allies spoke up for her at the United Nations, the western countries, alas, listened and agreed. They were all anti-colonialists as long as the colonies concerned were those of someone else!

Yet how difficult the Republican government would have found it to tighten its grip on the rest of Indonesia, if it had been left alone against the Dutch and against the other sections of Indonesia, was demonstrated in 1950, when Java tried to reverse the decision I had won in the Celebes. By their customary methods of intimidation, the Republicans attempted to seize power at Makassar. All that was necessary to foil them was a single courageous Indonesian captain, Abdul Assiz, and three hundred and fifty men—though it is true that the whole island was behind him. Having once tasted Javanese terrorism, the Celebes had no desire to experience it again. The natives clung to the peace the Royal Indonesian Army had given back to them. Remembering the lessons of self-defence we had taught them, they did not intend to be victimized once more.

The best evidence as to the feelings of the natives about the pacification of the Celebes was provided by the spontaneous testimonial they gave me when I said goodbye to their island. When the news that I was leaving got around thousands of the local inhabitants gathered near our camp to say goodbye and to thank me for what I had done for them—I had put an end to bloodshed by punishing the culprits without at the same time sacrificing the innocent. I had never bombed a village nor had I ever set fire to the huts of peaceful people. I had had criminals executed, but I had no undeserved or unnecessary deaths on my conscience.

Behind me in the Celebes I left thousands of friends.

CHAPTER XIX

In Self-Defence

I owe it to myself to take the opportunity at this point of answering some of the accusations which have been made against me in connection with the pacification of the Celebes.

I have been represented as a bloodthirsty monster, who attacked the people of the Celebes with fire and sword, subjecting to a pitiless campaign of repression all those who opposed Dutch domination in the interests of Indonesian national independence.

I have already explained my methods and the care which I took to avoid punishing the innocent with the guilty. I have also given the figures of the losses resulting from my operations—less than six hundred terrorists killed, three of my own men lost.

This is a far cry from the fifteen thousand dead which the Republicans of Java attributed at first to my activities. Even this was their most modest claim. Later their broadcasts swelled the figure to twenty, then to thirty thousand, and finally in their propaganda they were claiming that I had killed no less than forty-two thousand persons. These fantastic figures served for attacks on me which even reached the United Nations.

Not only do I maintain that I was responsible for no more than six hundred deaths—a figure which the Republicans multiplied by seventy, but I maintain also that by taking those lives I saved tens of thousands of others, both by stopping terrorism short and then by driving the Javanese off the island. The lives I took were those of criminals. The tens of thousands I saved were those of innocents.

With this much said, let me make something else plain: the figure which I have given is for the deaths for which I accept personal responsibility. It was not, however, the

116

total of the losses suffered from combat with the terrorists
or inflicted upon them. I was not the only Dutch officer
operating in the Celebes. I cannot charge to my account
the losses caused by the operations of others. Nor can I
be charged with the deaths—and this is the most numerous
single category—which resulted from the actions of the
natives in defending themselves against the Javanese or
from the executions which their local councils ordered of
their own accord, without our co-operation or knowledge.

But even if all the casualties are added together, the total
of deaths *on both sides* will nevertheless be only somewhere
between three and four thousand . . . still far less—not
one tenth—than the figures with which the Republicans
charged us.

Because of the attacks which have been made against me
personally, I think it important here to establish the exact
limits of my responsibility. It is true that on my arrival at
Makassar I had been asked to work out a plan for the
pacification of the Celebes. This I did. But though I provided the general plan for the operations, I did not command them. I had full liberty of action for my own troops,
my personally organized Commando. But I had no control
over the actions of the other captains or majors operating
in different sectors. I was only a captain—a captain given
that rank the very day that I was asked to produce a plan
—not a general. If I had been, if all operations had been
under my effective command I should not hesitate to take
full responsibility for everything that happened, including
excesses.

I differed from some of my colleagues on certain matters:
for instance, on the respect due to the Moslem religion
which is almost universal in Indonesia. One of my strictest
rules was that there were to be no armed incursions into
mosques, even though we had reason to believe that criminals
we were pursuing had taken refuge in one of them or had
caches of arms inside. The Javanese often took advantage
of the sacred character of mosques to hide their arms there.
In such circumstances, I always summoned the *imam* and

expressed to him my unwillingness to order a search of the mosque and requested him to surrender the arms in order to avoid it. The Moslems were grateful for my attitude towards their religion and co-operated with me whole-heartedly.

One day, when I was pursuing some guerrillas with a few of my men, we passed through a peaceful village, and reached the mosque at the hour of the evening prayer. Some thirty men were kneeling outside, while an old *imam* droned out passages from the Koran.

If it had not been for my sympathy for the Moslem religion, I would have hurried forward on the trail. But the beautiful ceremony of the evening prayer made me stop a few minutes to listen to the surats which the *imam* was repeating. To my stupefaction, I realized that he was mumbling the same words over and over, like a gramophone running in the same groove. And suddenly, I realized why the position of the group had seemed to me to be vaguely wrong. The faithful were turned towards the north; but a Moslem always prays facing Mecca. They were not pious followers of Mohammed, but the very men I was seeking!

If they had pursued their stratagem a little further and entered the mosque, they would have been safe from me— at least as long as they stayed inside, for I would not have entered the sacred building in search of them. But they were outside the mosque—at its door, but still outside. We surrounded them and arrested them so quickly that the operation was over before they realized that their ruse had failed.

In spite of the fact that my tactics in many respects differed markedly from those of some of my colleagues there was a tendency, during the periods of violent attack against me, to throw up at me various cases which the investigating committees cited with disapproval, even though I had nothing to do with them. The reason they concentrated particularly against me was because I was the Republicans' most effective enemy. Precisely because I was careful to associate myself with the population against the terrorists and not to allow myself to combat all Indonesians because some Indonesians were combating us, I made it difficult for the Javanese to maintain that all whites, all the Dutch, in fact, were the enemies Number One of Indonesia and that a tight union (under Java) was necessary to fight us. It was less because I was militarily a thorn in their side, than because I was politically and ideologically a danger to their thesis, I imagine, that they vented their wrath especially upon me. In the long run, it would have suited their aims perfectly if in retaliation to their behaviour Dutch forces had made indiscriminate attacks upon native villages, for it would have ranged the local populations on their side. As it was, I managed to win over the local populations to our own side. That was why the Republicans acted as though every case cited against the Dutch were my personal doing. As a matter of fact, most of the incidents noted unfavourably in the reports of the investigating committees concerned tactics of which I myself disapproved.

For instance, here is one case concerning a captain who was a highly courageous officer—his offence, indeed, being a product of his courage and his zeal.

He was a strange combination, a half-breed whose mother was Indonesian and whose father was German. His father had been brought to Indonesia because the Sultan of Djocja-karta (father of the Sultan who entered Sukarno's cabinet), had returned from a visit to France with a carriage which had caught his fancy and which he had bought there. This purchase proved to have one disadvantage: the coachman's seat was, of course, higher than that which would have to be occupied by the Sultan; but the rigid caste system of Indonesia would not tolerate the seating of the Sultan on a level lower than that of any of his subjects. The Sultan got round this by importing a German coachman. Since the German was not only not one of his subjects but also, as a foreigner, not involved in the caste system, his higher position could be ignored without shocking local social morals, and it was all right for him to climb up on the coachman's box above his royal employer.

119

Challenge to Terror

The son of this European and his native wife was a curious mixture. Physically, he was an Indonesian, from his jet-black hair to the tips of his wide-spread toes—except for one striking feature. He had the clear blue eyes of the pure Nordic. As blue eyes never occur among pure-blooded Indonesians, these were a striking feature, which it was impossible not to note. Those blue eyes shining from the face of a man otherwise apparently a hundred per cent Indonesian had an instantaneous effect on everyone who met him.

Mentally, the captain was a German. He thought like a Westerner, felt like a Westerner and possessed the type of audacity characteristic of occidental soldiers, rather than the sort of madness which possesses the Indonesian warrior. It was his audacity that caused him to take the risk which led to the incident for which he was so severely blamed.

He learned one day that a secret society called the "Black Panthers" was operating in his sector. He was aware of my tactics of never proceeding without careful preliminary scouting by native informers. But the "Black Panthers" were so dreaded that he could not find any natives willing to make such a mission. He accordingly decided to go himself.

If he had been one of my men, I would have forbidden the attempt. But he was not. He was a captain, of equal authority with me—indeed he outranked me on the basis of seniority. For that matter, he was operating in a different sector, and I knew nothing about his activities. Of this incident, for which the responsibility later on was to be attributed, at least by implication, to me, along with several others of which I knew nothing, I was completely ignorant at the time. I had as little to do with it as you.

I would have forbidden such a scouting expedition on two grounds: the Commanding officer's function is not to serve as a scout. That is a ridiculous misuse of rank, an unjustifiable exposure of an officer with other duties too important for him to be wasted on such details. I admired the captain's courage, but not his judgment. Secondly, it

was foolhardy because of those eyes of his. His object was
to gain information without betraying to the bandits that
they were being spied upon. But it was hardly likely that
he could attain that object, handicapped by a feature that
made him a marked man. He should have anticipated
trouble, for trouble was what he got.

He made his way to the village, bare-footed and in a
sarong, in order to be able to pass as a native. Under the
sarong he had hidden a sub-machine gun. As chance would
have it, he found the terrorists holding a sort of meeting
under the shade of a banyan tree—not a secret meeting of
their society, for terrorists and villagers alike were seated
in a circle about the bandit chief.

The captain sat down quietly in the last row and listened
to the talk, his eyes fixed carefully on the ground, his eyelids
nearly closed.

He remained undisturbed for a few moments, but then,
as was to be expected, the chief spoke directly to him,
being naturally interested under the circumstances in knowing who this stranger was who had entered the village.
The captain answered—and unvoluntarily, in answering, he
raised his opened eyes towards the chief. The expression
of stupor on the chief's face warned him at once of his
mistake. His reflexes were European—thus somewhat
quicker than the chief's—and he was on his feet first. He
pulled out his sub-machine gun, fired a volley into the
crowd, and as the natives, taken by surprise, scattered in
panic, the captain escaped.

It was for this indiscriminate firing on villagers and
terrorists alike that the captain was blamed, and I agree
with that. I do not want to accuse anyone else, nor to dis-
charge any of my own responsibility upon others, for I
made it a point not to interfere with the activities of my
fellow officers, even though they might be applying the
tactics which I had laid down, unless they asked me formally
for aid.

I received such a request at one time from another Dutch
captain, a rather elderly man, extremely courageous and

conscientious, who had been trying to follow my methods, but had had no success in applying them.

He had two companies operating in a region about seventy-five miles from Makassar, a sector absolutely infested with bandits, who almost daily succeeded in carrying out coups under his nose. He had, in accordance with my precepts, set up a scouting service of natives, and this private police force showed itself excellent at reporting quickly on all outrages which occurred in his territory. Hardly had a native village been attacked than the captain would be informed of it, and would set out hot-foot with his men after the guerrillas, guided by his zealous informers. The result was always the same. The scene of the crime was invariably discovered, but the criminals had fled. The captain's men were near exhaustion from marches and countermarches, and their morale, as can be imagined, was none too good, none of their efforts having produced the slightest result.

I responded to my fellow officer's call for help. But the fact he was practising my tactics seemed no reason why I should not also follow them independently of him, and, I should remark, without mentioning it to him. I thus began by sending a few of my own best scouts into the region.

For a few days, I took part in a number of his pursuits of phantoms who were never on the spot when we arrived. Then, one morning, I called on him at his office.

"I have caught several of the terrorists' leaders here," I informed him, "and I am about to have them shot. Would you like to come with me?"

He came out into the courtyard where the convicted prisoners whom I had tried a little earlier were lined up against a wall before the firing squad.

"But what are you doing?" he cried. "You're shooting my chiefs-of-police!"

"Exactly," I said. "Your informers were the terrorists' leaders. It's not surprising that they were able to report crimes to you quickly. They had just finished committing them."

It is one thing to know what methods to use. It is another to know how to apply them.

For those who applied my methods and applied them correctly, I am willing to accept responsibility, as well as for those activities which occurred under my direct command. But I can go no further. Since 1947, it has been convenient for the Dutch Government—which has not, however, had the good faith to publish the various official military, judicial and parliamentary reports on the pacification of the Celebes—to make of me, since I am no longer in its service, a scapegoat for the abuses and excesses committed by all those who operated under its authority.

I cannot prevent the Dutch from casting me for this role. But I am not obliged to accept it.

I do not expect governments to be grateful for services rendered. In that sense, the government of Holland has not disappointed me.

CHAPTER XX

Good Words, Bad Faith

After the pacification of the Celebes, my men and I were returned to Java, not directly from Makassar to Djakarta, but by way of New Guinea.

New Guinea, as everyone knows, belongs half to Holland and half to Australia. It is not a part of Indonesia. It constitutes indeed, a different world. The people are not Malays, but Papuans. Neither the flora nor the fauna are the same. The volcanoes and the trees, the birds and beasts, are quite foreign to what is to be found in Indonesia. Nevertheless at about this time the Javanese nationalists began demanding this territory, which had never been Malay and over which they had no rights whatsoever.

Why this Javanese interest in what was unquestionably an alien land? Was it a case of colonialism being reborn immediately in the breasts of these anti-colonialists, as soon as they themselves became the rulers, and thus possible collectors of colonies themselves? Were the Javanese nationalists, hardly liberated as yet, inspired by dreams of empire on their own account, that they should want to acquire the hostile jungles of this island, which was so inhospitable that the Dutch had already been obliged to give up their plan of installing there the two hundred thousand Eurasians of Indonesia who wanted to flee from Javanese persecution?

I see another reason for the appetite the Javanese displayed for this extra morsel of territory. They were acting, I believe, on the recommendation of Moscow, the influence of which had always been strong in the Republican government and which counts on achieving some day a Communist Indonesia. If the situation is regarded from the point of view of Communist tactics and ambitions, the importance of New Guinea becomes plain.

The islands of the Indonesian Archipelago stretch across the sea like a great fleet of aircraft carriers steaming towards the west, a fleet from whose decks it is possible to command the whole of Southern Asia. But the principal ship in that flotilla is not an Indonesian island. It is New Guinea. And if the strategic importance of the Indonesian Archipelago is not to be neutralized, it is essential that New Guinea should be in the same hands as those which hold the power in Indonesia. Hence Java's interest in New Guinea. Ethnically, historically, politically, geographically, Java has no claim on New Guinea. Strategically, it has every interest in securing it.

An Indonesia considering only its own truly national interests, concerned only for its own independence, would have no particular military ambitions which would make the acquirement of New Guinea desirable. But an Indonesia conceived as a bastion of Communism in Southern Asia, and a possible spring-board for aggressive Communist action, would have vital need of New Guinea.

At this point, a consideration arises which must have escaped the Australians when they made themselves the

advocates of the Indonesian Republican government before
the United Nations. This is that the Javanese nationalists,
if they wish to secure New Guinea as a base for future
operations, can hardly content themselves with the western
half, which belongs to Holland. They will want also the
eastern half, Australia's half. No admiral would be willing
to confine himself to half an aircraft carrier, leaving the
other half in the possession of a potential enemy.

It may be that the Australians today are beginning to
regret their championship of the Republican government.

On my return to Djakarta I found that the situation had
developed considerably since I had last seen that city. The
greater part of Java and Sumatra was under the control of
the Republic and its marauding bands. The British had
withdrawn their troops, but the Dutch who had replaced
them had been able to take over only a small part of Java,
about Djakarta, Bandung and Surabaya.

These small zones which the Dutch held were the con-
stant prey of terrorist raids, which were now being carried
out by much larger groups than had formerly been the case.
Whole battalions of the T.N.I. (the Republican army) were
attacking at a time. Atrocities even more frightful than
those committed under the occupation by the Japanese
were ravaging the island, the guerrillas, whether in uniform
or not, behaving like bands of homicidal madmen.

These excesses continued in spite of the fact of the agreement reached at Linggadjati, while I had been in the Celebes,
which had supposedly fixed the status of Indonesia and its
relation to the Netherlands. The islands of Indonesia were
to constitute a federation, of which the Republican government of Sukarno would be only one of the constituent parts.
It was to be associated with Holland by its allegiance to the
Dutch crown. Although it had seemed politic for the
Republican government to join the other local governments
in agreeing to this arrangement, they did not abandon their
attempt to impose the rule of Java on the other islands.
Instead of ordering a cease-fire, the Republicans only increased their terrorist activity. On paper, they had accepted

federation, but in practice they sabotaged it. Far from wanting a federal government in which every other Indonesian community would have the same rights as themselves, they wanted a single strong centralized government, which they were to boss.

So the hapless archipelago entered upon a long and a painful period during which the Republican government went through the motions of negotiating the details of the establishment of the Federation whose creation it was resolutely determined to prevent. The situation might have been comic, if it had not been tragic as well.

The acts of this bitter comedy took place as follows:

On November 15th 1946 the draft agreement for the creation of the United States of Indonesia, under the Dutch crown, was initialled at Linggadjati. The Dutch Government was the first to declare that it accepted the arrangement, on December 10th. The Republican government remained stand-offish. Worse, on December 26th, the Commander-in-Chief of the Republican army, General Sudirman, declared in a radio speech: "The fight goes on."

This seemed to write off not only the Linggadjati agreement, but even the armistice of October 14th, which had preceded it. At that time, the Dutch had issued a cease-fire order, while the Republicans had not. The Dutch Lieutenant Governor-General of Indonesia, van Mook, pointed out in alarm that such statements as Sudirman's could only result in new bloodshed. Two days after van Mook's observation, on January 4th 1947, the Republican defence Minister Sjarifuddin seemed to be adopting a conciliatory attitude when he stated that the Sudirman speech should not be considered as an incitement to break the truce (which the Republicans were not respecting anyway), but three days later he joined Sudirman in accusing the Dutch of breaking it themselves.

On January 12th 1947 Sukarno himself spoke before a Youth Congress, stating: "The final aim of the Republican struggle is the unity of Indonesia, by which I mean all territories of the former Netherlands East Indies." But what did he mean by unity? A federal government, on the lines of the Swiss Confederation? Or a centralized Java-dominated Republic which the Linggadjati agreement had supposedly ruled out?

It seemed, a few days later, that this could be interpreted as a federal government. For on January 14th the Indonesian delegation was authorized to sign the Linggadjati draft. But it transpired that this was only one more phase of the "blow hot, blow cold" policy by which Java kept the Dutch hopeful (and thus reluctant to take repressive measures) while actual effective implementation of the agreement was regularly postponed. Thus, though the signing had been authorized on January 14th 1947, on February 8th the Republican government objected to doing so on the ground that it did not agree with the interpretations of Linggadjati expressed in the Dutch Parliament. A week later, on February 15th, this obstructive move was followed by a conciliatory one—the Republic at last issued a cease-fire order. On March 17th, conciliation was again followed by obstruction—Sjahrir repeated, "I am only authorized to sign the original agreement."—his position being that the Dutch Parliament's interpretation had modified its terms.

But pressure to accept what the world had hailed with relief as a solution of the Indonesian question was growing too strong to resist. Foreign Secretary Bevin had told the House of Commons in London on February 27th that it was regrettable that Linggadjati had not yet been signed. Minister Jonkman on March 21st reminded the Dutch Second Chamber that the Netherlands Commission General had been authorized to sign it. The West Borneo Council came out for it on the same day. The Sukarno government found itself appearing in public opinion as the sole obstacle to the conclusion of an accord which it was generally believed would end the bloodshed and anarchy which was martyrizing Indonesia. The occupation of such a position was not considered likely to promote its policies, and on March 25th 1947 Linggadjati was signed.

But if signing the agreement was one thing, putting it into effective application was another.

The first indication that the signature which had been generally considered as meaning the end of dissension actually marked only the beginning of a new phase of it, came with an argument over the foreign representation of Indonesia. Minister Jonkman pointed out that it had been set down in the Linggadjati agreement that Indonesians would be employed in the Netherlands foreign service during the interim period before the complete establishment of the United States of Indonesia (tentatively set for January 1st 1949) but that the Republic could not meanwhile have its own foreign service. The more or less official Republican Antara news agency retorted that the Indonesian delegation had always considered that the Republic should have its foreign service, even before the establishment of the United States of Indonesia.

The Dutch responded to this assertion by publishing some correspondence between themselves and the Republicans which had laid down the principle that there could be no formal international representation of the Republic before the establishment of the United States of Indonesia. At the same time, they reminded foreign consuls that under the Linggadjati agreement, the Republic had been recognized as possessing authority only over Java, Sumatra and Madura. Thus, though it tried to speak for all Indonesia, it actually had no right to do so. It was in this sense—as the government of these three areas only—that America recognized the Republic on April 17th 1947.

Meanwhile various sections of Indonesia which had no taste for the Republican government were doing their best to consolidate their status as autonomous states within the United States of Indonesia. South-east Borneo was organizing its own administration; West Borneo had its statute signed on May 12th; the Moluccas, Minahassa and Timor— the half-Dutch, half-Portuguese island—put forward their claims for incorporation as separate units in the new Netherlands Union on the following day. And in Java itself, revolt was developing against the Sukarno government which had fastened itself on the island.

This was in Pasundan, or West Java, that part of the island of which Bandung is the principal city, where resistance to terrorist pressure had been gathering momentum. On December 12th 1946 the Sundanese People's Movement had called for an independent state of Pasundan, which would have meant subtracting this part of Java from Republican territory. This had led, on the 18th, to skirmishes with Republican troops in Buitenzorg in the same region. And on May 4th 1947 the Partai Rakjat Pasundan proclaimed in Bandung the independent state of Pasundan. It was more than an empty pronouncement. On May 23rd, the supporters of Pasundan autonomy carried out a *coup d'état* against the Republican government in Buitenzorg, where it took over all administrative buildings.

At this point the Dutch demonstrated the good faith which they were bringing to the implementation of the Linggadjati agreement by stating, on May 29th 1947, that actions such as that taken in Buitenzorg would not be tolerated. They had opposed the Republican attempt to speak on behalf of all Indonesia at Linggadjati; but in consistent support of that document, they had also to oppose any attempt to diminish the territory there attributed to Sukarno. If the Republican government had been motivated by a similar good faith, the sequence of future events might have been different.

That it was not so motivated had been publicly recognized by the Dutch two days before their own statement on Buitenzorg. Ministers Jonkman and Beel had just returned from Indonesia. The latter reported that they had been convinced that the other native states were doing a good job of organizing themselves for participation in the Federal United States of Indonesia, but that they regretted they had found the Republican attitude over the implementation of Linggadjati unsatisfactory. As a result of these findings, the Dutch government issued a warning to the Republic on May 27th, the day after Beel's statement, in which it said that the Netherlands government considered that the Linggadjati agreement was the firm foundation of its policy and that it expected the Republic to adopt the same attitude.

The Republic, however, clearly did not. New points of contention continued to arise between Java and Holland. On May 30th the matter came up of the evacuation of the unfortunate internees of the ex-Japanese camps. While the Republic announced that all of them had been released, the Hague was still concerned about two thousand of them who were unaccounted for.

Then, on June 8th (five days after the authority of the Republican government had been re-established at Buitenzorg), Java answered the Dutch warning of May 27th. The Sukarno government insisted that the interim administration of Indonesia should consist of representatives of the member states only—thus ruling out the delegate of the Dutch Crown—and that *half of the members should be appointed by the Republican government!* This was equivalent to throwing Federal status overboard. The Republican government would need only one vote from the other states to have everything its own way and in fact generally impose the rule of Java. In addition, Java also stated that, immediately after its formation, the interim government would appoint its own representatives abroad.

"Blow hot, blow cold." After this inauspicious communication, Sjahrir made a radio speech on June 19th which included a notable concession: a representative of the Crown would be accepted as *de jure* head of the interim government. There was, of course, this important difference between the two manifestations: the note answering the Dutch communication was official and binding, but the radio speech was not. And the more conciliatory attitude which the broadcast seemed to indicate was immediately contradicted by a new statement: on July 27th Sukarno declared that the Dutch demand that a combined gendarmerie be maintained to police the islands was unacceptable.

Bewildered, the Dutch tried to pin the Republic down to specific propositions. On June 29th van Mook repeated the

Good Words, Bad Faith

Dutch demands, of which the chief points were acceptance of Netherlands sovereignty, foreign representation under Dutch responsibility and the constitution of a combined gendarmerie, and asked Sukarno to explain his stand on them. He also demanded, as a token of good faith, suspension of hostilities—for in spite of the ostensible issuing of the cease-fire order, terrorist attacks had not ended.

The last Republican step had been on the obstructive side. It was therefore to be expected that the next one would be conciliatory. And so it was: on July 6th the Republic accepted all the Dutch demands except that concerning the combined gendarmerie, and two days later, as an after-thought, it even expressed a willingness to admit the gendarmerie point—provided each state have its own police under its own control, and restricted to operations in its own area only. In other words, Java did not propose to admit a truly Federal police, which might have cracked down on its own police-terrorists.

This was the stumbling-block. On July 11th van Mook made a radio speech demanding acceptance of all the Dutch proposals. As that for a combined gendarmerie was the only one still outstanding, his broadcast was in fact simply a reiteration of Dutch insistence that the Republican government agree to this stipulation.

On the following day, Sukarno went on the air in his turn: the Republic still rejected the combined gendarmerie.

It was a stalemate. Neither side would budge from its position on this point and there seemed to be no solution.

At the same time as this interminable and apparently futile argument was going on, the Dutch were being plagued by difficulties on the international and commercial plane. On January 28th 1947 an accord had been concluded on import and export regulations. Except for native produce, exports were subject to the license of the Director of Economic Affairs, while the importation of military equipment was forbidden.

The object of these regulations was to prevent the illicit traffic which the terrorists had been carrying on, and was to serve the double purpose of discouraging their pillaging by cutting off the market for their booty and making it difficult for them to get the arms for which they had been bartering part of their loot. It was hardly to be expected that they would easily abandon an activity so profitable for them; and as the Republican government did nothing to end the pillaging and smuggling out of the resulting plunder, it continued unchecked in spite both of the truce and of the new regulations.

The day after the announcement of the new regulations, the *Kitakami Maru*, flying the British flag, was detained and on the following day, January 30th, another British ship, the *Empire Mayrover*, was also stopped. Both were loaded with estate rubber.

On February 20th the British sent a protest note to the Dutch about the detaining of their ships. Meanwhile the American *Martin Behrmann* of the Isbrandtsen Line was stopped on its way to Cheribon, and its captain was warned about the new regulations. He proceeded to Cheribon nevertheless, arriving on February 20th, and on March 5th the United States protested against interference with that vessel.

British fulminations against the Dutch finally reached the House of Commons. The American reaction caused a threat by union leaders to institute a boycott against the Dutch. The harassed Netherlands finally decided to permit the *Martin Behrmann* to continue its voyage with a new cargo and to compensate the company for the delay. The Dutch must have been thoroughly bewildered when the State Department declared on March 22nd, the day after this decision had been announced, that Holland had been within its legal rights in the *Martin Behrmann* business. They were, however, not too bewildered to take advantage of this puzzling change of front by the United States, and on April 3rd, the *Martin Behrmann* finally left for Singapore *without cargo*.

But these difficulties of the Dutch with foreign countries could only strengthen the Sukarno government in its

Good Words, Bad Faith

obstruction to the effective implementation of the Linggad-jati agreement. It was plain enough to Sukarno that this was not a moment when the Netherlands could expect support from other countries. This no doubt contributed to the obstinacy of the Republicans in blocking the establishment of the federal United States of Indonesia. As we have already seen, a stalemate had been reached. In desperation the Dutch decided to break it.

Events moved rapidly. On July 15th van Mook handed the Republican government two draft agreements. One called for the institution of a gendarmerie to police Indonesia, the other called upon the Republican government to issue a cease-fire order—this time, it was to be hoped, one that would be obeyed—for midnight.

These agreements were at first tentatively accepted, subject to confirmation. The Republicans then asked for a delay of twenty-four hours and a simultaneous cease-fire order from the Dutch. The Dutch answered that they had already given their order and had kept it. On the 18th, a governmental radio broadcast rejected the Dutch demand for a cease-fire order, at which time the deadline set by the Dutch had already been passed. Nevertheless van Mook waited two days more before issuing his final warning: the Republican proposals being unacceptable, the Netherlands Government was being forced to take a decision.

The answer to that, on the 19th, was the departure of the Republican representatives from Batavia. It was clear that Sukarno was not going to permit the implementation of the Linggadjati agreement. On July 20th van Mook crossed his Rubicon. He sent a letter to the Republican government notifying it that the Dutch government had decided upon military action.

It was the announcement of what is known in contemporary Indonesian history as the First Police Action.

CHAPTER XXI

Hostilities Resume

At this time I was in Java, still in command of the same force which I had directed in the cleaning-up of the Celebes. We were stationed on the outskirts of Djakarta when the First Police Operation began.

The note to the Republican government in which Governor-General van Mook warned President Sukarno that since all attempts at conciliation had proved unavailing, he had given his troops instructions to restore order, was sent to the latter at Djocjakarta.

This fact deserves some explanation for it throws a good deal of light upon the Republican position.

Djocjakarta should not be confused with Djakarta. Djakarta was the new name given to Batavia, the largest port and, under the Dutch, the capital of Java. Although some of the offices of the Republican government remained at Djakarta, the headquarters of that government had been established in Djocjakarta.

Djocjakarta was located in the centre of Java. It was the capital of a small sultanate, ruled by a family which enjoyed great prestige throughout the island. The contemporary sultan was a young man named Amengku Buwono who had been brought up in The Hague and educated at Dutch universities. An officer in the Dutch Army, he was a young man of ambition and talent, remarkably intelligent and the natural person to employ to play a conciliatory role between the legitimate nationalism of the Indonesians and the Dutch, when they returned to their former colony.

The valuable services which this exceptional personage might have been able to render to both sides, the part he might have played in keeping an independent Indonesia in the Netherlands Union, were allowed to go by default, according to common opinion, because of contempt shown him by the local Dutch authorities. In their anxiety to appease the extremists and to arrive at an accord with the bitterest enemies of the former colonial regime, they neglected the importance of the great families of Indonesia and made no attempt to employ the influence they still possessed.

Thus a very curious situation developed. The Dutch, represented as the oppressors, the anti-Republicans, refused to ally themselves with the former ruling families, whom they must have known to be also, by definition, anti-Republican, and hence automatically unwelcome to the resurgent Republicans of Indonesia. And so it came about that numbers of native rulers were picked up by the Republican side and their influence added to it.

In the case of the Sultan of Djocjakarta what happened was that the unstable vulnerable government of Sukarno, seeking a safe centre in which to instal itself, found the Sultan offering it the hospitality of his own capital. It was accepted, and Djocjakarta immediately became the capital of the Republican government.

Its great attraction for Sukarno was this: the Sultan had a small private army, which he paid from his own revenues. That was just what the Republicans needed. They had, of course, their own "army" mostly composed of those terrorist bands which often had only allied themselves with the Republican government because they could thus dignify their marauding as "military" operations carried out with some purpose other than simple brigandage. But the control the government actually exercised over these outlaws was highly theoretical. Its members were not anxious to be at the mercy of its own "troops". The chances were that in such a case, it would not have been the government which ruled the terrorists, but the terrorists who ruled the government. Sukarno and his followers felt themselves much safer protected by the rifles of the private army of the Sultan of Djocjakarta than they would have been surrounded only by the machine-guns of their own terrorists.

Thus the Republican government found itself secure, protected by a kinglet whom the Dutch had had the bad judgment to offend.

One of the administrations which had remained at Djakarta was the Republican foreign ministry. At the beginning of the First Police Operation, I was ordered to seize this Ministry, as well as the Republican headquarters at Pangang-Sahang East.

Foreign Minister Sjahrir was away. His guards were there, however—for by virtue of the agreements reached between the Indonesians and the Dutch, he was authorized to maintain a guard of thirty armed men. Within an hour I had rounded up not only the thirty uniformed men but thirteen hundred civilians. At the same time, we captured a regular arsenal, which included not only rifles and machine-guns, but even hand grenades.

We also arrested a number of extremist leaders—but it was hardly a rigorous arrest, as we installed them in the most comfortable hotels of the city and invited them to consider themselves the guests of the Dutch government.

The First Police Operation lasted only two weeks. During that period it was enormously successful. Everywhere the Dutch Indonesian Army was sweeping the terrorists away. In a few weeks, if the movement had been allowed to continue, we would have gained control of all Java. Terrorism would have been stamped out there as it had been stamped out in the Celebes. We were well on the road to pacification, to the restoration of normal conditions.

But the Police Operation was not allowed to continue. Although the Dutch government and Queen Juliana herself declared publicly that the establishment of the independent United States of Indonesia could only be accelerated by this restoration of order, which was the first condition for the establishment of an effective government, international sentiment was mobilized against the Dutch. At Lake Success, the Soviet delegation succeeded in convincing the western countries at the United Nations that the Dutch Indonesian Army, the legal military force of the country and the only police organization on the spot, was an aggressive weapon being used against the Indonesian people. International criticism was so strong that The Hague dared not continue its successful campaign. Governor van Mook was obliged to order his troops to end their advance and to observe a cease-fire order beginning at midnight, August 4th 1947.

This was the beginning of a long period of futile argumentation at the United Nations and of equally futile attempts on the spot to cope with the anarchic situation which the Dutch had been prevented from ending. A Good Offices Commission was formed by the United Nations, which sent neutral military observers to Indonesia to establish a frontier between Dutch and Republicans for the maintenance of the status quo, an action which had no effect on terrorist activity.

During this period of comparative peace, the race against time continued beneath the surface. While the local governments of the various Indonesian regions continued to try to consolidate their authority with a view to assisting the establishment of the proposed federal state. Sukarno's terrorists continued to sow chaos and confusion so as to prevent the establishment of any stable government.

I had played a fairly active part in one of the two games which were being played simultaneously to decide the fate of Indonesia—that of military action in the archipelago. Now, surprisingly, I found myself a figure in the other— the manœuvres which had the United Nations as their terrain.

Both for the operations which I had carried on in the Celebes and for those which I had conducted during the First Police Operation, I had become the Number One Bogeyman of the Republican government. The Sukarno government flaunted my name before the United Nations. I was granted the unenviable privilege of being described before that body as a bloodthirsty butcher who had slaughtered forty-two thousand innocent Indonesians. All the crimes of the terrorists were brought up at Lake Success—

and attributed to me! To me, whose whole career in Indonesia had been that of a fighter against terrorism!

The attacks against me were only part of an extravagant spectacle which was being staged at the United Nations. The great strength of the Indonesians, in the play they were making for international support, was not derived from their own small group at Lake Success, but from the opposition which the Soviet delegation in particular and, for quite different motives, the great western nations as well, were putting up against a return of the Dutch to their former colony. United Nations observers were later to discover on the spot, however, with some astonishment, the following disturbing facts:

1. The entire educated upper crust of Indonesia, the only persons capable of staffing the administration of a new state, numbered some seven hundred persons. About five hundred were doctors, two hundred lawyers, with a handful of engineers, like Sukarno himself. Small as this potential governing class was, it was still only partly for Sukarno. In fact, those individuals who appeared at Lake Success and gave the impression that they *represented* the brainiest Indonesian nationalists instead *were* the only brainy Indonesian nationalists to be had. Virtually all the most brilliant persons of the Sukarno faction were paraded before the United Nations where it was assumed, of course, that there were many others like them at home capable of taking up the reins of office.

2. The Indonesian Republic, the "government" of Java and Sumatra, was a group of adventurers, without effective power and without a police force—except for that private army of the Sultan of Djocjakarta. Only in that sultanate and in the areas controlled by the Dutch was there any semblance of order.

The "officers" of the Republican army (that is, the ex-leaders of the terrorist bands) had no intention of giving up the perquisites they had enjoyed for so long, controlling the ports and selling abroad crops stolen from the peasants and from the plantations, machinery removed from the refineries, and even rails pulled up from the railway tracks. Those were Java's exports. As for imports, handling them was providing such handsome profits for the officials of the government and for their friends that there was no chance of their giving up this lucrative commerce.

An anti-Dutch propaganda before which the Dutch seemed petrified was successfully presented before the United Nations. Certainly they took no effective action to refute these accusations, letting the case go almost by default. Yet they had sent four different commissions to the Celebes to establish the truth regarding the pacification of that island, so blatantly and so brazenly distorted by their opponents. General Spoor signed a military report which completely justified all my actions. The Parliament of The Hague sent an Investigating Commission to Indonesia, which made a minute study of the matter. None of these reports were ever published. It appeared that rather than defend both itself, and me its agent, the Dutch government preferred to adopt the tactics of allowing the hate and the fury of the Indonesian Republicans to be crystallized against me, in the hope that I would serve as a scapegoat, and perhaps distract attention from the accusations made against them by not rebutting attacks on myself.

If this was the calculation, it proved erroneous since, by failing to exonerate me, the Dutch government gained no greater tolerance for itself.

I may have remained blackened in the eyes of world opinion, but my stock had not diminished in the eyes of those who knew my work at first hand. Accordingly, I was entrusted in 1948 with the task of creating a Special Corps, divided into Commandos and paratroopers, and with giving it intensive training in the methods which had succeeded so well in the Celebes. This group, which was garrisoned in Bandung, was built up to a strength of twelve hundred men—a force, that is to say, of a size which would normally be commanded by a colonel.

At the end of 1948, after the campaign of vilifications directed against me had reached its height, I was nevertheless called to Djakarta by General Spoor, Commander-in-Chief of the Royal Netherlands Indonesian Army, and entrusted with the mission of pacifying West Java, where terrorism had passed all bounds. In giving me my orders, General Spoor told me that the reports of the investigators had justified me completely in my actions in the Celebes and that he was proposing me—for the fourth time—for the highest Dutch decoration.

I had hardly begun, however, my purging of the terrorists of West Java than Spoor recalled me to Djakarta. The so-called "truce"[1] which was supposedly in force under the auspices of the Good Offices Commission of the United Nations was a farce. The Sukarno government was systematically avoiding every effort to reach any permanent effective agreement. Extremist gangs were multiplying, their misdoings being reported from every area. The situation was rapidly becoming uncontrollable. It was impossible to sit idly by and allow Indonesia to be martyrized.

"A Second Police Operation is going to be necessary shortly," General Spoor told me. "Get your men ready. You are going to lead an important operation."

I was not told then what the important operation was to be. It turned out that the role of my unit was to be to take Djocjakarta and imprison the members of the Republican government.

I foresaw what would happen. I would carry out my mission—and a week later the ministers would be released again, for Sukarno had more influence with the United Nations than the Dutch government.

Consequently, I informed General Spoor that I would accept the mission with which he wished to entrust me—but on two conditions:

1. The arrested leaders would not be freed again as on previous occasions, but would be tried in accordance with their personal responsibilities for collaborationism and for the common crimes which they had committed or ordered.

[1] The Reville agreements, signed on board U.S.S. *Reville* on January 17th, 1948. (Publishers' Note.)

140

Hostilities Resume

2. The soldiers of the Dutch Indonesian Army would not be made the scapegoats of another compromise which would in reality mean another Dutch capitulation, but would constitute the future army of the United States of Indonesia for which they were fighting.

General Spoor was unable to give me any assurance on these points. It was hardly likely that he could. But I was weary of the futile task of winning military successes which were then nullified by political defeats. If the conditions which would guarantee to me that my efforts would not be wasted could not be met, than I preferred to abandon my thankless activities.

I told Spoor that I could not participate in the Second Police Operation and handed him my resignation.

The place where the news of my impending departure from the army caused the most consternation was West Java. I had spent just one week at the task of cleaning out the terrorists there, and the inhabitants had already felt the beneficial effects of my activities. They had looked forward with hope to being delivered from their tormentors, but their hope turned to despair when they learned that I was not going to finish the job, and they hurriedly dispatched a delegation to General Spoor to beg him to refuse my resignation.

"Captain Westerling enlisted for the duration of the war," Spoor told them. "The war ended three years ago. Captain Westerling has served seven years. He has the right to resign if he wishes to."

The delegation insisted.

"Why don't you see Captain Westerling himself?" Spoor asked them.

They came to me. It was difficult for me to resist their entreaties, nevertheless I didn't yield. I knew in advance that no definitive success was possible under the banner of the Dutch. They did not know how to hold the victories their fighters might win for them. Something could be done for the Indonesians, something should be done for them, but it was not the Dutch who were going to do it. These former masters of Indonesia were now vanquished in advance. The only way to win any permanent amelioration would be by working, not with the Dutch, but with the Indonesians themselves.

On November 11th 1948, during a dress parade, I transferred my command over the Special Corps to Lieut.-Colonel van Beek in the presence of General Buurman van Vreede, Chief of Staff of the Commander-in-Chief, and retired to a little bungalow, lost in the open country, where there was no European within miles.

For the first time in seven years, I was no longer a soldier. I was a civilian. But for the moment, I did not miss my chosen profession of arms. I had something else to preoccupy me.

I was going to marry.

CHAPTER XXII

Brief Interlude

I had been busy in Java, but not too busy to succumb to the charms of a young Indonesian woman, whom I had first met in 1946 and whom I now determined to make my companion for life.

My wife bore the non-Indonesian name of Yvonne Fournier, for she was not a pure Indonesian, but a Eurasian, her mother being Javanese, and her father a French hotel-owner who had been in Java for thirty years.

I was not Yvonne's first husband. She brought to our marriage two young children and was destined to become later the mother of my own daughter, Cecilia.

With her I began a period of domestic tranquillity which was a welcome change from my long period of soldiering. Although I had to wear uniform for six months after my resignation from the Army, I was now a civilian, and I resigned myself happily to the quiet charm of the married civilian life which was normal for most people but which for me was a novel and idyllic experience.

I believed that I had put adventure and military matters behind me for good and that I had settled down to the delights of domesticity. How surprised I would have been if I had been able to look into the future!

Yvonne and I set up housekeeping in our isolated bungalow, surrounded by native huts, in the depths of a valley. It was not a strategic location. We were shut into our depression among the hills, with no avenue of escape and no point from which we could expect help in case anyone should attack us. No one did. If I had been the ogre the Republicans had painted me, we would have had our throats slit the first night.

The terrorists might have been happy to get rid of me, but I was under the protection of my native friends, the villagers among whom we lived. Their recognition of the services I had rendered to Indonesians was the proof that the Republican accusations against me as "butcher of the natives" were unfounded. I was now protected by my loyal Indonesian comrades in the same manner in which the terrorists themselves had been protected. At the first approach of danger, the tomtoms gave warnings. We were able to go safely into hiding and to ignore the fact that I had made a few enemies, because at the same time I had made thousands of friends.

I returned to one of the delights of my boyhood—the taming of pets. I doubt if many of my European acquaintances would have felt entirely at ease in my Indonesian home. It was full of trained lizards and snakes. I had a twelve-foot python which would come to me when I called it and drape itself about me like a living scarf. I had green snakes, and even a cobra, which lived on milk that it drank out of a saucer, like a pet cat. Less startling for Europeans was my collection of butterflies, which I caught in the fields and in the jungle.

My pets did not disturb the natives, and our house was always full of visitors. Natives came to see me from the farthest parts of Java and even from Sumatra. Most of them wanted me to come to their villages and help them organize the self-defence units which had made it possible for so many *kampongs* to defend themselves. At first, I evaded these requests. I had withdrawn from military service, I had no official status, and I did not want to have any. I thought I had earned the right to repose, to enjoy the quiet pleasures of a home and a wife.

But the natives ordained otherwise. They knew my reputation, thought of me as the man who had saved whole populations from terrorism, and looked to me as a counsellor, almost as a father. Though I attempted to hold myself aloof, to live quietly in my little valley among the friendly villagers, I found myself besieged more and more by visitors who came to ask my advice on all sorts of questions, the most intimate and the most insoluble. One man would ask me how to improve the character of a difficult wife. The next would want my advice on the best means of preventing a drought. They had child-like faith in me, and I felt almost guilty at not being able to solve all their problems. My failure to do so, however, did not at all seem to affect their belief in me, but they continued to come to me for counsel, with a touching belief in my abilities.

I lived among them according to the rules I had set for myself from the beginning in my relations with the natives. As always, I refused the offered chairs which would have placed me on a higher level than themselves. When they offered me a fork, I refused too, and helped myself to their rice by dipping my hand into the common dish, just as they did.

They accepted me as one of themselves. When I came to their homes, the women did not flee my presence, as is usually the case in a Moslem home when a stranger approaches. I sat down on the ground in the middle of the *tanis* and we chatted together as equals.

But though I refused to accept the signs of respect offered

to whites as superiors, I was careful not to fall short of
what the natives expected of white men. Thus, I was
extremely careful never to make a promise I could not keep
and, once I had made a promise, never to fail to keep it.
Among white people, one might promise a service and then
excuse oneself for not having been able to perform it, without
causing any great repercussion. But an Indonesian never
forgot an unfulfilled promise made by a white. For him the
white, a superior being and more powerful person than
himself, was always able to fulfil any promise, however
rash, if he wished to. If he failed it was because he did not
wish to. There was no possible excuse which would exonerate him, in the mind of the native, from the fault of having
wilfully broken his word.

While I lived quietly among my native friends, I followed
the progress of the Second Police Operation, which had
begun on December 19th 1948, by radio. With me no longer
at their head, my Commandos struck like lightning, seized
Djocjakarta, and took Sukarno, Hatta (then Premier) and
other Republican leaders prisoner.

The developments which followed were in complete
conformity with the prediction I had made to General
Spoor. The brilliant efforts of the men I had trained, which
had led to an apparently decisive victory, were rendered
futile and fruitless by the political manœuvres which
followed.

The political prisoners, who were very well treated and
were placed in supervised residence in comfortable hotels,
became by gradual degrees not prisoners, but solicited
partners to negotiations on the future status of Indonesia,
then representatives in these negotiations at the Round
Table Conference held at The Hague, and finally, as a result
of that conference, they emerged as victors pure and simple
and masters of Indonesia. By the end of 1949 the Netherlands had formally handed the sovereignty of Indonesia over
to the Republican government and President Sukarno was
able to make a triumphal entry into the old Dutch capital of
Java, Batavia, renamed Djakarta.

This was the result of the international pressure applied to the Dutch, chiefly through the United Nations.[1]

The beginning of this gradual evolution which transformed the conquered into conquerors was conducted by the young Sultan of Djocjakarta. When my old Commandos arrived in his capital, he was wise enough not to allow his personal army to fire on them. He shut himself up in his *kraton* or palace and was allowed to remain there unmolested, unlike the members of the government to whom he had given refuge. As soon as he sensed the propitious moment, he burst from his *kraton* like a jumping jack popping out of its box, and constituted himself the intermediary between the prisoners, their embarrassed Dutch jailers and the investigators whom the United Nations had sent to the spot.

I followed these events from afar with interest, and indeed I could hardly fail to retain interest as an outsider in matters in which I had once been so active a participant. I had no intention of mixing in them again, however, having become disgusted with politics. On the contrary, I was engaged in setting myself up in private business, in starting what I expected to be a new life, a permanent undertaking which would keep me thereafter a private citizen out of the public eye.

My demobilization from the army had become officially effective on January 15th 1949. As soon as I was free I bought several lorries with the help of friends who proposed becoming my customers, and proceeded to establish a lorry service for freight.

This may have seemed pure folly at such a time and place, for the countryside was still infested with bandits who had paralysed ordinary traffic. A lorry driver was lucky if they did no more than confiscate a portion of his load in each village through which he passed, as a sort of tribute to the local brigands. He might quite as easily, on the other hand, lose either his freight, his lorry, or his life.

[1] On 21st January 1949 the Security Council called on the Dutch to release all political prisoners and to arrange for the transfer of sovereignty by 1st July 1950. (Publishers' Note.)

Brief Interlude

But I was not entirely crazy nor were those friends who thought it their interest to support me in this venture. They believed that I could restore normal communications and get their goods through where formerly they had not dared try to transport them. This calculation proved correct. It was not necessary for me to put into play my knowledge of anti-terrorist tactics; the reputation I had acquired was enough. My lorries went through on the strength of my name alone.

If a group of bandits tried to stop one of my shipments, the driver had only to shout: "Westerling lorry!" to see them leap quickly aside. If they had placed an obstacle across the road, my name was enough to set them to work removing it. Perhaps they considered me a super-natural character. That would have explained many things to them —how, for instance, I had gained the Spirits of the Night to my service. None of them cared to risk a midnight visit from these same spirits which, they knew, had carried away the Terakan and many others in the past, and which might take it into their heads to visit them as well if they dared molest a Westerling lorry. So my vehicles rolled merrily in every direction throughout Java, delivering their untouched cargoes safely to their destinations.

The immunity of my vehicles was the finest kind of free advertising I could have—and in which the whole population co-operated. Whenever a cloud of dust appeared in the distance, someone was sure to say, "That must be a Westerling 'fire cart'." What other vehicles could move through the anarchy of this terror-ridden country without being fired on or otherwise molested? The name "Westerling" became a household word for safe transport. The fear I inspired in the bandits, the friendship by which I benefited among the natives, conspired to give me a virtual monopoly of safe-conduct for merchandise in the island of Java.

Naturally, business flourished. I could not find enough lorries to carry all the goods proposed to me. In a year, my profits had reached six hundred thousand florins—nearly thirty thousand pounds.

CHAPTER XXIII

The Prince Justice Legion

My attempt to be a peaceful private citizen lasted just three months.

It was the natives who succeeded at last in overcoming my desire to be, for the future, a businessman rather than a soldier. It was they who turned me aside from a course which was rewarding me richly to one which beggared me.

I would like to point this out to those who have criticized me so bitterly for the activity I now undertook: I had set up a thriving business which was rapidly making me rich. I had only to continue in it, only to continue to think first of myself and of the profits I was making, to secure a happy personal future. It was because I did not pursue this selfish course that I became a target for vilification and attack. I not only gave up the pursuit of private profit, I poured all the money I had gained into the cause which I now embraced —that of the harassed people of Indonesia, who came to me imploring that I help them.

For the number of suppliants who came for my aid increased daily. Terrorism was rampant. Looting, kidnapping, rape, arson, threats, extortion, torture, massacre were the commonplaces of life for the Indonesians. With monotonous similarity, the unfortunate inhabitants of this island, helpless before the bandits who martyrized them, recited to me over and over again the same list of outrages. There was only one exception, one case of normal activity in the general chaos—the Westerling lorry service. Its immunity provided for the peasants one more agrument to bring to bear upon me.

" 'They' are afraid to fire on your lorries," they told me. " 'They' would not dare attack our villages if you were protecting them."

The Prince Justice Legion

Their argument shook me. After all, if I alone could impose some sort of respect upon the terrorists, had I the right to use that gift for my own personal profit alone? Was it not an obligation to put it at the service of my neighbours, to protect their peace, their property and their lives?

I began to give serious thought to the organization of self-defence among the *kampongs* of West Java (Pasundan) as I had already organized it in the Celebes.

Before making any final decision, I went to Djakarta to ask the advice of General Spoor, and told him what I had in mind.

"If village militias are established in each *kampong*," I pointed out, "they will not only serve to protect the villagers from bandits, but will also provide a force to defend the small states of the Federal Union. Of course, the Republic has promised to respect their separate existence, but you know and I know that it will suppress all rivals to its own domination as soon as it can."

"You were right before," Spoor said. "You were absolutely right when you resigned before the Second Police Operation. You said it wouldn't lead anywhere, and it didn't."

He paused for a moment, as he turned over my suggestion in his mind. Then he nodded slowly:

"I think your present idea is excellent," he said. "Of course, I can't do anything officially. My hands are tied. But if you choose to go ahead on your own responsibility . . ."

He left the sentence unfinished, but he had said all that was necessary. It was clear that I had the approval of my former Commander. My doubts were banished. In March 1949 I set to work.

My sphere of action was limited to Pasundan, the now theoretically independent state of West Java. After some months of conflict, of which a few incidents, like the brief capture of Buitenzorg, have already been mentioned, the principle had finally been established that Pasundan was to

149

enter the Federal Union as an autonomous unit, divorced from the "Indonesian Republic," which still spoke for the rest of Java and for Sumatra. But the brand-new existence of this little state was still perilously fragile. It was for this reason that the terrorists who wished to bring it back under the rule of the Republicans had intensified their attacks on the hapless *tanis* of West Java.

To save this infant state and to save its people, I set to work alone, with no resources save those which I possessed as an individual. I had no money except that which I had earned myself in my transport business. I had no arms. I had only one asset, but that an important one, the unlimited goodwill of the simple village peoples who looked trustingly to me for their deliverance.

I began by organizing self-defence groups in the villages nearest to my own, teaching them the tactics of protecting themselves against intruders, and then moved outwards, farther and farther from my home, creating an ever-widening circle within which the *kampongs* and plantations were securely organized against interference. In the midst of this region given over to bloodshed and anarchy, there grew gradually a zone within which peace and quiet reigned once more. And as the peasants outside that zone saw the restoration of order within it, they clamoured all the more loudly for me to extend its boundaries to take them in as well. Like a drop of ink spreading through a sheet of blotting paper, the clear zone absorbed more and more of the previously blood-stained map of Pasundan. I worked feverishly, organizing militias in village after village. In a few weeks I found that I had eight thousand uniformed men under my direct orders, and twenty thousand others, village militiamen, in the *kampongs*.

These last had no uniform. They did not even have shoes. They went bare-foot, and for arms, brandished lances and *machetes*. I had no money with which to pay them. My feeble resources enabled me to give them only rice and fish.

But their spirit was wonderful. They were determined to defend their own villages and they were leagued with one another, so that all the militiamen of any given region would come jointly to the defence of any *kampong* which was attacked.

Yet these bodies of fighters with their antiquated arms remained feeble. By sheer courage and superior numbers, they might be able to repel the isolated bands which attacked them. But political developments pointed to the success, sooner or later, of the Republican government. If that government, to break up the federal system, launched attacks in force against these villages, threw against them considerable bodies of men armed with modern automatic weapons, they would not suffice to defend the individual liberties of Pasundan and preserve the state of West Java.

We had a militia. We needed an army.

How could I build this necessary force? What means were available to provide this spinal column for the body of defenders I had already given to the state of Pasundan? Where, to begin with, was I to get the men?

I could think of only one answer to this question : I would use the terrorists.

After all, putting terrorists to work as a defence against terrorism was not a new, untried idea. I had put it into effect successfully in the Celebes. What had worked there should work equally well in Pasundan. I set to work to prove that it would.

To place this activity in its perspective within the over-all developments of the Indonesian affair, I should note here that this was at the time when Sukarno was a "prisoner". That is, he was living in a hotel to which he had been assigned by the Dutch who had captured him, under their watchful eye. But very much unlike a prisoner, he was receiving, in his "captivity", foreign diplomats who came to consult him on the settlement of the Indonesian problem. It was not very difficult to predict that his rather theoretical incarceration would not last long.

Some of the terrorists whom I now approached represented themselves as acting more or less vaguely under the authority of Sukarno. Others were operating for their own private profit. They were organized into small groups, their headquarters hidden away in the bush, generally in inaccessible spots. To some I sent messengers, inviting them, in spite of their previous record, to join the forces of order. Others I visited myself.

In my penetration of the wild country where these guerrilla fighters had their lairs, I went alone, or with a single guide, in civilian clothes, unarmed. On foot, I climbed into the mountains or pushed my way through the difficult jungle country. Nothing would have been easier than to strike me down in this wilderness. But no one ever dared attack or even threaten me.

When I had ferreted out one of these bands in its hiding place, I would talk to them along these lines:

"You are nationalists," I would say, "you want your independence. Good! You have a right to independence. All parts of Indonesia have a right to that. Only fight for it as soldiers, not as criminals. I invite you now to become soldiers of an independent Pasundan."

By these means I rallied to my standard groups which professed a more or less close adherence to no less than eighteen different political, religious or cultural groups. Some of them were lost battalions of the Mohammedan Darun Islam movement. Some of them were dissidents from the rule of the government of Djocjakarta, others were even Republican squads acting on their own—legally part of the Republican army, but actually largely independent groups.

My visits to detachments of these last gave me a chance to see on the spot what discipline was like in this so-called army—or more exactly, to discover that it was non-existent. Every man was a law unto himself. He could, on his own initiative and according to his own whim, chop living men into little pieces, rape women, loot and burn native huts. The officers would make no objection, *dared* make no objection. The supposed representatives of the Republican legality, if there was such a thing, they were without effective control over their men. For that matter, they behaved themselves in much the same fashion.

The Prince Justice Legion

From these bands of former malefactors, I drew recruits at such a rate that I soon found myself at the head of twenty-two thousand men. The new soldiers from the ex-terrorist groups were a particularly precious addition to my forces, for they brought their weapons with them. About a third of my force was thus armed with modern western equipment, although, unfortunately, we were extremely short of ammunition for our rifles and machine-guns.

To these men, I added also some of my former Commandos, who enlisted under me willingly in memory of our former joint exploits—some of them Europeans, some from Amboina, some from Minahassa, some Malays. Not only were we beginning to be an army, but we had by now a very substantial area to defend, with a population of nine million.

The first thing I had to do was to impose discipline upon this force—a particularly important task, not only because of the diverse nature of the individuals who composed it, but also because of the previous unruliness of a large proportion of my troops. My regulations were strict. I did not permit my soldiers to abuse their uniform: the penalty for pillaging a *kampong* or raping a native girl—privileges which my ex-terrorists had once allowed themselves as a matter of course—was execution.

But in three years of command, exercised to a large extent over men who had committed almost every conceivable crime before I took charge of them, I only had to sentence ten men to the extreme penalty. And my troops were the best disciplined and the most zealous soldiers that I have ever encountered anywhere.

It was only in extremely rare cases that it was necessary to be really severe. For the ordinary minor military offences, we operated according to a simple code. A warning first, and expulsion from the service if the warning were not heeded. Ordinarily, this was as much punishment as was required. The *esprit de corps* of my soldiers was extraordinary. Expulsion was considered a bitter disgrace and the threat of so dire a punishment was usually sufficient to persuade any offender to mend his ways.

Challenge to Terror

The most common cause of disorder within our ranks was fighting between soldiers of different race or religion. I worked out an excellent, if somewhat spectacular, manner of diminishing inter-racial and inter-religious frictions and promoting tolerance. Whenever two men got into a fight, guards immediately collared both of them and took them to a gymnasium which I had established. They were given boxing gloves and invited to settle their differences there and then.

But it was not a question of boxing a round or two innocuously. The fight went on until one of the two quarrellers had been knocked out properly and was ready to be carted off to the infirmary. It was not rare for the stretcher on which the vanquished left the ring to be followed by that carrying the victor.

This sort of trial by combat quickly put an end to fighting among the men. Once they understood that anyone who picked a quarrel with another was not likely to end it short of the infirmary, they became extremely conciliatory with one another. The boxing was a sovereign remedy.

With the recruiting, disciplining and training of my men proceeding in this way, one fine day I discovered that I was at the head of a genuine army, small but efficient. It had an ensign—the symbolic scales of justice. And it had a name. It was known as the A.P.R.A.—initials which stood for the Legion of Ratu Adil—The Prince Justice Legion.

The name of my private army was the result of a visit from some natives who brought to me the *Book of Prophecies of Jojo Boyo.*

These prophecies had been written by a saint of Panjalu, in the Kedirilang region, in A.D. 1150. The natives maintained that up to the present time all the rest of its predictions had been fulfilled. They asked me to read the following passage:

> *When carriages move without horses,*
> *When wires are stretched about the earth,*
> *Then Whites will be in Java,*
> *Who will be put in cages by the Yellow men.*

The Prince Justice Legion

The Whites will suffer, then they will be freed.
The Yellow men will disappear and hard times will come.
Pointed hats will float in the Serayu[1]
But the better times will return.
The corn crop will be the sign of it.

The age of the automobile and the locomotive, of telegraph and telephone, seemed plainly enough indicated by
this prophecy. The whites of Java, the Dutch, had indeed
been caged by the yellow Japanese, had suffered and had
been released, and the Japanese had gone. Very hard times
had indeed followed the war. But the pointed hats? What
could that mean? I still ask myself that question and I am
still without an answer. The only image which rises to my
mind is that of the hats of the Chinese communist soldiers.
Could they be really called pointed?

The prophecy continued:

When the Serayu River becomes the red river,
The white buffalo will return to his stable.
The Chinese will no longer know what to believe.
Those who remain will be those who agree
With the new state of things.
And then will come the Ratu Adil,
The Prince Justice,
Who will be of Turkish birth.

The natives who brought me this prophecy pointed
triumphantly to this last sentence.

"And you were born in Istanbul!"

It seemed to be their argument that I was the Prince Justice
of the ancient prophecy, the promised deliverer of the Indonesians from tyranny, almost a messiah. They thought it
only natural that I should have come to their aid. Had it
not been ordained that I should do so eight hundred years
ago?

[1] A river of central Java.

This belief in the fore-ordained success of my mission was too precious an asset to be ignored. I read a few passages of the prophecy. It made up my mind for me. That very day I baptized my force the "Prince Justice Legion."

CHAPTER XXIV

The Growth of Power

When I began to build up my private army I had not the slightest intention of taking any part in politics. The Prince Justice Legion began purely as an instrument for the defence of the peasants and establishment of police power in an area where before there had been none. It might reasonably have compared with the Vigilantes organizations which arose in the west of the United States in the pioneer days, before the establishment of a reliable governmental police. Indonesians needed the same sort of protection, which the Prince Justice Legion was born to provide. I had no visions of myself as a leader who proposed to build up military strength as a means of seizing political power. On the contrary I was inspired by what might be called a kind of Robin Hood spirit. I wanted to help and protect my Indonesian friends, and apart from this I had no other object.

I have been accused of having been impelled by personal ambition, by the desire to hew out a kingdom for myself, to create a new state of which I would have been the dictator. This is completely inaccurate. If the military power which I built up, little by little, somewhat to my own surprise, without any previous realization of the proportions it was to assume, led me on to participation in politics, it was because of an unplanned development of my movement which was forced upon it by the nature of the situation and by events which occurred after the constitution of the Prince Justice Legion.

The Growth of Power

Looking back, it seems inevitable today that my movement should have taken on political meaning, whether I intended it or not. There was to begin with the simple power situation. At that place and time, a disciplined force of twenty-two thousand trained men could easily be decisive, especially since it was the only armed force in the country which enjoyed popular support. Neither the Dutch nor Republican armies could appeal to the people as we could. And though the Republican resources were of course incomparably superior to my own, the lack of discipline among them and the inability of their government to control its own troops, meant that any resources turned over to them were likely to be quickly dissipated.

The fact was that without intending it, almost without knowing it, I had gathered into my hands enough power to enable my taking decisive action in Indonesia.

Whether I intended to use that power for political purposes or not, anyone else who proposed to take such action had necessarily to take into account the potential power I wielded and to find out whether it was likely to be thrown into the balance before making any plans for the future.

It was also inevitable that the peasants who looked to me for protection should attribute a political character to the military power I represented. Thus, bit by bit, the Prince Justice Legion began to take on the colour of a political party, and one to which thousands of Indonesians were devoted. If it had ever formulated a platform, which of course I never did, it would have called for local autonomy, for the Federal organization of Indonesia which had been agreed upon at Linggadjati. That it came to stand for this in the minds of the Indonesians was also the result of a logical and inevitable evolution of the situation.

The one thing which was preventing the establishment of effective local government was the anarchy purposely created by the Republican terrorists. The disorder was so great that no new government could succeed, in such an atmosphere, in setting up stable administrative bodies. Though our primary purpose was simply to stamp out

157

terrorism for the protection of the community, our suppression of it also created the circumstances in which it was possible for orderly local governments to be born. The Prince Justice Legion and the self-defence militias I had created brought peace to Pasundan. And with peace came the opportunity to set up local administrations. What we were doing in Pasundan could be done as readily in the other supposedly independent states of Indonesia. And that purely police action, given the basic situation, would inevitably bring about as its result a strengthening of the Federalist movement.

Local governments were indeed being established and consolidated in those peaceful states of Indonesia which had been lucky enough, so far, to have been spared the horrors of the guerrilla warfare imposed upon the regions nearest to the stronghold of Java and most important in the creation of an independent Indonesia, either from their size, position or wealth. In the other islands, governments were being improvised, some good, some mediocre, some more or less strong, some more or less weak, but governments all the same, which needed only time and peace to become authorities capable of holding their heads up in the Federation which was gradually coming into being.

But it was precisely the prevention of the creation of a genuine Federation which was the primary objective of the Republican government. Since the other parts of Indonesia, given peace and order, would create local governments capable of playing a role in the Federation; and since my organization was engaged in bringing peace and order to Indonesia, the Prince Justice Legion necessarily took on the political aspect of a pro-Federal organization hostile to the anti-Federalism of the government of Djocjakarta.

This was the actual situation, though not the admitted one. At the moment that my power was growing, Dr. Hatta, representing the Republican government at the Round Table Conference in The Hague, was himself accepting the principle of Federal government. Yet nothing was more odious to the Republican government than the Federation which would give them rivals in the control of Indonesia. Actually, they were accepting this principle with the determination of violating it as soon as possible. Once they could eliminate the Dutch influence and the Royal Dutch Indonesian Army, which was a sincere supporter of the accepted Federation, from the Indonesian picture, they counted on being able themselves to dominate the fledgling United States of Indonesia.

To this end, speed was necessary. Java needed to be able to operate in Indonesia with a free hand before the other governments had time to consolidate themselves. Hence the willingness to accept, on paper, principles which it was not intended to apply in fact. In order to be able to override these abstract ideas, it was necessary to get into the driver's seat before they crystallized into concrete organizations capable of maintaining them. Thus the Republicans did not lose time battling against principles which in reality they opposed. They accepted the principles, in order to gain time, but they had not the slightest intention of ever implementing their acceptance.

The difference between acceptance of a formula and the translation of the formula into fact was clearly indicated, for instance, in the discussions at the Round Table Conference on the future army of the Federal government. Obviously, the Federation had to have an army to maintain its authority and make it an effective government, not a paper one. Such an army already existed in the form of the Royal Dutch Indonesian Army, the K.N.I.L., the regular native army of the former Dutch East Indies.

Unfortunately, from the Republican standpoint this was an army which, if it had been mustered into the service of a Federal government, would obviously have considered it its duty to defend the Federation. It was commanded by Dutch officers or by Indonesians who had been educated in Dutch military schools. Its native soldiers were largely professionals, almost a hereditary group, for many of them were from families who had sent their sons for generations into the service of the Queen. Most of them were from the traditional suppliers of warriors, the islands of Amboina and Minahassa, to which the Spaniards had long ago brought Christianity, and which had supplied the army with soldiers, from father to son, ever since Dutch power was first established in Indonesia. This army had already been in the service of Federalism from the time that régime had been agreed upon for the area. Its long established tradition of loyalty would lead it to continue to defend Federalism. This made it a hostile force for the Republicans, who, as I have said, were accepting the principle for the sake of avoiding a long argument, with the intention of sabotaging it later. They could hardly hope to succeed if they accepted at the same time an armed force which would take seriously the engagements they were themselves accepting with their tongues in their cheeks.

Still, to engage in another long argument about the army would also have meant loss of time, a fatal matter for the success of their policy. So they accepted the army—which was looked upon as the guarantee of their fidelity to their promises and at the same time added a proviso which quite vitiated the effect of their acceptance.

It was agreed that the Royal Dutch Indonesian Army and the Army of the Republican government should be merged, to become the army of the Federal United States of Indonesia. This could have been all right—except for one thing. The merging of the two forces was to be left for execution by the new Federal government.

It was easy to predict what would happen. The Republican government, calling itself the Federal government, would never actually bring about an effective merger of the two forces. The experienced and disciplined soldiers of the K.N.I.L. would be left in their barracks, while the Republican terrorists and the guerrillas would be re-entitled "the Federal Army." And in their new status, they would be able within a few weeks to end the independence of the other states and to establish the dictatorship of Java over the entire region. What it all amounted to was not a merger of the two forces but the subtraction from the scene of the

K.N.I.L., the only force sincerely trying to serve the Federal government which had been agreed upon.

The only force, that is, except the Prince Justice Legion.

CHAPTER XXV

Recognition of Power

The importance which the Prince Justice Legion had assumed as a force automatically supporting the Federal principle and as a factor to be reckoned with in Indonesia was quickly recognized on every side.

One of those who realized that this unofficial army might play a leading role in shaping the future of this part of the world was the Dutch Commander-in-Chief, General Spoor. Nor was its meaning lost on the champions of Federalism in other parts of the archipelago. A number of the Federalist leaders invited me to visit their territories and organize there self-defence militias and new battalions of the Prince Justice Legion.

I was too busy in Pasundan to answer these calls immediately. If the negotiations at The Hague had dragged out longer, I might have had time to extend my movement throughout the islands until the Federal cause possessed a force so strong that subsequent developments would have been different. Again, if an unexpected trick of fate had not removed from the scene the one man who might have been capable of securing respect for the engagements undertaken regarding Federalism and who, I am sure, would have looked upon the extension of my movement with a benevolent eye, the course of history might have been changed.

This catastrophe was the sudden death of General Spoor on May 25th 1949.

This dramatic removal from the scene of one of the most important actors on it occurred in so abrupt and strange a

fashion that many of the staff officers of the K.N.I.L.
believed that General Spoor had been poisoned. This was
not an absurd assumption, for poison was a means frequently
used in Java to get rid of embarrassing persons, and the
Javanese are past masters in the poisoner's art. They have
developed vegetable poisons much more subtle than the
toxic chemicals with which the West is more familiar. They
leave no trace of their action, or at least none obvious to
Western doctors familiar with the effects of such poisons
as arsenic or strychnine but not with the deadly oriental
concoctions whose secrets are jealously guarded by the
initiate.

General Spoor was succeeded by General van Vreed.
The new Commander-in-Chief did not by any means share
the ideas of his predecessor. It was, in fact, for that very
reason that he was in Indonesia. Maybe the Socialist
government of Holland had appointed him to be Spoor's
aide partly in order that he might serve as a brake on him.
One of van Vreed's functions was to see to it that Spoor's
political ideas were not translated into decisions in which
The Hague might not concur.

On one point, however, van Vreed had to agree with
Spoor—the importance of my movement. By now it had
assumed a scope which had surprised even me, so it was not
odd that van Vreed also should not fail to recognize it.

In November 1949, I received a message from the
Dutch General Staff Headquarters. General van Lange,
General Buurman van Vreed's Chief-of-Staff, wanted to
see me.

"I am no longer a member of the army," I answered.
"If the general wants to see me, he knows where I
am."

General van Lange therefore put himself out to the extent
of paying a call on ex-Captain Westerling. He visited me
at Bandung, where at the time I was occupying room No.
101 in the Preanger Hotel.

"We understand," he told me, "that you are at the
head of a rather important movement. We hope that it is

not your intention to take any action before the transfer
of sovereignty to the United States of Indonesia. If you
should do so, you might do great harm to the interests of
the Netherlands."

"Give me the assurance," I answered, "that the Federal
states and their populations will be protected against the
violence of Republican guerrillas and that the soldiers of
the Royal Dutch Indonesian Army will not be simply
abandoned to their fate."

"You have the guarantee of the Dutch government on
these two points," General van Lange assured me.

But within a few weeks, the trust which had been placed
in the Republican negotiators at the Round Table Conference on these two points was to be betrayed.

The Republicans fully recognized, of course, that the
force I controlled could be an obstacle to their plans to
reject Federalism, and they thus thought it necessary
to assure themselves as to my intentions before going
ahead.

It was towards the end of 1949 that I received a message
from the prefect of Bandung, the capital of Pasundan, whose
local government looked to the support of my Legion to
safeguard its independence. He informed me that the
Republican military authorities wished to send an emissary
to talk with me.

It was five days before the date set for the transfer of
sovereignty to Indonesia—the Round Table Conference had
agreed that this ceremony should take place on December
27th—that I received Colonel Sutoko, Chief-of-Staff of
the Silivanghi division of the T.N.I., the Republican army.
This was the best division of that army and the only one
that was more or less a regular military unit.

Sutoko showed himself extremely courteous, even
affable. His division, he told me, was assigned to keep
order in Pasundan after the transfer of sovereignty. Could
he collaborate in that task with the Legion of Ratu
Adil?

I told him that I was entirely willing to co-operate with

the Republican troops for the maintenance of order. However, I continued, I had to put two conditions. They were these:

1. The Republican troops must cease maintaining the prevailing anarchic conditions and sabotaging the Federal régime established by the agreement reached at The Hague.

2. Rigorous discipline must be instituted among the Republican troops. My forces were disciplined and orderly. Their reputation could not be compromised by association with troops which were undisciplined and disorderly.

Colonel Sutoko was voluble in giving me every assurance on these two points.

I thus had assurances as to the protection of the native population and respect for the engagement taken to institute a genuine Federal government from both the Dutch and the Indonesians. They proved to be of exactly equal worth—that is, none at all.

Of course, the promises of politicians have never been looked upon as particularly worthy of trust. And it was too much to expect of the Republicans in particular that if they had not hesitated to accept at The Hague commitments which they had no intention of honouring, they should boggle at making with me, a private individual, engagements entered upon in the same bad faith.

Indeed, at the very moment when Colonel Sutoko gave me his word on my two stipulations, the group whose very composition was evidence that the Republican government had already been formed was waiting in the wings to play its designated role.

The transfer of sovereignty was pronounced by Queen Juliana on December 27th 1949. My interview with Colonel Sutoko occurred on December 22nd. But two days earlier, on December 20th, the cabinet which a week later was to become the first government of the United States of Indonesia had already been consituted.

It will be instructive if we take a careful look at that cabinet.

CHAPTER XXVI

Rape of a Government

There were sixteen constituent states in the Federal United States of Indonesia to which sovereignty over the former Netherlands East Indies was transferred on December 27th 1949, one of which was the Indonesian Republic of Djocjakarta—that is to say, Java.

The administration which had been set up in advance to govern these sixteen states comprised a President, a Premier and seven ministers—nine persons at the head of sixteen states. However equitably the new régime might have tried to divide the offices, seven states had to be without immediate representation.

But it was hardly necessary to leave thirteen out of the sixteen unrepresented!

Yet that was what the new government did.

Seven of its nine members came from the Indonesian Republic—which was only one out of sixteen states!

Two of its members represented the other fifteen!

The mere mention of the names of the new cabinet was evidence that the Federation had been stillborn.

Sukarno, President of the Republic of Djocjakarta, became President of the Federation.

Dr. Hatta, Premier of the Republic of Djocjakarta, became Premier of the Federation.

Of the seven ministers, five—one of them the Sultan of Djocjakarta, whose private army had protected the infant Republic from the beginning—were from the Republic of Djocjakarta.

As though this were not enough, the personalities of the two sole representatives of the other fifteen states guaranteed no effective opposition on their part to the ruthless manœuvres of the tough, determined ministers from the Republic of

165

Djocjakarta. They were both charming, pleasant men—but that was not what was needed to oppose the Sukarno forces. They would have had to have been as tough as their opponents to be able to block their manœuvres—in fact tougher, for they were outnumbered. Pleasant men, affable men, reasonable men—men who were not fighters—were conquered in advance.

One of the two outsiders represented West Borneo—Sultan Hamid of Pontianak. He was a friend of mine, a most agreeable companion at social functions or officers' clubs.

His father had been that ruler of West Borneo who had courageously resisted the Japanese invasion in 1942—a resistance which had cost him his life and that of Hamid's brothers (there were eleven of them), decapitated by Japanese sabres.

Hamid had been fortunate enough to avoid this untimely end. He was absent from Pontianak at the time of the invasion and of the executions which followed. A lieutenant in the Dutch Army, he had been made a prisoner after having valiantly distinguished himself, and had been interned along with his Dutch brothers-in-arms captured with him on the field.

A brilliant officer, and extremely handsome young man who was adored by women (they called him Handsome Max), and husband of a blond Dutch girl, he was not taken very seriously in his state, which he ruled as an absentee. He was a good jazz-player and an excellent dancer—in short, an escort much in demand and a decorative high society Sultan. But he was no politician, although events had conspired to make him the official representative of the Federated states at the Round Table Conference.

There he might have played a decisive role, for he represented the majority of Indonesians, whether counted as individuals or as states. Nevertheless he permitted the Republicans to take the lead in the conduct of negotiations. Having found him malleable at The Hague, they had no fear that he would make any difficulties for them within the

Rape of a Government

Federal government. Rather he served to provide a semblance of representation for other states than the Republic, while at the same time he could be counted on to follow meekly in the Republican wake.

If the Republicans knew him, so did I. I had talked with him often and I knew in advance that he would not be able to steer Indonesia away from the disaster the Javanese were preparing for it.

The other non-Republican member of the cabinet was likewise a sultan, Anak Agung Gne Agung, son of a rajah of Bali. He had become the premier of President Sukawati, the leading spirit in the government of the Celebes. Anak Agung Gne Agung was a distinguished man, with an excellent Dutch education, but in no way a leader. Though a non-Republican, he was nevertheless, in the beginning at least, a pro-Republican.

Neither of the only two non-Republicans in the Federal government were capable of preventing the assassination of that government. Thus the very composition of the cabinet fixed the fate of Federalism before it had even begun to function.

Even these two innocuous hostages from the other fifteen states were not to remain in the government long. Anak Agung Gne Agung was removed from it in courteous fashion: he was named Indonesian Ambassador to Belgium. Sultan Hamid was less fortunate, for he was shortly afterwards imprisoned. It was in that fashion that he was repaid for his deference to Republican leadership.

Thus not one Federalist remained in what had been organized as a Federal government!

It was left to be administered by Hatta, the right-hand man of Sukarno; by the Sultan of Djocjakarta, who has been called the Bonaparte of Indonesia; and by the other anti-Federalist-Republican ministers who were dominated by these three.

One final observation on this curious cabinet:

We have already seen how the Dutch forebore from using the influence of the ruling families of Indonesia, in

167

the belief that a revolutionary government which called itself Republican would be antagonistic to the rajahs and sultans. But this revolutionary government had not been able to get along without three sultans among its nine leaders —one third of its membership.

On December 27th 1949 Queen Juliana proclaimed the transfer of sovereignty at The Hague and in Djakarta Dutch High Commissioner Lovink looked on as the Dutch flag was lowered and the red and white ensign of the new Indonesia rose to the top of the flagpole of the governmental palace, and immediately afterwards boarded a plane for Amsterdam.

The Federation was born.

On December 28th 1949 the Republicans began their assault upon the statute which they had accepted for the United States of Indonesia, and the Federation began to sicken.

The leaders of the other states received threatening letters. "Join the Republic," they were told. "Think of the safety of your wives and children."

Detachments of the Republican army, now renamed the Federal army, were dispatched to occupy the capitals of all the other states of the Federation. The assignment given to this "Federal" army was to stamp out Federalism.

This mission took several weeks to complete in those localities where neutral officers, serving as observers for the United Nations, were stationed. There it was necessary to apply discreet pressure to force the local governments, seemingly of their own free will, themselves to announce their fusion with the Republic of Djocjakarta. The Javanese colonel sent to the local capital was charged with negotiating this surrender with the authorities there, who knew very well what sort of fate was reserved for them if they held out. They were not obstinate long.

Where there were no observers from outside, it was less necessary to use persuasion. Simpler and more direct methods could be employed. How extremely simple they were, I had an opportunity to see for myself, one fine morning, when the Resident of Cheribon arrived in Bandung in his pyjamas.

At 11 o'clock the night before, four Republican soldiers and a corporal had broken open his door, had pulled him out of bed, and had simply thrown him out of his official residence, barring his office to him at the same time. He had not even been allowed time to take his trousers or to throw a blanket over himself. At midnight his Republican successor had already taken possession of his slippers and his portfolio, of his functions and of his bed, which must have been still warm when he climbed into it.

The transfer of authority here from Federalism to that of the Republic was thus unceremoniously concluded.

It was only a matter of a few days before the sixteen states of the Federal government had become a single state, the Indonesian Republic, administered by the Javanese. To maintain that power in the stolen territories, the terrorist régime, whereby the peasants were subjected to the orders of Djakarta (for the Sukarno government now returned to the former capital), was reinstated throughout Indonesia.

The process was not quite so easy at Pasundan, for there alone was there a force capable of preventing this rape of the local government—the Prince Justice Legion.

The co-operation of the Legion had been promised to Colonel Sutoko for the support of the Federal government and the maintenance of law and order. It had not been promised for the destruction of the Federal government and the return of the terrorism which the Legion had once banished from Pasundan.

Hardly had the colonels of the Republican army, who had installed themselves in Bandung, assumed their functions, than they began to violate the formal assurances which had been given me by Sutoko. Their so-called military companies were exposed as bands of unrestrained terrorists, which set to work at once, under the leadership of their political commissars and their piratical officers, to loot private dwellings, farms and plantations, assault the officials of the local government, arrest those who dared oppose them and kidnap others. Attacks were made against our under-armed and outnumbered self-defence groups in their villages and captured militiamen delivered to torture by the Republican "soldiers".

There was no other force anywhere capable of checking these outrages except the one which I controlled. There was no one except myself in a position to protect the peaceful peasants whom I had once freed from the terrorism and extortion and who were now doomed, if I remained inactive, to be subjected to it again.

Possession of that power imposed a duty upon me. So long as I was able to do anything about it, I could not sit idly by and allow tyranny to be established over my friends and neighbours by default.

I had to act.

At the beginning of January 1950 I sent an ultimatum to the government at Djakarta.

CHAPTER XXVII

"Arrest Westerling!"

The ultimatum which I sent to the government at Djakarta was exactly that. It had the two characteristics of the sort of ultimatum which one government sends to another—it made specific demands and it set a time limit for conforming to them. I was hardly a government. But I possessed, in Pasundan, the most essential attribute of a government—I controlled a police power capable of enforcing governmental measures. This was more than either the West Java or the Republican governments could claim in this territory for the moment. They could legislate, but they could not enforce. I was not a government but I could govern—if I wished. They were governments but they could not govern.

In my ultimatum, I addressed the "Federal" government as Commander of the Prince Justice Legion and of the self-defence organizations of Pasundan. I demanded of that government that it cease its anti-Federalist propaganda, that it put an end to the terroristic exactions of its troops and that it recognize the Prince Justice Legion as the official police force of this territory. I gave it six days to execute these measures.

At the same time as I dispatched this communication to Djakarta, I sent two copies to addressees who had every interest in supporting me. One went to the United Nations observer at Bandung, for the benefit of the foreign observers as a whole. Since the function of these observers was to see to it that the conditions of the Round Table Conference —of which the keystone was the Federal organization of Indonesia—were observed, and since the whole meaning of my ultimatum was adherence to the Federal principle and opposition to the Republican attempt to sabotage it, it should have been welcome to the neutral observers.

The other copy went to the local government of Pasundan at Bandung. The very life of this government was threatened by the actions of the Republicans. If the issue were to be settled by force, I controlled the only force which could save it. I felt, therefore, that the West Java government also should be on my side. More precisely, I was on its side.

Reaction from the two sources interested in maintaining Federalism was direct and comparatively prompt, but that from the recipient of my ultimatum was only indirect. It is difficult, indeed, to see how the Republicans could have answered me without embarrassment, unless they were prepared to keep their engagement to establish a Federal Indonesia, which was the one thing they were obstinately determined not to do.

The first response came from Major Simpson, the United Nations observer in Bandung. He notified me at my head-quarters that the time I had allowed the Djakarta government in my ultimatum was not long enough to permit it to take a decision. He asked me to extend the time limit.

I answered that I was quite willing to do so if the Republicans put an immediate end to the outrages committed by their forces. Obviously it was impossible for me to accept an indefinite continuation of their régime of terrorism. That would have meant presenting the Republicans with victory in advance. But if they wished to call a truce during their deliberations, I was prepared to meet them half-way.

Following the initiative of Major Simpson, I received a message from the West Java Parliament. On January 10th, five days after the dispatch of my ultimatum, this body invited me to come to Bandung to confer with the cabinet. On the following day, therefore, I went to the capital and participated in a cabinet meeting.

Republican propaganda has chosen to represent me as an adventurer, an irresponsible individual. But here I was accepted as an at least semi-official personage, with whom the members of a government could talk on equal terms. I sat with the ministers, on the right of President Wiranataku-suma, an old prince of a very ancient noble family, facing Premier Anwar Tchokro Aminoto, one of the chief leaders of the Islamic movement, and discussed with them the situation in which West Java found itself.

I explained my personal position to them. My sole aim, I said, was to protect the Federal states and to defend their peace against Republican terrorism. My disciplined troops and the village militias of the self-defence organization, I pointed out, were much more capable of constituting a police force for Pasundan than the lawless guerrillas of the Republican government. I offered to put the Prince Justice Legion at the disposition of the Pasundan government, for the maintenance of order and as a guarantee that the independent status within the Indonesian Federation established for it at The Hague would not be violated.

It was salvation that I offered them. If they had accepted at once, they would have possessed the force necessary to maintain themselves—but, afraid, they hesitated. In their debate, they showed themselves badly divided as to the safest course to pursue. The bold one, of thus providing themselves with an armed force which would permit them to face the Republicans on equal terms and bargain with them in

"*Arrest Westerling!*"

the knowledge of solid armed support, was too forthright for them. They compromised—but in such a situation compromise was fatal.

They agreed with my proposals in principle, but were unwilling to give them immediate practical effect. If they were terrified at the excesses of the guerrillas, they were even more terrified at the prospect of taking any direct action against them. Premier Aminoto announced finally that he would go to Djakarta himself, taking one of the other ministers with him, to attempt to reach an agreement with the central government.

He was putting his head in the lion's mouth. He might, perhaps, have gone safely to Djakarta if he had first accepted my organization as the official police of his state. He would then have had the possibility of answering force with force, if the Republicans chose to employ it—as they did. But to go before a Pasundan force had been established was to give Djakarta the chance of acting immediately to forestall its establishment. And act immediately was what Djakarta did.

The two Pasundanese ministers went to Djakarta, but they did not return. As soon as they arrived, the anti-federalist "Federal" government had them detained.

This was the answer to my ultimatum. These detentions were a declaration of war against me. Prime Minister Hatta made its significance even more plain by declaring to newspapermen: "If Westerling attacks us, we will defend ourselves." In other words, he had supplied the provocation and was now challenging me to answer it. The Republicans had not directly rejected my demands; but it was obvious that they could never accept them. Instead, they had undertaken this aggressive act against Pasundan and had said to me, in effect: "What are you going to do about it?"

Their tactics were not unskilful. They wished to force me to take the initiative. Then I could be made to appear the aggressor in the eyes of public opinion. And if they chose simply to maintain their position, how could I avoid taking the initiative? To fail to act meant surrendering to terrorism. The Republicans had only to wait, without

173

proceeding directly against me, to force me to proceed against them.

That this was the way they wanted it was clear in the developments of the next few days. The extremist newspapers fulminated against me, demanding my arrest again and again. But Hatta issued no warrant. It took a violent press campaign (his own journalists apparently did not understand the secret intentions of their government) to force him at last to issue the order for my arrest. Did he at the same time warn his police officers confidentially that if they actually did arrest me, that would be highly embarrassing for the government? Certainly they acted as if arresting me were the last thing they desired to do.

During these troubled days, when my name was being shouted from the front pages of all the newspapers coupled with the most violent invectives, I made three trips to Djakarta—and back. I was able to enter the enemy's capital and leave again, openly, something which the legally appointed ministers of Pasundan had not been able to do. Not a single Republican policeman or soldier made the slightest move to arrest me. Yet everyone knew me. I made no attempt to hide.

My immunity was no doubt due in part to the Republicans' desire that I should be forced to act first. But it must also have been due to the knowledge that the Prince Justice Legion stood behind me. If they had arrested me, they would have held one individual, but how would the Legion have reacted? Would the Republic not have had an immediate war on its hands, conducted by what was now, since the departure of the foreign troops, the best-trained and best-disciplined force in Indonesia?

The Prince Justice Legion was my protection, which permitted me to enter and leave Djakarta freely, even though my arrest had at last been decreed. It might have served as protection also for the Pasundan ministers, if they had been wise enough to accept the services of my soldiers when they were offered.

"*Arrest Westerling!*"

My freedom from arrest was not without its comic side.
Two episodes in particular were especially amusing.

One day I found a military road block in my way—one
which could hardly have had any purpose except to serve
as a defence against a possible movement of my troops.
As my jeep drove up to the block and stopped, a dozen
armed men surrounded the car. I reached into my pocket
for my identity card and held it out to the officer in charge
of the block. As I did so, my sleeve caught my revolver, which
was pulled out of my pocket by the same motion with which
I withdrew the card, and fell with a clatter on the ground.

The officer looked at the card.

"Captain Westerling?" he exclaimed, in surprise. He
had perhaps been prepared for my arrival with a troop of
soldiers ready to storm his barrier, but not for this peaceful
presentation of credentials.

He seemed nonplussed for a moment. Then he made up
his mind, saluted, handed back my card, and gestured to his
men to open the block.

"Go ahead, Captain," he said.

And he bent over, picked up my revolver and handed it
politely to me.

Two days later I made another trip to Djakarta. I called
on some friends who were terrified at seeing me. They
told me that my photograph was displayed in all the police-
stations and that I would certainly be arrested unless I
managed to slip out of town at once without being spotted.

I got into my jeep and drove to the central station of the
military police. I walked straight into the Chief's office
and tossed my automatic on his desk.

"I hear you want to arrest me," I said.

The Chief of Police jumped up and came to attention.

"Not at all, Captain, not at all!" he stuttered.

I glanced significantly at the poster bearing my photo,
tacked to the wall behind his head.

"A mistake, Captain," our police chief explained. "Just
a mistake. No one wants to arrest you."

"As you please," I said.

I picked up my revolver and headed for the door. The Chief of Police hastened after me and opened it for me. "Good luck, Captain," he said, as I left.

CHAPTER XXVIII

Coup d'état

No answer had been returned to my ultimatum. The time limit having expired, the moment had come to act.

I knew, as I have already explained, that the Republicans preferred that it should be I who took the first overt action. But I had to oblige them. There was no other possible strategy. The only alternative was to do nothing, and that meant letting the anti-Federalists win by default.

I determined therefore to launch a *coup d'état*.

This was to be a movement on a larger scale than anything I had yet attempted. I had been operating hitherto in West Java, where I headed an effective police force, but it was not simply for West Java that I intended to act now. It was for all Indonesia. The question was not simply that of governing Pasundan. I proposed nothing more nor less than the seizure of the Federal capital—Djakarta. It was my plan to overturn the so-called Federal government, and take over for the entire archipelago.

Here I must set the record straight once again on my personal role in this movement. It was not my intention to take over in my own name. I had no ambition to become the white rajah of Indonesia, and it was for the benefit of the people, not for my own, that I was preparing to overthrow the government which had betrayed them. Federalism was a mere façade; the few Federal members of the government were only hostages. This was not what Indonesians had meant by independence, it was not what the Netherlands had purchased for them by their relinquishing of sovereignty, and it was not what the United Nations, as the sponsors of the infant nation, had meant the Indonesian people to have.

These exploiters of the people I intended to replace, not by the dictatorship of a single man, however well-intentioned, but by a government of genuine Indonesian nationalists, made up of men who had neither collaborated with the Japanese in the past, nor were preparing to collaborate with Moscow in the future.

This government was ready.

You will understand that it is still not possible for me to reveal all the details of this movement. That would mean sacrificing those who were ready to support it. I cannot set down the names of the Indonesians who were prepared to assume political responsibility and create a government of Indonesians, by Indonesians and for Indonesians. They would immediately be sacrificed to the vengeance of the oppressors.

But it was Indonesians who would have governed as a result of my *coup d'état* if it had succeeded. Not I.

The government was ready. How was it to be invested with power?

I had no fear of the ability of my disciplined troops to seize the administrative machinery and take over the capital if they could act by surprise and act quickly. The action could succeed with one blow, if that blow were struck quickly, firmly and accurately. We could not lose time storming the city, fighting our way in. We had to begin from inside. If I once succeeded in slipping my armed forces into Djakarta, I was confident that we would succeed.

But how to get them in? I could hardly march armed formations openly into Djakarta and expect to be allowed time to get my men into place to strike the decisive blow, which had to be a surprise blow, when I was ready. I needed some ruse like the wooden horse which brought about the fall of Troy.

I decided to let my men slip into the city separately, unarmed, like ordinary innocent peaceful citizens going about their routine affairs, and to arm them in Djakarta itself at the last moment, when we were ready to pounce.

The first part of this programme was easy. My soldiers had no trouble infiltrating the capital. They were inside the enemy's headquarters, ready to seize them as soon as I should distribute their arms. It was arming them that was the hard part.

I analysed the situation carefully. The final arrangement would have been to seize the arms somewhere in Djakarta and equip my men on the spot. But this method appeared impractical. The possibilities for laying hands on enough weapons in Djakarta were strictly limited. The K.N.I.L. which should have been merged with the Republican forces to constitute the Federal army, had instead turned over all its major equipment—planes, lorries, jeeps, automatic arms, etc.—to the Republicans which it had so long fought. Such members of its daily shrinking units as still remained kept only their individual arms.

Even these meagre weapons which the soldiers of this vanishing army might have been quite willing to let us take without opposition, would be guarded jealously by the remnants of the Dutch command, still not entirely liquidated. I noted in the last chapter that foreign troops had been withdrawn. This was true in so far as their operations in Indonesia under foreign command were concerned. But the evacuation of the Dutch soldiers from the archipelago had not been completed. Until they had all been safety transported home, the Dutch general staff, which continued to function as long as any Dutch troops remained, quivered in its boots at the very thought of doing anything which might annoy Sukarno—and this at the moment when the press was accusing the Dutch of clandestinely encouraging agitation against the Republican government! Not only could I expect no aid from this source, but the touchiness of the Netherlands army commanders had communicated itself to the Dutch officers of the Royal Indonesian Army, the K.N.I.L.

These Dutch officers, who still remained in the ranks of the dwindling force which the Republicans, instead of merging into the new national army, were engaged in liquidating, were taking good care that the remnants of their forces should not be employed by anyone else against the Republicans. The latter were the legal heirs to the government and though they were violating the spirit of the law which had made them that, it was no business of the military men to look beyond the letter of the law in attempts to preserve its spirit. Thus they did not raise a finger to prevent their own destruction or to preserve the form of government—Federalism—of which the army was intended to be the defender. Instead, obedient servants of the legal fiction, they would infallibly oppose any attempt to use their troops, or their arms, against the established government, even by opponents who wanted to maintain respect for the principles which the government was flouting.

The men of the K.N.I.L. would have followed me, I am sure, and would have turned over their arms to me if I had asked for them. After all, they were drawn from the population of Indonesia, and the government which I proposed to install in Indonesia was one which was assured, from the very make-up of its membership, of genuine popular support. The native officers also would have sided with me. But the Dutch officers, frozen in their tradition of unquestioning obedience to authority however that authority might have been established and regardless of the use it was making of its power, were sure to block any attempt of mine to secure what arms might still remain anywhere with the K.N.I.L.

Yet there was where I planned to get my arms, but by sidestepping the Dutch officers.

There were enough arms for my projected operation at the K.N.I.L. arsenal in Bandung. It was easily accessible and our plans were laid to pick up the weapons we needed there, drive them to Djakarta and distribute them to the men I already had inside the capital. It was only a question of driving three innocent-looking lorries into the city, which I judged we could manage without difficulty. After that—one blow, and power was ours. We would hold the lines of communication. The Republican ministers would be cut off from their followers, and unable to transmit their instructions, but we would be able to transmit ours.

Once again, it is impossible for me to reveal those through whose complicity we benefited. I can say only that it was arranged that a few of my soldiers, with the lorries, were to come to the arsenal after ten at night, when no Dutch officer would be present. The native guards would make no opposition. My men had only to load the arms they needed on to the lorries and drive away, and no one would be any the wiser.

With this arranged, it remained only to set the date.

It was a case of the quicker the better. The Republicans were making rapid progress in the destruction of the Federal organization of Indonesia. Unless I acted quickly to save the Federation, there would be no Federation left to save. I set the date January 23rd 1950 for the *coup d'état*.

The plan of action comprised three principal movements. Two of them were to be simultaneous. One was the seizure of power in Bandung, capital of Pasundan. This was a comparatively simple matter, in which there was no chance of failure. We were already the chief organized force in Pasundan, my centre of operations, incomparably more efficient than the undisciplined Republican troops. I therefore confided the execution of this part of the plan to one of my lieutenants.

I was to command myself the second and the more important of the two simultaneous operations, the capture of Djakarta, capital of all Indonesia. Only after the Djakarta operation had succeeded and the capital was occupied were we to proceed to the third, the seizure of Buitenzorg, about forty miles from Djakarta, where some minor administrative headquarters were located.

The timetable of the affair was as follows:

10 *p.m. January 22nd*: Seizure of arms at the Bandung arsenal of the K.N.I.L.

11 *p.m.*: Delivery of the seized arms to me at a rendezvous about fifteen miles from Bandung, and distribution of them to my men inside Djakarta at 2 p.m.

5 a.m. January 23rd: Simultaneous seizure of garrisons, police stations, administrative buildings, communications and other focal points in Bandung and Djakarta, making prisoners of the Republican soldiers and arresting the Republican politicians.

Probably later the same day, depending upon the success of the first two movements: Similar seizure of Buitenzorg.

On the eve of the day set everything was ready. All my men were in their places. On January 22nd the sun set on the anti-Federal Republican government. I hoped that it would rise on January 23rd on a new Indonesian government, Federalist and nationalist, devoted to the best interests of the people.

CHAPTER XXIX

Success at Bandung

The attack at Bandung was scheduled to move at 5 a.m. from Tjimahi, about three and a half miles from the West Java capital. The force which participated in this action consisted of about five hundred men of the Prince Justice Legion, plus a few squads of the K.N.I.L. which joined my troops spontaneously when they learned what was up.

This small group left Tjimahi according to plan promptly on time. It should normally have entered a sleeping city, have taken the garrisons and administrations by surprise and found itself in control almost without fighting. But hardly had the column of the Legion formed to move from Tjimahi than it ran into a disagreeable surprise.

A motorized corps of the famous Silivanghi division, the crack unit of the Republican army, whose men should at this hour have been sleeping peacefully in their barracks, attacked the Legion almost at the doors of its own quarters.

What had happened? The surprise movement was no longer a surprise—the Republicans, somehow forewarned, were ready for the attack. The whole situation was transformed in an instant. My lieutenant commanding a few more than five hundred men of whom he was sure, plus the few K.N.I.L. volunteers, whose reaction was unpredictable, found himself attacked by surprise when he had expected to gain the same advantage over his opponents. He knew that with Bandung warned, he had to face four thousand five hundred of the best men in the Republican army, for, in tribute to my forces, it was in Pasundan that they had stationed their crack troops. This force, which outnumbered the Legion nine to one, had tanks and artillery; it was, moreover, a certainty that barriers would have been set up to guard the approaches to Bandung.

My lieutenant did not know what had miscarried, apart from the evident fact that the surprise was no surprise. What's more, he could not communicate with me.

At this moment, according to our plans, I should be marching with my men against Djakarta. He was thrown on his own devices, compelled, in this unexpectedly threatening situation, to make his own decisions. With an apparently overwhelming force opposed to him, ready and waiting, he might easily have been excused for abandoning the operation, for yielding to the Silivanghi division and treating for the best terms possible. He might have been excused for not engaging an operation which in advance looked like a forlorn hope.

But there was no need to excuse him. He chose to undertake the forlorn hope.

That was the kind of men I chose for my legion and the way I had trained them. Their original merit coupled with the sort of military education I had given them explained the effectiveness of my force. How effective it was became clear as the action of the forlorn hope developed.

In a quarter of an hour, the small force of the Prince Justice Legion had destroyed the crack motorized corps sent against them.

Pushing on to Bandung, my men took just one hour to liquidate all opposition and occupy the city.

Success at Bandung

At 11 o'clock, a courier—a woman—reached me in Djakarta with an urgent message. It was from Colonel Sadikine, commanding the Republican troops in Bandung. He wanted to negotiate the terms of his surrender.

It was a brilliant success for the Prince Justice Legion. Too busy elsewhere to have the satisfaction of following this operation myself, I only learned of its details later. How it looked to one witness I can set down here from an account I heard some time afterwards.

This informant happened to see a considerable part of the action because he had business in Tjimahi, the starting point of my troops early in the morning. I will call him Schmidt, though that was not his name. A friend who was going to Tjimahi with him called for him in his car very early on this fine Monday morning. It was the monsoon season, and the sun rose with tropical suddenness, converting night immediately into bright day.

As Schmidt and his friend rolled through the streets of Bandung, most of whose citizens were still asleep, they saw nothing to mark this date as any different from any other. Workers coming into town from the neighbouring villages were moving through the streets. Some early-rising Dutch school children were pedalling by on their high bicycles.

The scene became more animated as the car started out along the Tjimahi road. The usual early morning throng began to assemble—rickshaws, pony carts, peasants walking into market, carrying the vegetables they were going to sell in baskets suspended from the ends of the long bamboo poles balanced across their shoulders.

A mile and a half outside Bandung, Schmidt and his friend were obliged to stop. A double barrier thrown across the road made it impossible for cars to pass except by slowing down almost to a halt and describing a sharp Z first round one barrier, then around the other. The road block was guarded by T.N.I. (Republican) soldiers, heavily armed. One of them came up to the car.

"You can't go through," he said. "There's fighting going on at Tjimahi."

Schmidt found this incredible. How could there be fighting at Tjimahi, only three and a half miles from Bandung, when the capital had been so quiet? How could there be fighting only two miles from this spot, from which nothing was to be seen or heard?

A young lieutenant came forward. He was trembling all over.

"Captain Westerling's Ratu Adil Legion has provoked a battle at Tjimahi," he explained; adding: "They've already been beaten."

"If they have already been beaten," Schmidt said, "why shouldn't we go on?"

The young lieutenant had probably made his last remark chiefly to reassure himself. But having made it, he had no argument to oppose to Schmidt.

"All right," he said. "Go ahead if you want. But it's at your own risk. You've been warned."

The car in which Schmidt was riding threaded its way through the barrier, and the two men continued on their way. Five minutes later, rounding a curve, they found themselves suddenly in the middle of a military movement.

On either side of the road a long column of Indonesian soldiers was moving forward. They were dressed in dark green uniforms, and were carrying rifles at the ready. They moved forward so calmly, however, that they appeared to be training rather than engaged in a military operation.

Moving slowly up the road ahead, keeping the same pace as the soldiers, were several heavy lorries on which machine-guns were mounted. Riding on one of them was an Amboinese, wearing the green beret of the parachute troopers. Schmidt's friend hailed him.

"What are you?" he asked. "K.N.I.L. or T.N.I.?"

"Neither," was the answer. "A.P.R.A."

The Prince Justice Legion, which the T.N.I. lieutenant had described as defeated!

The car with the two men in it continued towards Tjimahi, in the opposite direction from the double column of men marching, obviously, on Bandung. Realizing that they would encounter three complete battalions of the Republican army, equipped with the modern arms turned over to them by the Dutch, Schmidt wondered how they could move so calmly towards certain suicide.

Schmidt and his friend entered Tjimahi. They found it deserted, save for one or two natives standing before their huts, who followed the car anxiously with their eyes as though fearful that the battle of the morning was not yet over and that this solitary vehicle was the harbinger of new fighting.

Abandoned disabled T.N.I. lorries stood in the road, their tyres flat, machine-gun holes in their bodies, from some of which drops of blood leaked slowly to the ground. A few tatters of uniforms lay in the dust. These were the only traces of the battle which had just been fought. But Schmidt and his friend thought the surroundings unhealthy. Behind the bushes survivors with nervous trigger fingers might still be lurking. It was also clear that they were not going to be able to transact their business in Tjimahi this morning. They turned around and started back to Bandung.

Their car covered ground much more rapidly than the marching men of the Prince Justice Legion. Just before the barrier where they had been stopped before, they caught up with the A.P.R.A. soldiers. As they drew up level with the rear of the columns, one of the men in dark-green uniforms waved them back, gesturing to them to throw themselves down in the road-side ditch. Remembering the machine-gun at the barrier, Schmidt and his companion lost no time in obeying.

A few shots were fired. Peering cautiously over the top of his hiding place, Schmidt saw the little lieutenant run suddenly across the road, aiming with his revolver. The crack of a rifle sounded, seemingly in Schmidt's left ear. The officer threw his arms skywards and fell.

"*Madjoe!* Forward!" a hoarse voice shouted.

The dark-green uniforms rushed the barrier. Schmidt ducked his head, waiting for a withering burst of fire from the machine-guns to mow down the charging men. But there was no sound except the beat of running feet. Cautiously he peered once more over the edge of the ditch. The men of the Legion were tearing down the barrier.

The little lieutenant, terrified as he had seemed that morning, had nevertheless been braver than his men. They had run off, abandoning their machine-guns, and leaving their officer to die uselessly before the advancing troops.

Schmidt and his friend climbed out of the ditch, got into their car, and proceeding at a walk, followed the double column towards Bandung, passing the body of the lieutenant lying by the side of the road where it had fallen. The scene had again become peaceful. The soldiers moved forward calmly and quietly. Could this be war, Schmidt asked himself? Now Bandung was in sight in the distance, peaceful, normal, undisturbed. Pedestrians could be seen walking unconcerned through the streets. And ahead were the two lines of soldiers, walking likewise unconcerned, peaceful promenaders on a fine morning.

Suddenly a military jeep darted out of a cross street, turned towards the marching column and then stopped short with a squeal of brakes as its occupants spied the men approaching it. Realizing that there was no time to turn, the driver started up again and tried to run the gauntlet of the A.P.R.A. troops too fast to allow them time to react. The manœuvre failed. From one of the Prince Justice lorries a Bren gun coughed once or twice. A body was projected from the jeep, as though thrown by the hand of an invisible giant. The car, out of control, wheeled crazily towards the side of the road and overturned.

Ahead, the men of the Legion wheeled into a street at the right. With relief, Schmidt's friend stepped on the accelerator and plunged straight ahead, happy to be free of the soldiers' dangerous company. The car stopped before the Grand Hotel Preanger.

On the terrace of the hotel, customers were seated, drinking their morning coffee or chocolate as though this were a day like any other. Inside, a couple could be seen at the desk paying their bill. Civilian cars were passing in normal fashion, and though an occasional military vehicle mingled with them, they ran along at a moderate speed, untroubled, apparently unaware of any emergency.

Schmidt and his friend wondered if they could have been victims of a joint hallucination. Nothing in this normal everyday scene accorded with what they had just witnessed. They sat down on the terrace, feeling as though they were living through a dream. The air of unreality was so strong that Schmidt hesitated to tell anyone else what he had just seen. He felt that he would be laughed at. No one would believe him. He wondered if he believed himself.

But the dream was not over. As he sat there on the terrace, wondering how to break to his neighbour the news he felt he should pass on, he saw the column he had been following emerge from a side street in the distance.

The Dutchman sitting at the next table said: "What are those devils of the T.N.I. up to now?"

Before he could answer, a volley broke out. Bullets hissed and pinged across the terrace, coming, it seemed, from all directions. Schmidt got out so fast and with so little reflection that he had no idea where he was going until he found himself, in the middle of the cream of Bandung society, lying flat on his stomach on the tiles of the hotel lobby. Get in and get down had been the common reaction of everyone.

The firing stopped as suddenly as it had begun. It became possible to take stock of what had happened. The advancing men of the Legion had been met by several Republican lorries. The lorries, and the men in them, had been liquidated.

Still marching at a normal pace, our troops entered the T.N.I. headquarters, took possession of it, and then emerged again to occupy the centre of the city. Republican soldiers were fleeing in all directions. In full view of the city's citizens, who scrambled madly about, seeking shelter in a panic, the Prince Justice men picked off the running Republicans as deliberately as if they were in a shooting gallery. Hardly would a running figure appear around a corner than a rifle would crack and the man go down.

Two motor cars turned into the street before Schmidt's eyes. A civilian car was ahead; with a Republican military vehicle behind it. In the twinkling of an eye, the occupants of the military vehicle were dead, while the civilian car in front continued on its way, its driver apparently unaware of what had happened just behind him. War was going on in the midst of the city's day-to-day civilian life, independently of it, almost without disturbing it, almost without being noticed.

T.N.I. soldiers were pulling off their shoes, in order to be able to run more swiftly—for the Indonesians from whom these forces were recruited were unused to shoes. Others pulled off their trousers as well and took to their heels in their drawers. This not only rid them of an encumbrance to their running; it served to end their identity as targets. Without their uniforms, they appeared in their underwear as dressed in the normal everyday costume of the Indonesian peasant, and thus escaped into the safe civilian anonymity.

As he passed before the Silivanghi division headquarters, Schmidt saw in gleaming fresh black paint on its walls the letters "A.P.R.A." The Prince Justice Legion was master of the barracks, and, with it, master of the city.

The sounds of shots had ceased. Calm had been restored. Civilians emerged from the doorways and buildings where they had taken refuge, surrounded the victorious soldiers, and began chattering happily with them. Some of the conquerors came up to the vendors' carts on the sidewalk to buy something to eat. They not only found that they were not allowed to pay, but merchants from nearby stores came out to give them presents of small sums of money.

Schmidt was watching these scenes of celebration, when a very small T.N.I. soldier appeared. He was a mere boy, lost in a uniform several sizes too large for him, loaded with his full pack, and with a heavy Sten gun tucked under his left arm. He moved along the sidewalk gazing at the ground, straight in front of him, as though he saw no one about him.

The crowd gazed in stupefaction at this solitary remnant of the Republican army. The Prince Justice Legion soldiers broke out into guffaws. Then one old native sergeant grasped the boy by the arm, separated him from his gun and his pack, and ordered gruffly:

"Get out of that uniform!"

Still not daring to look up, the boy obeyed and stood silently before the sergeant in the white underwear which was the normal dress of the Indonesian peasant.

The sergeant gave him a sharp whack on the buttocks and the boy took the hint. He broke into a jog trot and disappeared to the accompaniment of the laughter of the soldiers. The sergeant grinned at the crowd.

"Too young to die!" he explained.

Thus disappeared the last Republican defender of Bandung.

The city was ours. The operation had been a complete success. How it looked to an outsider has been set down in Schmidt's personal account of what he saw. To that may be added a few details.

One of them was that the cost of the fight which had made the capital of West Java ours was relatively low. There were about one hundred dead, almost all of them Republicans. We ourselves suffered practically no casualties.

Another was that most of the higher Republican officers deserted their men and left them to their fate. Some of them, at the very outbreak of the action, turned over their uniforms, arms and valuables to inhabitants of Bandung, taking civilian clothes in return for them. The colonels took refuge in a Dutch barracks, where an Australian journalist reported later that he had seen one of them reading a detective story while his four thousand five hundred men were being dispersed by my five hundred and twenty-three.

CHAPTER XXX

Failure at Djakarta

At eleven o'clock on the night of January 22nd, I was waiting at the agreed rendezvous on the Bandung-Djakarta road for the three lorryloads of weapons with which my men in the capital were to be armed.

The lorries were to load at the K.N.I.L. barracks at ten. By eleven, they should have reached me. Then we had only to drive into Djakarta, equip my men and duplicate there what you already know the Legion was able to do in Bandung.

But at eleven there was no sign of the lorries.

I waited impatiently. Everything depended on the arrival of those arms. With them I had no doubt of the outcome. Without them, there was nothing to be done.

Eleven-thirty. No lorries.

Midnight. Still no lorries.

Something must have gone wrong. I dared wait no longer, in the hope that the lorries would still turn up, with some explanation for their delay. I had to find out myself, and accordingly I dispatched one of my cars to Bandung.

It returned quickly—too quickly. It had not been able to reach Bandung, for it had been stopped at a road block. The driver, pretending innocent surprise, had asked what was happening. The answer given was: "Westerling is trying a *coup d'état*."

I was stupefied. What could have happened to give me away? My surprise operation was no longer a surprise. Something had gone wrong. But what?

I was in exactly the same situation as my lieutenant at Bandung. Like him, I knew that our attempt to take the enemy by surprise had failed, and also like him, I had no idea how the secret had come out.

Failure at Djakarta

I was only to learn later what had happened. For the sake of clarity I will relate now what I was not to know myself until after the end of our operation.

My three lorries, with their team of members of the Legion, had arrived as scheduled at the K.N.I.L. barracks. Everything was going ahead as planned. The lorries were being loaded without hindrance when suddenly a Dutch officer who normally should have been elsewhere at this time turned up and discovered what was going on.

Once again, I cannot go into details at this point, as I do not wish to incriminate others. I cannot explain exactly why the appearance of a single officer who shouldn't have been there was able to upset the whole carefully arranged scheme for giving us the arms we needed. Suffice it to say that the arrival of this man, at a time when we believed we had arranged things so that no one unfriendly to us would be on the spot, changed the whole aspect of the affair. He took one look at the lorries being loaded by my soldiers and raised the alarm.

The lorries were seized, my men arrested, and the officer who had by so unfortunate a chance turned up at the wrong time and place—ten minutes more and the lorries would have been away leaving nothing for him to see—phoned to the General in command of the city. As soon as General Engles learned of the attempt to seize the arms of the Bandung arsenal, he phoned in turn to the Indonesian government. An hour later—by the time I sent my messenger towards Bandung—road blocks had been set up everywhere, machine-guns were installed beside them and Republican troops were waiting for us.

That was why my lieutenant, instead of attacking Bandung by surprise, had himself been attacked by surprise at Tjimahi. But he had one advantage over me. He had *armed* troops under his command, who were able to react and snatch victory from what had seemed the jaws of defeat. How successfully the Legion could act even though its plans had gone awry was demonstrated at Bandung. How futile were the road blocks Schmidt's account of the action there has shown.

There was no reason why, in spite of the loss of the advantage of surprise, the same thing could not have been done at Djakarta—if, at Djakarta as at Bandung, there had been an *armed* force of the Legion to act.

But their arms had not come.

I stood there in the night on the road, after receiving the report from my scout, and considered the situation. I was ignorant, of course, of what I have just related as having happened at the Bandung arsenal; but I took it for granted that the arms on which I had counted were by now not coming.

I knew, of course, that our Bandung force, already armed, could move as planned, even though it no longer had the advantage of surprise. But the Bandung operation would be meaningless without the move on Djakarta. Unless the nerve-centres of Djakarta could be seized, the Republicans could react and organize to send against us a force superior to anything we could muster. If I could not move at Djakarta, it would be better not to move at Bandung either.

But I could not call off the seizure of Bandung. There were now only about three hours left before that operation was to begin. If the road had been open, I could have sent a car to annul the movement, but the road blocks meant that I would have to send a courier on foot, across country to dodge patrols. There would just not be time.

As my men were going to move at Bandung, I had to try to find some means of making the projected attack on Djakarta also.

I climbed into an empty lorry and we headed for the city.

My only hope was to find weapons in the capital itself. It was a slim hope—in the middle of the night, with no more than three hours at my disposal, to acquire enough arms in this hostile capital to capture it—it might have seemed impossible. But under this régime of corruption and bribery, everything was possible—even to buy arms at short notice under the eyes of the government to use against it. My problem actually was not to find arms. It was to find money. If I could get the money, I knew where to locate the arms.

Unfortunately, I had no money. I had poured everything I had made from my transport business into feeding the Prince Justice Legion. I had sold my bungalows and mortgaged my lorries. Everything I owned had been converted into rice and fish for my followers. My means did not permit me to buy arms and equipment. I did not even have enough money left to pay the living expenses of my wife and our three children.

It was a small force indeed which was now speeding towards Djakarta with the object of mastering it. One empty lorry, myself, a lieutenant of mine who was with me, and the drivers of the lorry—two Bandung policemen who had joined my movement. Armament: our revolvers.

The car which had scouted the road towards Bandung had reported a road block in that direction. There would certainly be at least one ahead before we entered Djakarta. How were we to pass it? This time I was sure to be arrested. No one would be pulling any punches now.

I decided that to get into Djakarta, the best bet would be to use our two policemen as camouflage.

I stopped the lorry. My lieutenant and myself got into the back, and I had the policemen put their handcuffs on us. Then we got going again.

As we approached the city, we came, as we had expected, to a road block. Our lorry stopped, and was instantly surrounded by men with levelled rifles. A Republican captain came hurrying up.

"Police!" the driver announced. "We're taking in a couple of prisoners we found on the road after curfew."

"Let's see your papers," said the captain.

The driver handed over his identifying documents. The captain looked carefully at the photograph, compared it with the driver's face, and then walked round to the rear of the vehicle.

He was going to compare the number-plate of my lorry with that of the car the policeman was ordinarily permitted to drive! And of course they would not tally.

Sitting in the shadow in the back of the lorry I held my breath. If the captain should look into the body of the truck, he could not fail to recognize me. I was tense, every muscle ready to act. I had handcuffs on, but they were laid on, not locked on; and my revolver was ready to be drawn.

The captain seemed to be taking a long time. He was peering, puzzled, first at the card, then at the licence plate, then back at the card again.

Finally he walked around to the front of the lorry, handed his papers back to the driver, and ordered his men to open the block and let us through.

There could be only one explanation. He hadn't been able, of course, to make the numbers on the card check with those on the licence plate—but he hadn't trusted himself to act on it because, like so many of the Republican officers, he couldn't read!

This was a case where ignorance was more than bliss. If he had been better educated, he would be dead now. I was ready to fire at the slightest sign of suspicion.

We entered Djakarta and I set feverishly to work, getting people out of bed in my hunt for arms. I had scaled down my demands tremendously. I was no longer thinking in terms of three lorry-loads of assorted weapons. I was willing to settle for one hundred automatic rifles—just one hundred rifles. With as few arms as that, I was ready to attempt to take Djakarta. If I had only a five per cent chance of winning, I was prepared to risk it.

My men were waiting to march. Some of them had been told off to take the garrisons, others to seize the presidential palace. A few rifles for them. That was all I asked.

It seemed to be too much to ask.

Failure at Djakarta

I did not even try the Dutch. I knew there was no help to be expected from them. But I found no help from others either.

Once again, I cannot tell whom I went to, or even give details sufficiently precise to permit guesswork. But I roused a good many persons in a short time—without success. Some had no way of getting arms, others were afraid. They had always thought of me as a man who guaranteed success—I had come to them with power at my back and offered to be of service to them and they had accepted. Now that I came to them to beg for the means of maintaining that power, they suddenly envisaged the possibility of failure, and lost their nerve. It had not occurred to them before that Westerling could fail. Now they realized that I was fallible like other men. Perhaps I was not Prince Justice!

It was a heart-breaking night. I went from door to door, as the minutes sped by and it became later and later, to begin an operation which must be undertaken now or never. The means of success were so slight and so near—and I could not lay my hands on them. It was maddening.

At four o'clock, I was still without any promise of effective help, still without those few rifles which were all I needed. If one hundred of my men had those in their hands, we would know how to take whatever other weapons we wanted.

Five o'clock! I knew the force at Tjimahi must have started for Bandung. I could wait perhaps one hour more before launching my movement at Djakarta. After that it would be definitely too late.

But six o'clock came and I still had no rifles. It was too late. "For want of a nail, a shoe was lost. . . ." In my case, it was want of a hundred rifles, of a few hundred dollars, that lost a battle for democracy.

My effort was over, but my work was by no means finished. I had to disperse my men and instruct them how to get away safely. I had to warn the political leaders who were to have formed the new government that the *coup d'état* had failed, the operation cancelled. I had hardly finished attending to these matters, when the courier arrived to report to me the capitulation of Colonel Sadikine —at Bandung.

It was the announcement of a victory and it brought me the bitterest moment of my life.

For it was a useless victory, a futile victory, a victory which no longer had any meaning, a victory I must throw away. And it accentuated the chagrin of the failure of Djakarta, for it demonstrated that that was a failure due to chance alone. We had won, and won easily, at Bandung. We could have won just as easily at Djakarta—except for the unlucky circumstance that a single Dutch officer had turned up unexpectedly at a spot where we had every reason to believe he wouldn't.

Because of that one unforeseen detail, Indonesia was delivered over to the terrorism and the Federation of equal self-governed Indonesian states disappeared—temporarily, at least—from the register of history.

There was no point in my treating with Colonel Sadikine now. The victory at Bandung, unsupported by victory at Djakarta, could not be maintained. All I could do was send a secret message to my commander at Bandung to end the occupation of the city and to withdraw to his quarters, taking with him whatever vehicles, weapons and supplies he had captured from the Republicans.

Schmidt, sitting on a terrace in Bandung, was astonished, at five o'clock in the afternoon, to see the soldiers of the Prince Justice Legion form again and march out of the city, discomfited. Timidly, the Republicans began to reappear. He was stupefied. The Legion was in full control—and then, without being attacked, without even being challenged, it had relinquished its victory. Such a reversal was incomprehensible!

Incomprehensible as seen from Bandung. For it was in Djakarta that the *coup d'état* had failed.

196

CHAPTER XXXI

The Fate of Sultan Hamid

In spite of the defeat of my attempted *coup d'état*, I did not give up at once. I hoped it might still not be too late, that the operation might still be tried again, this time with success. But I seemed the only one who held this opinion.

My former friends had been thoroughly alarmed by the failure at Djakarta. They had no appetite for exposing themselves once more by taking the risk of helping me, and they were afraid of being compromised by contact with me. Ready enough to triumph with me when they looked to me as the future master of Indonesia, now that I was beaten, they were not willing to fall with me. I could rely on no help from them, either in the form of arms or money.

Yet if they were frightened, so were the Republicans. In the panic of the attempted *coup d'état*, they would certainly have arrested me—because they were momentarily more afraid to leave me at large than to lay hands on me—but once the day of the *coup d'état* had passed, their apprehension dropped to its former level and I once again enjoyed my astonishing immunity from arrest. I did take the precaution of changing the licence plates on my car. But that was all I did in the way of disguise. I moved freely through the streets of Dkajarta and no policeman or soldier made the slightest move to apprehend me.

It was not because the Republicans now considered me harmless. The success of my movement at Bandung had frightened them gravely. A state of siege had been proclaimed. And how serious a threat the government still considered me was indicated by a curious offer which was now made to me.

Challenge to Terror

The Republican government offered to pay me a hundred thousand dollars and pledge itself to take no action against me if in my turn I would agree to renounce for ever all political activities in Indonesia!

I didn't have enough money to buy myself a lunch, but I refused.

For a month I continued to attempt to find support for a second attempt to unseat the government—always in vain. Meanwhile the Republicans were gradually undoing my work and eliminating the elements which might make such a second attempt feasible.

My Legion, back in its quarters, deprived of my leadership, gradually disintegrated. When the Republican troops appeared to disarm its members, no resistance was offered. I had not ordered them to resist. Under the circumstances, how could I? That would only have meant exposing them to reprisals. I had no reason for believing, on present indications, that I could protect them. As it was, about a hundred of my officers and men were arrested, and were imprisoned in the dungeons of the palace of the Sultan of Djocjakarta. They may be there still.

Another arrest which followed from my revolt, some weeks later, was that of a man who had had no connection with it—Sultan Hamid of Pontianak. My movement provided a pretext for the anti-Federalists to get rid of one of the two Federalists admitted to the government. Since Sultan Hamid was considered the head of the Federalist movement, he represented the principal obstacle, though he was never a particularly formidable one, to the swift betrayal of that ideal. It was therefore handy for the Republicans to accuse him of complicity in the "Westerling coup", in order to get rid of him.

It was the Sultan of Djocjakarta, then Defence Minister of the Federation which he was engaged in suppressing, who struck this particular blow against the constitution he had sworn to defend. It was by his orders that police arrested Hamid at his quarters in the Indies Hotel.

The accusations which were made against him were

fantastic. He was represented as having entered into a plot with me to assassinate all the other members of the cabinet—the conspirators were to have surrounded the building where the cabinet was meeting and to fire through the windows to liquidate both Republican Federalist leaders at a single blow. Why, if this plot existed, had it not been tried? The accusers had a ready answer. The cabinet meeting during which the attack was to have been made had broken up half an hour early!

It was not a very good invention, but it served its purpose, namely of eliminating the Federalist representative in the cabinet, and with him the Federated United States of Indonesia. And perhaps the Sultan of Djocjakarta, the immediate author of the arrest, was not displeased, on the personal level, at the fact that it also eliminated his old rival of the ruling caste, the too brilliant Sultan of Pontianak.

There was a good reason for the fact that Sultan Hamid had nothing to do with the movement which I had prepared against Djakarta—simply that we were not at all in agreement and the idea would never have entered my head to confide in him or to seek his aid. He believed it possible to trust the Republicans to maintain and defend the constitution which they had accepted. I was of the opinion that they had only accepted it in order to be in a position to destroy it. Time has shown that I was right.

Over the course of a year, there were periodic announcements that Sultan Hamid, "Westerling's accomplice," was about to be brought to trial. Three times the date was fixed, three times it was postponed. No doubt the Republicans were not able to work out a sufficiently convincing scenario for the trial for them to dare to display in public the flimsiness of their "evidence".

In the meantime, the most contradictory reports were bruited about in Indonesia on the imprisonment of "Handsome Max". One story said that he had become insane as a result of the tortures to which he had been submitted in the dungeons of the *kraton* of Djocjakarta. Other accounts represented him as being not only still alive but also in good health.

Although the Sultan of Djocjakarta gave up the War Ministry at the end of 1950, he then took over that of the police. His rival was thus his personal prisoner, as well as the prisoner of the government.

It was curious that while Hamid was arrested and imprisoned simply on a charge of conspiring with me, I, the avowed, undisguised and confessedly guilty author of the abortive *coup d'état*, was still able to move about unmolested. It was a situation that could not long endure. As the Prince Justice Legion gradually melted away, as the self-defence militias which I had established in Pasundan grew weaker, it was obvious that the time was coming when the government would feel itself strong enough to arrest me. Once it felt it could master any popular repercussions which would follow my apprehension, it would not hesitate to lay hands on me. I had an idea that the sort of imprisonment which would be prepared for me would be rather less than pleasant. I decided that it would be wiser to lie low, until I could get away.

It had become evident that I could expect no further aid in Indonesia—at least, not until I could demonstrate by my own means that I was about to make a comeback. I thought that if I could get to Singapore where I had friends, I might be able to enlist support there.

There had been a time when the Republicans would have been very happy to have seen me go. They would willingly have closed their eyes to my "escape" from the country. But would they be so ready now to let me get away, perhaps to organize further plots against them? Nevertheless I decided, beyond doubt, that I must get to Singapore. There was only one little question.

How?

CHAPTER XXXII

Escape from Indonesia

My escape from Indonesia was arranged with the aid of one of my friends. The reader will again understand that I cannot give precise details which might compromise others. Let me only say that the plan was to fly me secretly to Singapore by sea-plane.

Dressed in the uniform of a Dutch sergeant, and carrying false papers, I set out for the harbour where the plane was waiting. I had my excellent British Commando training to thank for the false papers. I had learned all that anyone needed to know about the art of producing faked documents, and flattered myself that the ones I was carrying were models of their kind.

I had, however, a moment of doubt at the entrance to the harbour of Prick.

The Indonesian guard at the gate scrutinized the papers I handed him with the greatest minuteness. He carefully examined the photograph which it bore and then myself, suspiciously inspecting the stamp and signature. Beyond him I could see the sea-plane which was to bear me away. I knew it was the one because nothing had been left to chance, everything foreseen. I recognized both the machine and its position, and could make it out now, its propellers ready spinning. I watched the guard closely. At the first sign that he had pierced the secret of my papers, I was prepared to shut his mouth, hurry across the beach to the plane, and be off before he came to or the alarm was otherwise given.

The guard handed back my papers and stood aside. My Commando training had been vindicated. Also the guard, though he did not know it, was a lucky man.

I moved unobtrusively across the port and slipped into

the plane, I think without anyone seeing me. My friend wasted no time in friendly greetings. He opened up his motor; the sea-plane taxied across the water and in a few seconds we were in the air.

I felt free already—free to resume my struggle for the independence of the people of Indonesia. For the first time since the failure of the Djakarta coup, I felt optimistic about the possibility of wresting an ultimate victory from the setback I had suffered. I had lost a battle, yes; but the cause was by no means lost entirely. The success at Bandung had proved the fragility of the Republican military organization. It had demonstrated the popular support which any attempt to end the terroristic rule of the Djakarta government could expect. These were two fundamental factors, possibly decisive factors, which were not going to change overnight. If I could find support in Singapore, I would try again.

The Catalina was not going to take me to Singapore itself. A secret landing there would be out of the question—and though I hoped to find aid in Singapore, it was not from official sources that I would get it. I meant to give officials as wide a berth as possible. I saw no particular advantage in letting the authorities know that Captain Westerling was on their territory.

So, although we were heading straight for British Malaya, we were not planning a landing. Instead, the Catalina was going to come down on the sea, and I was going to row ashore, using the collapsible rubber boat which had been put aboard the plane for the pilot in case he were forced down. It was not even our intention to approach near enough to Singapore to run the risk that our plane, with the identifying circles on its wings, might be sighted from there. Finally, as a last precaution, we would not come down until just before dark.

First, therefore, we flew along the coast to pick up a propitious spot for my landing later. Then we went on to the Dutch base of Tandjung-Peinang in Sumatra, where we refuelled. We killed time there until five in the evening, which we judged would be late enough to bring us to the point we had chosen by dusk. We reached it, in fact, at 6.45 p.m. almost at the moment when the sudden tropic night was falling.

The Catalina swooped down on the water. We were three miles off the coast, opposite Pontian, about thirty miles from Singapore. I got out the rubber boat, inflated it, shook hands with my friend and climbed in. Hardly had I pushed off from the sea-plane when it began moving away, gradually gathering speed, left the water, and, after a final circle of goodbye over my head, turned away towards Java.

I was alone in the sea and the dark, about to attempt a surreptitious landing on an unknown coast, but I was unworried and confident. I was familiar with this sort of craft, which was of exactly the same type as those I had used for our expeditions across the swamps and marshes of Indonesia. I pointed it towards the distant shore and began paddling.

It was only a matter of minutes when I became aware of an uncomfortable sensation. I realized immediately, without looking, what it must mean. My eyes confirmed the report of my skin. I was sitting in an inch of water!

My boat was not air-tight. Somewhere there was a minute leak. The air which gave it its buoyancy was slowly escaping and water was seeping in!

Three miles, which had not seemed too much of a row when I had light-heartedly started, suddenly became a terrific distance. I began paddling frantically.

The sea, fortunately, was calm; but it was not that that worried me. What worried me was that I knew these waters to be infested with sharks.

I wielded my paddle like a madman. I was suddenly conscious of the minute dimensions of the paddles carried by these rubber boats—it seemed as though I were trying to make time with a teaspoon for an oar. The land, almost invisible now—it was only because of a light showing here and there that I could tell where it was—seemed to come no nearer. I was thrashing about in my circle of darkness without making visible progress, and I felt the craft beneath me sinking deeper and deeper into the water.

Through the dark swells about me, I began to distinguish disquieting movements. Shadowy shapes swooped by, beneath the surface. Once or twice a triangular fin passed so close that I could see it even through the gloom. The big fish were becoming intrigued by this intruder who had invaded their domain in a hip-bath. For that matter, the interest was mutual.

My bark had by now become so indistinguishable from the water that surrounded it that several flying fish landed in it. A big shark swished by. I thought the disturbance of his passage would finally swamp the boat. But it still kept afloat, though barely, its rim just clearing the surface.

I cast another desperate look towards those distant lights on the shore, when suddenly something that looked like an enormous bat's wing blotted them out as it imposed its black silhouette against the almost equally black sky. Beneath it a dark hull floated slowly over the water. A unk!

I let out a yell which would have waked the dead—with whom I was already beginning to feel associated—and it did the trick. The junk veered towards me, bumped my boat with what should have been its last shock but miraculously was not, and a rope dropped down from its deck. I grabbed it and went up hand over hand.

The parting push of my feet finished my boat. It was sinking slowly beneath me as I went up the side of the junk. Over it a black form swirled by, and I heard the rasping scrape as the shark brushed the junk. Then I was over the side and on deck.

My saviour was an old Chinese fisherman. He smelled more like fish even than his catch—his odour reminded me, indeed, of an old, a very old, cask of herrings. I found him charming.

He had a number of good points. One of them was generosity. He had only one blanket, but he offered freely

to share it with me. I might have put up with the fisherman
and his rich aroma, but the blanket was too much for me.
I have seen dirt in my time, but nothing to compare with
that blanket. It was the filthiest piece of cloth—assuming
that there was somewhere a basis of cloth under the filth—
that I have ever encountered. I thanked him for his kindness,
but refused to deprive him of half of his blanket.

Another merit of my host was lack of curiosity. He showed
no surprise whatever at having discovered a white soldier
in a sinking boat two or three miles off the coast. It is
true that so many curious things were happening in the
Far East at this time that the natives learned to take them
in their stride. The old fisherman asked me no questions
and I offered no explanations.

Instead, I shared with him the concentrated army rations
I had with me. He agreed without difficulty to put me
ashore at Pontian.

CHAPTER XXXIII

Jailed in Singapore

After a slow and tedious passage during which my Chinese
fisherman lost some of his charm but none of his odour, the
junk landed me at Pontian. I found a rickshaw at the port
which took me to a taxi stand where I was able to hire a
car to take me to Johore. The chauffeur was not too anxious
about this drive—there was a danger of being ambushed by
Communist guerrillas on the way—but I offered him a good
price and he decided to take the risk. It might have cost me
more if he had known that while he was worried about
one danger en route—Communists—I was worried about
two—the Communists and the British police.

The latter were there all right. We were stopped twice
by Malay police between Pontian and Johore. Both times
they looked carefully over my forged papers and both times

they waved me unsuspectingly on. I seemed to have done a good job.

At the crossing from Johore to Singapore, I was stopped again. Once more my false papers were checked, and once more they stood the test. I mentally congratulated the British instructors who had taught me to forge papers so well that they fooled even the British police.

Safely inside Singapore, I had, I thought, nothing more to fear. I took a bus to a hotel where I registered under my new identity as Herr Rentéenbeeck. Captain Westerling had temporarily ceased to exist. Herr Renteenbeeck, I felt, would bring trouble neither upon himself nor on his friends.

I went at once to visit an old friend who was waiting for me, and busied myself with searching for help to renew my activities in Indonesia. Using his home as my headquarters—the registration under my assumed name at the hotel having been only a blind—for three days, I was able to operate undisturbed. On the fourth day—February 26th, at five in the morning—I was woken up by two officers of the Intelligence Service, come to arrest me. Someone had given me away to the Sukarno government whose Minister of Police had immediately telegraphed to the British authorities in Singapore, demanding that they arrest me and extradite me as a criminal who had caused hundreds of deaths in Bandung and had "killed forty-two thousand people" in the Celebes.

The English were highly embarrassed. It was true that I had entered the territory of one of His Majesty's colonies under a false name and with false papers, which was against the law. Although I was subject to arrest on this count alone, to arrest me at the request of the Indonesian government, for extradition, involved certain complications. For one thing, I had fought in the ranks of the British Army (and just to make the situation a little more absurd, against the very terrorists who now, elevated to governmental status, were demanding that I be delivered to them for having fought against them) and was therefore entitled to claim British citizenship.

Jailed in Singapore

Furthermore, at this time, no extradition treaty existed between Indonesia and the Malay States. The new state had as yet had no time to make any. Indeed, it had not yet even named its ambassadors to other countries. This situation gave the British an easy way out. They could always refuse to extradite me on the grounds of the absence of a treaty, without having to commit themselves to any point of view on the intrinsic merits of the demand for my extradition. But at the same time, in view of their own delicate colonial situation, the English did not want to annoy the Indonesian government by refusing it anything, however excellent the pretext, for Indonesia was on the best of terms with India, which was more than the English could claim to be.

The reasons why the English should say "No" seemed to be balanced very evenly by the reasons for which they should say "Yes." They would very much have preferred not to have been put into a position where they had to say either.

While thinking the matter over, however, they decided to keep me handy for future reference. Hence the visit of the two Intelligence Service officers, who proceeded to take me to the nearest police station.

While I was sitting on a bench there, waiting to be called in, I fell into conversation with the man sitting next me. He was an Indonesian student, whose position, legally, was also not quite in order. While we were chattering amicably together, a constable entered and called out:

"Captain Westerling!"

I rose.

"Westerling!" the Indonesian exclaimed. And in an instant, his whole manner changing, he began to abuse me violently.

When he stopped for breath, I managed to get a word in myself.

"We may have fought on opposite sides," I said, "but the fight's over now. Let's forget it."

And I held out my hand to him.

207

Challenge to Terror

He spat on my wrist. I doubled up my fist and wiped it dry on the side of his jaw. He hit the floor and rolled over to the wall.

This little incident enabled the police to add assault and battery to the charges already listed against my name. I was probably due for a cell anyhow, but this settled it.

I was held for two days in the police station and then was moved to the model prison of Shanghi, in the north of Singapore Island. If I had to be in prison at all, this was not a bad one to be in. I had a cell to myself and I was well fed, considering the sort of hotel I was in.

My former comrades of the Intelligence Service were extremely courteous towards me and I can only be grateful to them for their attitude. Towards the governor of the island, however, I felt differently; he overdid what is ordinarily accounted a virtue: hospitality. I had been condemned to a month in prison for illegal entry and another month for the speed of my reaction to the insult of my Indonesian fellow prisoner.

Therefore, I should have been released at the end of two months. But the time came and went and I was still in prison. The reason given for my continued detention was that there was an outstanding demand for my extradition on the part of the Indonesian government.

Legally, however, there was no such demand. In the absence of a treaty, there could be none. The Indonesian government could ask the British government to hand me over as often as it liked; but in the eyes of the law such requests were non-existent in the absence of a convention in the light of which they could either be accepted or refused.

Even if a treaty had already existed, it could hardly have justified my extradition. It is a standard feature of such agreements that they apply only to ordinary crimes. One country may demand that another country surrender to it a person who has violated its criminal codes; but exception is always made for political offenders. No country engages to surrender to another persons who have been in political conflict with the latter, as was my case.

208

Jailed in Singapore

It was also standard practice, in the treaties which other states had concluded with the British authorities holding me, that a demand for extradition had to be followed within six days by a detailed account of the charges against the person wanted, to permit the country which held him to assure itself that there were indeed valid reasons for extraditing him. But within the two months allowed, and for that matter within the six months during which I was to be held, the Indonesian authorities never communicated to Singapore either any formal list of the charges against me or the customary submission of proofs as to their validity which accompanies all regular requests for extradition.

Perhaps the Indonesians might have done a better job in trying to get hold of me if they had been more experienced and more competent in the art of government. It was probably literally true that there was no one in the offices of the Indonesian authorities who knew how to go about making a formal demand for extradition. One might have thought that during the period that I was held they would have had time to find out. But they never did. It may have been that the English authorities would have been willing to turn me over to the Indonesians if it had been legal for them to do so. But it was not. Embarrassing prisoner though I was, I was protected against deliverance to my enemies by British law and British respect for law.

I was not protected quite so adequately against being held in prison in spite of the expiration of the term to which I had been regularly sentenced. Six or seven times I was led, handcuffed, to court for a ruling on my case. If the court always refused to permit my extradition, it did not on the contrary order my release. Each time I went back to my model prison, which, model though it might be, was nevertheless still a prison, of which I had had more than enough.

CHAPTER XXXIV

The Rape of the Celebes

It was while I was in prison in Singapore, helpless to do anything about it, that the last of my work in Indonesia was undone.

I had given peace to the Celebes. I had freed it of terrorism, had driven the Javanese back to their island, had made it possible for an independent local government to install itself and to function in the manner foreseen by the Federal organization of Indonesia. My work had at least this effect, that the Celebes held out against the attacks of the Republican government. But with no defenders left, this region could not hold out forever.

The Celebes and its dependencies were known as the State of East Indonesia. Of all the constituent parts of the United States of Indonesia, this region, which I had pacified, was the most firmly opposed to the unification which the Republican government was forcing, willy-nilly, upon the other parts of Indonesia. It had been able for a time to maintain its own autonomy and its own independence. But only for a time. The central government could not permit it to continue in this course indefinitely.

Once it was ready to act, the government at Djakarta dispatched a force of seven hundred men to Makassar, under the command of Colonel Sunkono, of the "Federal army." Sunkono was a former sergeant in the Indonesian army, who had already come to the fore in 1926, in the movement known as the "Revolt of the Seven Provinces." His second-in-command was Colonel Mokoginto of the military police.

With their arrival in Makassar, these two worthies immediately began to apply pressure upon the East Indonesian President, Sukawati, to proclaim the attachment of East Indonesia to the Republican government and then himself to resign. President Sukawati failed to oppose an energetic resistance to these manœuvres—his weakness could only encourage the Javanese.

The troops sent by Djakarta, together with the guerrilla fighters who had been imported with them, began to put into effect the tried and tested methods which they had used with so much success in so many localities: the methods of terrorism. They fomented disorder in the cities, wherever they scented opposition, setting to work to eliminate it with the aid of Dutch grenades of the latest model.

But they did not have everything their own way. There was a garrison in Makassar—a garrison of the former Royal Dutch Indonesian Army which, according to the constitution which had been accepted, should have been incorporated into the Federal army. But as it had not been so incorporated, it was free to act against the imported trouble-makers—provided it had brave enough officers.

It did have one officer of this kind—Captain Abdul Assiz, once a parachute trooper in the British forces in Europe. He had only three hundred and fifty men under his orders, as against the seven hundred of Colonel Sunkono, plus perhaps another two hundred guerrillas in the Makassar region. But in spite of being outnumbered, he did not propose to permit the terrorists to have everything their own way without opposition.

Abdul Assiz marched his men against the seven hundred Republican soldiers and their guerrilla supporters, actually attacking them in their own quarters. In a matter of a few hours, the men of the Federal army had mastered the terrorists, outnumbering them nearly three to one.

Stung to the quick, Djakarta reacted violently. The central government announced that a rebellion had taken place. A blockade was proclaimed against Makassar, and it was announced that an expeditionary force was being dispatched to quell the rebellion.

President Sukawati was terror-stricken. He had no idea which way to turn. On the one hand, Abdul Assiz was defending the legality of the Federal constitution, which guaranteed the autonomy of East Indonesia, and denied to any other of the Indonesian states the right to subject its partners to its own rule. But on the other hand, the Javanese soldiers and guerrillas sent to Makassar were part, officially, of the "Federal" army—even if their mission was that of destroying Federalism. In desperation, Sukawati sought some means of conciliating the government of Djakarta.

Meanwhile Abdul Assiz, who had seized the offices of Colonel Sunkono, had been making some very interesting discoveries. He had found there a number of highly intriguing documents, copies of which reached me later. There were, for instance, some letters from a Communist leader attached to the Republican intelligence service, which outlined the means for destroying the "capitalistic" régime in Indonesia. Then there was a memorandum of Mokoginto, advocating the establishment of an independent military government in the Mollucas. In addition, there were various papers inspired by the Communists setting forth a plan for the Sovietization of Indonesia under cover of the Sukarno government. These last insisted on the necessity, from the point of view of Moscow, of the rapid unification of Indonesia—that is, the establishment of a centralized as opposed to a Federal government—behind the façade provided by the Republican administration. They set forth the means for ruining the "capitalist" organization of the country by the most direct means, for liquidating the local upper classes etc. . . . All of this was to take place through the Sukarno government so that what went on would appear to be a purely national movement, and not what it was—an activity planned and directed by Moscow.

Knowing so much, and having in his hand so many proofs of the duplicity of the Republican government and of Moscow, Abdul Assiz was no doubt badly advised to accept the offer now made to him—to come to Djakarta to "negotiate" concerning the situation in the Celebes. He was given a safe-conduct signed by Sukarno and an officer of the United Nations Commission for Indonesia, and a private plane was put at his disposal. But a safe-conduct granted by the masters of Djakarta was hardly a sufficient guarantee. It proved not to be in the case of Abdul Assiz.

The moment that Abdul Assiz stepped from the plane which brought him to Java, he was arrested, safe-conduct or no safe-conduct, by the Sultan of Djocjakarta, who imprisoned him in his private jail. Of his fate thereafter, there is no certain trustworthy information.

His sacrifice was not completely vain. For the documents which he seized, which did not disappear with him, as the Sultan of Djocjakarta had no doubt hoped they would, served to lift a corner of the veil which disguised the interference of the Soviets in Indonesia.

With the elimination of Abdul Assiz, the Celebes were left without a defender. It was a simple matter thereafter for the Republican government to swallow the Celebes as it had swallowed the other states of the "Federal" United States of Indonesia.

CHAPTER XXXV

Two Flights

After I had been in jail in Singapore for six months—four months longer than I should have been—held on the two charges of illegal entry and assault and battery which had been made against me, my lawyers decided to put my case before the Singapore Supreme Court. The judges of this tribunal ruled that I was being held illegally: my sentence had terminated and I could not be considered as a prisoner subject to extradition since there was no extradition treaty between Indonesia and the Malay States. They, therefore, ordered my release.

I was thus freed from jail—yet not completely free.

From the prison I was taken directly to the aerodrome, to be deported to Holland.

This was the solution the English had found to get out of their dilemma. They would avoid annoying the Sukarno government by transferring custody of my embarrassing person from themselves to the Dutch, instead of simply releasing me. Technically, it was a thoroughly legal procedure. Having entered the country illegally, I could be sent out of it again—and where to except to the land of my formal nationality, Holland? I hardly knew the country, I had seldom heard its language until I went to war, but my passport said I was Dutch. Therefore I was put on the plane for Amsterdam.

The Dutch government had not asked for my extradition, but it had a welcome prepared for me nevertheless. Anxious not to be compromised itself by my activities, it had issued a warrant for my arrest on the charge of "incitement of soldiers to rebellion." It was a highly dubious charge. I had not seen a Dutch officer since 1949. As for the "soldiers" I had incited, if my men were to be considered technically as soldiers answerable to a military authority other than my own, and against which they had rebelled—a doubtful point in itself—they must be Indonesian soldiers. My action had taken place on Indonesian territory after it had ceased to be Dutch territory. What jurisdiction could a Netherlands court possibly claim in the matter?

But however shaky the legality of the Dutch charge might be, it seemed clear that I was only leaving one prison to enter another. I had a pleasant trip ahead of me, but the arrival seemed likely to be less pleasant.

My presence on the plane caused a certain amount of excitement, and it was therefore only natural that when it turned around after having taxied only five hundred yards along the take-off strip, the word went round among the other passengers that someone had tried to sabotage "Westerling's plane." All that had happened was an oil leak, which the plane had turned back to have fixed. But the incident made some of the passengers a trifle nervous. I suspected most of them would have preferred not to share a plane with a man who had so many enemies—particularly

among terrorists—who would not boggle at a little thing
like causing a plane crash.

Our first stop was Colombo, our second Karachi. This
latter being in Pakistan, a Moslem country, and Moslems
everywhere considering me a champion of their co-religionists
in Indonesia, it was not surprising, therefore, as I prepared
to leave the plane, that I learned a horde of journalists was
waiting to interview me. I didn't think it was a politic
moment for talking to the press, so I persuaded another
passenger to represent himself as Westerling and divert
the attention of the newspapermen to himself until I could
slip away from them. He agreed and went off in a swarm of
them, while the airport officials, anxious to show themselves
agreeable to the Ratu Adil, danced attendance on him.

This little comedy meant a surprise for the Passport
Control Officer, who started when he saw the name on mine,
and demanded suspiciously:

"How many Westerlings are there on this plane, then?"

In another Moslem country, Egypt, I was met at Cairo
airport by two persons who invited me to dine with them.
No one responsible for delivering me to Amsterdam saw
any objection to my having dinner at the airport, pending
the departure of the plane, with my two hosts. This let
them in for a little surprise some time later.

When the plane in which I had arrived was ready to take
off, its crew discovered that Captain Westerling was not
on board. What was more, he was not to be found anywhere
about the airfield.

The fact was that I was already in the air en route for
Europe. I had taken the liberty of making a slight altera-
tion in the programme. I had slipped quietly aboard a
Belgian plane of the Sabena line instead of the plane which
expected me. I had decided that I would prefer to land in
Brussels rather than in Amsterdam.

The rest of the flight was without incident, except for
a minor pleasant surprise at Athens. At the airfield there,
where we made a brief stop, I heard someone hail me by
my first name, and I turned to recognize the local manager

of the Sabena company, Mr. Philipucci, who had been a schoolmate of mine in Istanbul. I had time for only a few words with him, however, before I was off on the last lap of my flight to Brussels.

The Belgian police received me at the airport with great courtesy. Indeed, they pushed hospitality so far as to offer me a shelter at the Petit Chateau, where political refugees were interned. I told them that my housing demands were modest. I did not require a chateau, big or little. A simple family pension would do.

They pointed out that it might be difficult for me to find suitable quarters with a Belgian family. What would I think of going to live in Luxembourg? It was a charming country, and the climate healthy, very healthy.

They seemed to think so highly of Luxembourg and even more highly of the idea that I should go there to live rather than Belgium, that I could make no objection. I had not selected Belgium deliberately anyway, as my desire had been less to come to Brussels than to avoid Amsterdam. So I plumped for Luxembourg.

So my two guides produced a comfortable car and we started out for this charming, healthy land.

We stopped for lunch at Bastogne. After we had disposed of a sumptuous steak accompanied by French fried potatoes, my policemen friends excused themselves in order to telephone. They returned to announce that it was not necessary, after all, for me to go to Luxembourg unless I absolutely insisted upon it.

Accommodating as ever, I remarked that I did not insist upon it by any means. After all, Luxembourg had been their suggestion in the first place. It was a charming country and it had a healthy climate.

Belgium, they remarked, was a charming country too, and the climate, on second thoughts, was very much like that of Luxembourg.

In other words, the Belgian government, after thinking it over, had decided to take a chance on my possibly explosive presence on its territory. I was asked, however, to engage myself, as long as I remained in Belgium, not to indulge in any political activity. I gave my word that I would not.

To avoid interviewers and unwanted publicity, I at first established myself away from the big centres, in the Ardennes, where I stayed about two weeks. To my great joy, my wife had succeeded in getting out of Indonesia and joined me three days after my own arrival. We suffered one disappointment: her two children and my two-year-old daughter Cecilia were not allowed to leave the country to join us.

After interest in my exploits had had time to die down a little, we ventured to move into Brussels, where we lived hidden away in a quiet family boarding-house, occupied mostly by elderly ladies, a far cry from the native hut with its tame serpents which had been our home in Indonesia.

During all the time of my Belgian sojourn I kept strictly to my promise not to carry on any political activity. But I had not forgotten Indonesia, nor lost my interest in it. My friends there continued to keep me informed and to plead with me to return. For there was work to do there, important work, not only for the well-being of the Indonesians themselves, but also for the peace and security of the whole world.

I have left Belgian territory now. I am no longer bound by any pledge to remain outside a struggle whose importance I am in a position to appraise. The stakes are large in Indonesia—how large, the western world does not seem to understand. I want, before I close this book, to help it to a larger understanding. Indeed it was only with that purpose that I wrote this book at all.

CHAPTER XXXVI

Will Prince Justice Return?

As I have already stated I have been asked many times by the friends I left behind me in Indonesia to return there and to resume again the work which I left unfinished.

217

Challenge to Terror

Will I do so?—Perhaps.

I feel myself very close to Indonesia and to the people of Indonesia. Without abjuring the Catholic religion in which I was brought up, I have become sympathetic to the Moslem religion, which corresponds most closely to my deepest emotions. It is a fraternal religion, and a religion for soldiers. And without abjuring my Dutch ancestry or the principles of the occidental civilization to which I belong, I consider myself as primarily, by my acquired interests and my acquired sympathies, an Indonesian at heart. I have made myself one with the gentle people of Indonesia. Their cause has become my cause. They have a right to the satisfaction of their national aspirations and of their desire for independence—which has been betrayed in the very name of that same independence. I will do everything possible to give them satisfaction.

From 1945 to 1950, the English, the Australians, later the Americans and of course the Soviets, by supporting the "Republicans" of Djakarta, represented as an effective and representative government, in practice prevented the Dutch from recovering their former colony and its fabulous riches. The West remained wilfully blind to the reality of the anarchy methodically organized by the conquered Japanese, the régime of terror created by uncontrolled and uncontrollable bandits, to whose horrors were delivered up not only the former colonists and two hundred thousand Eurasians, but also the 75,000,000 gentle, peaceful, defenceless Indonesians themselves.

The horrors of 1945 have continued for many years now, directed towards the liquidation of the entire upper class of the population—the administrators educated by the Dutch, the former nobles, the landowners, all those who would oppose the establishment of a Communist régime.

In many sections, the government possesses no real authority. Power is exercised locally by Communist agitators, disguised as majors or colonels of the Republican army. Get a few miles away from Djakarta and you are in territory where Sukarno's orders mean nothing. A mere lieutenant,

Will Prince Justice Return?

a leader of fifty men, can ignore scornfully the instructions of the government, and rob, kidnap, kill—and "purge"— at his own pleasure and on his own responsibility. Even individual soldiers are equally undisciplined. The prisoners they take are their personal property. No officer will intervene to prevent them from doing anything they want with them.

A large part of the Indonesian press itself calls daily for the end of "military administration". That means an end to the terrorism of the bandits masquerading as soldiers. But the theoretical government has had no means with which to destroy this anarchy, even if it had the will to do so.

Twice between 1945 and 1949, the Dutch started to sweep away these terrorists. Twice all the weight of the United Nations, all the influence of the other powers of the world, was thrown against them to force them to stop. Yet the task would have been an easy one. You have seen how I myself, with about five hundred men, was able to take possession of an important centre of Java, after having ended terrorism and maintained order in Pasundan with my own small Legion. You have seen how I pacified the Celebes with less than two hundred men. You have seen how close I came to liberating Java and thereby gaining control of all Indonesia, in order to make it possible for conscientious politicians to establish at last the free democratic federal constitution foreseen by the Round Table Conference at The Hague.

The Indonesians have not themselves yet given up the struggle. Their battle may seem to have been lost, but it has not been so entirely. There is still a strong and active opposition in certain parts of the archipelago to the anarchy over which President Sukarno presides—and in certain localities, that opposition has the upper hand.

The immense majority of Indonesians do not want to let themselves be Sovietized. The mass purgings and liquidations which are preparing the way for the proclamation of a Communist Indonesia are teaching the humblest rice planters

219

what they may expect from those who seek to make themselves their masters in the future and are already in part their masters of the present.

A widespread desire to shake off the rule of terrorism and to replace it by peace and order animates all Indonesia. The country will rally to the banners of anyone who promises to satisfy that desire.

Countless requests have been made to me to return to help in the liberation of the Indonesian people. It is possible that the development of events will send me back there some day.

But let me make myself plain.

If I ever return to the archipelago of the South Pacific, it will not be to aid in the re-establishment there of Dutch sovereignty. The last page in that chapter of Indonesia's history was blown away with the last leaf on the calendar of 1949. My countrymen have resigned as governors of Indonesia—or more exactly, they were forced to resign by a coalition of the Soviet Union and the Western nations.

That is ancient history.

The future of Indonesia now must be the future of Indonesian independence. But for Indonesia to become Communist would not mean independence. It would mean that the mild hegemony of Holland had been exchanged for the harsh domination of Soviet Russia.

There is today great danger that Indonesia will be subjected to that domination. The development of recent events proves it. All the documents in the case prove it. The speeches of President Sukarno indicate it. All that is required is a sign from China or from Russia to oblige the present government, whose authority is an illusion, to announce the adherence of Indonesia to the group of the popular democracies.

Do not forget that there are three and a half million Chinese in Indonesia. They control a great part of the country's trade and wield considerable influence. Some of them are millionaires, but they are Chinese first of all, ready to follow the lead that China has taken.

Will Prince Justice Return?

The government of Mao Tse Tung has accomplished a tremendous amount of underground work in Indonesia. Communist school teachers and college professors have been sent there to indoctrinate Chinese youth in Indonesia in the principles now accepted by Chinese youth in China. Secret Chinese militia forces have been organized, ready to act when the signal is given.

The peril for the Western nations, given the strategic situation of the Indonesian archipelago and its inexhaustible resources, is immense and imminent. But the peril is even greater for the Indonesians themselves, faced with a disastrous future, in defiance of the fact that a minimum of peace and social justice operating in this natural paradise would make them one of the world's most privileged peoples.

The Indonesians have a right to independence, as I have said. But that means all of them. Not only those of Central Java, whose domination over the other islands has been so cruelly exercised both in ancient history and in the last few years. The Indonesians of every island, of every religion, of every race. Their independence, within an Indonesian Union, is the dream of all those populations so brutally conquered in 1950 by the government of Djakarta.

If I ever return to Indonesia, it will be to serve that ideal of independence. It will be to aid the genuine democrats who seek to end the armed tyranny which now oppresses them in order to establish at last a régime based upon free popular elections. For did you know that the Indonesian people, in whose name Sukarno and Company profess to speak, have never yet been called upon to vote in a general election?

But if Indonesians have never had a chance to express by vote how they feel about the cause I espoused or how they feel about me, they have managed to do that without voting. They gave me spontaneously the title which pleases me more than any other honour which has come my way, more than the eight campaign ribbons I may wear, more than the four recommendations for the highest military decoration. It is a title not often accorded to a man of thirty-one.

Challenge to Terror

My friends the *tanis* call me Bapa. It means father.

And my friends the *tanis* are still waiting for the coming of Ratu Adil, Prince Justice, announced by their prophet—the deliverer born in Turkey. They saluted me by that name once. But I failed to deliver them.

Had the time of the prophecy then not yet come? When is Prince Justice to arrive?

When "pointed hats will float in the Serayu"?

Pointed hats? Could that mean those peaked caps bearing the five-pointed star of Communism?

Lightning Source UK Ltd.
Milton Keynes UK
UKHW010935120121
376889UK00003B/491